Waltz With Me, Alaska

Waltz With Me, Alaska

An Alaskan Love Story

by

Donna Blasor-Bernhardt

JADA

Waltz With Me, Alaska

All Rights Reserved © 2004 by Donna Blasor-Bernhardt

No part of this book may be reproduced or transmitted in any form or by any means, electronic or mechanical, including photocopying, recording, or by information storage and retrieval system except by a reviewer who may quote brief passages in a review to be printed in a magazine or newspaper without written permission from the publisher and the author.

Published in 2004 by JADA Press
Jacksonville, Florida
www.JadaPress.com

ISBN: 0-9747501-1-5
Library of Congress Control Number
LCCN: 2004100259

Printed in the United States of America

DEDICATION

I believe that most of us have the opportunity only once in our lifetime to experience true, complete love. If we are fortunate enough to meet that person and share some part of our lives together, however long or short it may be, then we are truly blessed.

It is with this thought that I gratefully
dedicate this book to my husband, Dick.

Waltz With Me, Alaska

CHAPTER 1:	Breaking Away	14
CHAPTER 2:	Anyplace But Tok!	19
CHAPTER 3:	Now The Work Begins	28
CHAPTER 4:	First Day Of School	38
CHAPTER 5:	Just An "Ordinary" September	42
CHAPTER 6:	Two New Bernhardt's	52
CHAPTER 7:	Winter ... Too Early	57
CHAPTER 8:	Settling In For Survival	65
CHAPTER 9:	Thanksgiving In Whitehorse	75
CHAPTER 10:	Swallowing Our Pride	83
CHAPTER 11:	Christmas	93
CHAPTER 12:	Poaching A Moose	109
CHAPTER 13:	Life In The Tent	135
CHAPTER 14:	Fire And Futility	145
CHAPTER 15:	Of Saws And Sutures And Science	160
CHAPTER 16:	Easter And The Woe Of Snow	184
CHAPTER 17:	The Race Of Champions	191
CHAPTER 18:	Paul Harvey Comments	195
CHAPTER 19:	Chinook	198
CHAPTER 20:	On Privvies And Privacy	207
CHAPTER 21:	Credit And The Tough Cookie	213
CHAPTER 22:	Bear Country	220
CHAPTER 23:	The High Price Of Credit	226
CHAPTER 24:	Windows And Stove Black	233
CHAPTER 25:	Katherine Takes A Dive	237
CHAPTER 26:	The Finishing Touches	242
EPILOGUE:	Farewell, But Not Goodbye	251

PROLOGUE

I can't remember a time when I did not love Alaska. Even before ever hearing the word, I loved something that later turned out to be Alaska.

As a five-year old, I recall standing in my mother's flower garden, the hot Kansas sun beating down unmercifully upon me. I loved the flowers, but even at that young age I hated the intolerable heat I had been born into. I watched mother clipping flowers, both our faces shaded with large-brimmed sun bonnets. We often took shelter under a shade tree and sipped iced tea for relief.

My Scotch-Irish grandfather, while working in his carpentry shop, stopped often to wipe his sweating brow. Using a well-worn handkerchief, he would run it over his face and through his thinning red hair before returning it to the hip pocket of his overalls. It was an automatic gesture. Taking up his work once more, he didn't seem to notice the closeness of the air or the lack of a breeze.

On those hot summer days, I often prayed for cooler weather. Like my grandfather, I am a redhead and while other children were able to spend hours playing in the sun, I could not. My fair complexion too easily burned, blistered and peeled. That was not the worst of it. Every time I sunburned, a million freckles seemed to follow. Grandpa was well-freckled, too, but it didn't seem to bother him. His face was always shiny red and blotched with big brown freckles. At times, I thought of him as a cactus. They both loved the heat, taking it in, soaking it up.

All I remember soaking was my clothes any time the opportunity presented itself. This was usually by way of the garden hose or grass sprinkler. Fully drenched, the world was once again bearable. I could continue my day's adventures, doing things any tomboy-in-training would be doing: catching bees, thrusting my arm halfway down a crawdad hole, climbing trees or swinging upside down on the trapeze my dad had fashioned for me. The breeze I could create on that trapeze was better than any dessert.

The biggest event of the day was waiting for the ice man to pull up in front of Grandpa's house. Sitting on the porch, the sun at high noon, I was careful to keep my bare feet off the hot brick sidewalk.

My dad had showed me once how hot it could get by dropping a raw egg on its surface. The egg had sizzled, then slowly solidified.

Peering down the brick-paved street I'd watch the ice truck slowly moving toward our direction, its image mirage-like in the heat waves rising from the road. As it neared, I made a point to help.

After unlocking the van's gigantic door, the ice man would swing it wide open. If a certain small child positioned herself just right, she could feel the momentary blast of cold air issue from the inside of the van before it was quickly closed again. This knight of white ice always wore gloves when handling the ice tongs that were kept inside with the ice. I suppose after handling those tongs and a truck full of ice day after day, he really needed them, but to me, just touching the tongs or the ice was a delicious refreshment.

Hurriedly, he carried the dripping ice block across the yard, up the steps and hoisted it into place inside Grandpa's little ice box. I was always two steps ahead of him, opening the door in precision time. For my thoughtfulness, I received a shard or two of ice from the back of the truck. I relished those shards as much as popsicles sold from an ice cream truck.

That was about as much experience with ice as I would ever have had, had it not been for my dad. A twist of bad luck, hard times and no income sent my father, who was a pilot/aircraft mechanic, looking desperately for work. He learned of job opportunities in the territory of Alaska and was off in a flash. After spending nine months in the frozen north, sending every paycheck home to my mother and writing wonderful letters to his family, complete with stick figure representations of his life, for a daughter who wasn't old enough to read, he returned for Thanksgiving/Christmas vacation. In the course of those next six weeks, my life would be changed forever. My parents sold the house, almost everything we owned and prepared to move to Alaska.

I accompanied my dad into a farmer's cornfield where a forlorn-looking, old Dodge pickup sat with dried cornstalks sticking up around it. After kicking the tires and scrutinizing the engine, he paid the farmer in cash. This was to be the royal coach that would take us to Alaska.

Alaska! My heart burst with anticipation. I could barely wait to board that old truck and be off. Dad had told me of mountains, snow, glaciers, northern lights and days filled with starlight. It seemed like a magical world, and we were going to live in that world.

But, *where* was Alaska? I had no idea, so I asked my granddad. Since he wasn't happy about us moving, he answered, with much conviction, "You're going to the end of the world." Wonderful! I had never been to the end of the world. I wondered how long it would take.

January 15, 1951, seventeen days after leaving Kansas, we arrived in Anchorage. The trip had been an adventure of steep, winding mountain passes, blinding snowstorms, sub-zero cold and careening down a narrow, slick, newly-opened trail called the Alaska Highway. And I had loved every minute of it.

Driving down the streets of Anchorage in early afternoon that first day, the town seemed almost magical. Christmas lights glowed beneath snow, people were bundled in wonderful warm parkas, kids were ice skating, and we were going to live here. I took to Alaska, cold, outhouses and frosty eyelashes as though I'd been born to it. At the ripe old age of six I had fallen in love.

FOREWORD

While growing up in the wild and free territory of Alaska, I entertained great visions of someday marrying a rich, old geezer. He could buy me an entire mountaintop, build a fantastic log house for me and I would live happily ever after there while he lived in some distant city. *Very distant*, like South Africa or the Antarctic. That was Plan A. Then there was Plan B.

Plan B wasn't so practical, but rather romantic. Marry the man I loved and live with him wherever he went.

I kept an open mind. Actually there was also a Plan C. It involved no man at all. Just me and one hundred and sixty acres of land that I would homestead. Unfortunately, it looked as if Plan C would never work. I was not quite old enough to file for a homestead when the federal government put a freeze on most of Alaska's land. What was left was not choice land and was accessible only by air. The land was so remote it would take me years to reach it, build on it and prove up on it alone. I would have to work in the city, put money aside and look far into the future for Plan C. Admittedly, that was a blow, but I was not devastated.

I still leaned a little toward the Geezer Plan because I never figured I'd find a man I was willing to cook and care for. And Plan C, while I thought it was reasonably sound, was out of the question for a while. The Geezer Plan A seemed the best for now, at least on paper.

Then I met Dick. Three weeks later we were saying, "I do," in front of a judge in the Anchorage courthouse.

I remember wondering during that short ceremony, *What in the world happened to Plan A?* Before the "I do's" were over, though, I had forgotten Plan A completely. All I knew was, I loved this man and wanted to be with him the rest of my life.

Later, I would find that Dick had the same set of plans. We were alike in so many ways, both having been reared in Anchorage. Our life together, from the start, was a continuous love affair with each other and with a third party, the beautiful lady, Alaska.

But slowly we were saddened as we watched our friendly town grow into a bustling city. We saw dirt roads turned to paved highways. Trees were destroyed, shopping centers were built and herds of moose being replaced by multi-storied buildings. Unlocked doors slowly succumbed to locks. *Civilized* civilization had been born.

Then came statehood. For us, a pretentious word that turned our wild territory into a tamed state. I remember, as a teenager, watching a huge statehood victory bonfire celebration in Anchorage and wondering if it really was a victory. Statehood has since proven to be both good and bad for Alaska.

Dick and I were married in 1964, the year of the Great Alaska Earthquake. Our dream was to homestead our land, build a log house and rear our future children there. We kept hoping the temporary land freeze would lift soon. Two years later our son, Ricky, was born, and we still had no land. Three years after that, in 1969, the Alaska Native Claims Settlement Act was imposed, further dashing hopes of homesteading. Privately owned land was skyrocketing in value. We were barely getting by. There seemed to be no hope of buying land.

One more year saw the birth of our daughter, Katherine. We were still unable to get out of the rent trap. Anchorage kept getting bigger and bigger. Its problems multiplied. So did ours.

Katherine was one year old when we realized that our hopes for homesteading were quashed forever. Congress confirmed the Alaska Native Claims Settlement Act as a stark reality. Our wild, free and wonderful frontier dream was gone. Dick and I were saddened. We loved this land so much. It was our life. We wanted a part of it, to be a part of it.

Without the possibility of homesteading and existing on a normal income with two small children, we had to forget trying to buy land. Down payments on land within driving distance of work were out of the question.

We spent six more years living hand-to-mouth, paying rent, utilities, taxes, camping away from Anchorage to break the monotony and becoming more and more discontented. Dick worked a day job and another one at night. I was working a six-hour day. Most of my income went to babysitters and gasoline. I quit driving to work and began walking, just to save on gasoline.

We wondered what would become of our dreams. Then one spring day in broad daylight in Anchorage, on my way home from work, our dreams could have ended for us. A stranger pulled alongside the sidewalk curb and asked if I needed a ride. When I replied that I didn't, he pulled a little ahead of me, jumped out of the car and grabbed my left arm, pulling me toward the open car door. I was terrified. There had been a series of women kidnapped, raped, killed and dumped along remote roads — all by the same person or persons, so the police thought.

Could this be the man, I wondered? I screamed, with no one there to hear or care. Then, as he began pulling at me, I dropped my right hand. It thunked on the hippie carpet bag I had slung over my shoulder.

I love you, my paranoid husband, I thought as I quickly slipped my free hand down into the bag. Since I was slightly bent forward, my attacker did not notice, until I thrust my arm and a .38 derringer directly into his stomach ordering him to back off as I cocked it. He looked down at the .38 and then at me in amazement. Now his eyes were wide with fear. Immediately he released me, threw both hands into the air and stammered, "Don't panic, lady!" He backed toward his car, jumped in and hastily drove away. There was no license plate on the back of his car.

I returned home, locked the doors and called Dick home from work. We called the police and they sent an officer out to talk with us. They informed us that I could have been in trouble for carrying a concealed weapon. Dick was furious. The .38 had been his idea. He'd made me promise to carry it when the rape-murders began and it had paid off. I loved him and blessed that weapon.

Ricky and Katherine were pretending to be villain and victim. That was our turning point. We looked at that incident as something positive. Dick considered it proof enough that we had to do something, take some steps forward in our life. We were stagnating in the city.

Dick and I realized then that we did not want to rear our children in Anchorage or any other city. We decided to find the *real* Alaska.

CHAPTER ONE

Breaking Away

We began by selling everything that wasn't useful for the bush. Since we didn't know exactly where we would settle, we had to gather things around us for survival, independence and multiple uses. Being raised under not-so-modern conditions, this wasn't difficult for us. We already knew the basic things we needed.

Dick and I grouped things we were getting rid of. There was one corner of the apartment for things that would go to the auction. This included big items like furniture. We sold it all. Another corner was for items to be sold in a newspaper ad: most of the kids' toys, small appliances, all of the necessities of everyday city life and anything that was electric.

Things not to be sold were packed away immediately and occupied yet another corner. These included baby books and photos, mementos that we didn't want to lose. Those boxes were marked with a black felt pen. There was another set of boxes in the same corner. The second set contained things such as sewing material, spare chain saw parts, ax handles, etc., that we would probably need soon, yet would not be traveling with us immediately. Those boxes were marked with a red pen. We shipped them to Fairbanks, 350 miles away to be kept in storage until we could find a spot to call home.

The fourth corner was for things going with us: sleeping bags, axes, chain saw, clothing, cooking utensils, small camp tent and a complete medical kit made by a doctor friend. In the kit were sutures, penicillin, you-name-it-we-had-it, for any small disaster.

"Which corner?" Dick was standing in the hallway holding his electric razor, grinning from ear to ear.

"None. New pile. We'll start one for the Salvation Army and anything that doesn't sell at the auction or ads, they get. Okay?"

"Sounds good," he replied. I haven't had this thing out of the case for years anyway. Probably never will. It's like new."

It was true. Dick and I had been married for twelve years and during almost all of that time he had worn a beard. Even on the day we were married he had a beard. Once, when Katherine was tiny, she complained of it scratching her during a bedtime kiss. Dick promptly shaved his face and lost his little girl until it all grew back! She didn't like him, or know him, without it. Besides, I always liked his beard. Without it, he had little chipmunk cheeks.

Dick had already turned in his resignation at work and we would have to rely on money from the sale of our castoffs to finance our adventure. It was a big step, but we knew it was right.

The days flashed by. Soon Ricky was out of school for the summer, having just completed fourth grade. Katherine had not yet started. We made final preparations. Dick had a snowplow and winch mounted on our four-wheel drive truck. He beefed up the shocks, made a good sturdy bumper that we called a moose-gooser and put four brand new tires on the wheels. Big tires with lots of rubber. We had some traveling to do and he didn't want trouble.

His next project was to do the same thing with the utility trailer we would be pulling. It needed new springs and tires. He re-welded the trailer tongue because there would be a lot of weight in the trailer and built a dustproof canopy for the top. Dick also bought a portable welder, which he mounted in the bed of the truck, for whatever might break down.

Our second car was a small Volkswagen. I would drive it, trailing behind Dick. It, too, was loaded, mostly with clothes, an ice chest, the medical kit and our calico cat, Denali. There was room for me and one of the kids. Katherine usually went with me, Ricky with Dick, and occasionally they would trade off. Our canoe went on top of the Volkswagen, too.

Donna Blasor-Bernhardt

The day finally arrived when everything appeared to be ready. There was nothing left to do but leave Anchorage, and we lost no time in doing so. We had all summer ahead of us and were confident that the right spot for us would show itself.

The four of us spent weeks just relaxing, sightseeing, fishing, and enjoying our new freedom, all the while keeping a watchful eye for *our spot*. Winding our way along any little side road, we explored miles of land, all north of Anchorage since Dick and I had decided it was north we wanted to go — inland. After driving as far north as Fairbanks, we turned east toward the Yukon border, then north once again, thinking maybe the little town of Eagle, on the banks of the Yukon River, would be a nice place to live, or perhaps even some place near there.

We were shocked upon arrival. Evidently a lot of others had thought the same thing — there were as many Californians as there were Eagle residents. This was, of course, its summer population. The winter in Eagle would be practically devoid of outsiders. Eagle, though small, was already divided into small lots. In spite of it being a beautiful little town, we decided it wasn't what we wanted. It didn't have *our spot*.

North again to Boundary. Nice place, but no land for sale. I liked Boundary, though. It is cut off from the mainstream of civilization all winter. That appealed to both of us. All along the Taylor Highway which is more of a large trail the land was beautiful, but none of it was for sale. It was all tied up by the native land claims.

We camped off the Taylor Highway for a week or so, trying to get our bearings, hoping that somewhere, we would find the break we were looking for. We had our small camp tent as a home for us. Denali, the cat, resided in a large mailbox attached to a lightweight leash. The arrangement with Denali was quite convenient. She had a permanent home of her own while we were traveling and she couldn't get lost. We were all comfortable in our surroundings.

One night while sitting around the campfire, Denali began to pace in front of her mailbox. She was in heat and restless.

"Sorry, Denali," I said, patting her head, "there's no boyfriend for you out there."

Suddenly her eyes grew wide. The hair stood up on the back of her neck and shoulders. She peered into the darkness.

"Dick, look at this crazy cat!" My words still hung in the air when there came an ear-piercing yowl from somewhere out in the dark night. Denali froze.

"Guess I was wrong." There came another yowl. Denali bolted into her mailbox and huddled in the corner.

Yee-owwl! Closer this time. Denali began a low growl. Her eyes were big, black saucers.

"Lynx," Dick said, matter of factly. "All we need right now is a run-in with a lynx." He checked his rifle and laid it next to his side.

"Well, girl," I said to Denali, "you're quite the vamp, aren't you? Got a big lynx all stirred up and ready to court. What do you say to that?"

Her reply was a loud hiss as the lynx yowled again. He was moving in closer, but we figured he wouldn't come into camp. I closed Denali's mailbox with her safely inside and we all got settled in the tent. At first, it was hard getting to sleep, listening to Denali's growling and the lynx answering her. Finally, sleep surrounded us all.

Suddenly, we were jerked from our sleep to the sound of all hell breaking loose. True love had won out. The lynx was right in camp and batting Denali's mailbox around like a toy. So far, the lid hadn't popped open, but it wouldn't last much longer. Denali was screaming inside it; the lynx became more excited.

I jumped out of the tent and shouted, hoping to startle the lynx enough to scare him away. No luck. I heard Dick step out of the tent behind me. The rifle bolt clicked into place.

Suddenly a rifle shot pierced the night air. The lynx jumped and ran off into the brush. I whirled and confronted Dick, not noticing the baffled expression on his face.

"What are you doing, shooting from behind me?" I shouted. "Are you crazy?" I couldn't believe he'd done that. Not Dick.

"I ... I ... Uh ... didn't." Now I saw how confused he looked. The rifle was pointed into the air. "It went off all by itself. Honest. I never touched the trigger." He lowered the rifle slightly and pulled back the bolt to eject the spent shell. It didn't eject; the rifle was jammed.

"This is a first," Dick said. He sat down and patiently removed the cartridge.

"Can't understand it," he said, standing up once more. "All I did," he kept on, aiming at a sand bank, "was cock the rifle." He pushed the bolt forward. Instantly the rifle responded with another shot in the semi-dark. He had not touched the trigger, and it was jammed again. That's all it took for Dick.

"Damn!" he shouted. "I'll never trust this gun again. I'm getting rid of it." He unpacked a spare rifle, checked it out and loaded it.

We could still hear the lynx yowling in the distance. Dick fired several shots into the air. The lynx moved farther away as I tried to calm Denali. She was shaken, but not hurt. Several more shots in the air and the distant cat sounds became more and more faint.

"We've both learned our lesson tonight," Dick commented. "He won't be back for Denali, and I'll never rely on that other rifle again."

He was right.

CHAPTER TWO

Anyplace But Tok!

We weren't making any progress. Were all our dreams to go up in dust? I wondered this as yet another truck and camper with stateside plates roared by our camp. Layers of dust settled over everything.

It was early August. I felt time slipping away. So did Dick. The more time spent here, the less time we'd have to build once we did find land. Something would have to happen soon.

Dick threw another log on the fire. Both kids were in the swamp just below camp picking blueberries. We were having our standard breakfast since living on the Taylor Highway: bacon, blueberry pancakes and instant orange juice. The blueberries were so thick it didn't take Katherine and Ricky long to pick more than enough for the morning's breakfast. Sometimes we had more berries than pancakes.

"Well, we've exhausted all land possibilities in this direction," Dick said, "I'm open for suggestions."

I dumped the blueberries into the batter and lightly stirred them around. "How 'bout west of here?" I ventured.

"Tok?"

"No. Lord not Tok!" I laughed. "Any place but Tok. It's the last place I'd want to live. I was thinking, between Tok and Delta, maybe. Lots of bush country there. Miles and miles of it. If we can find any for sale." I turned over one golden brown pancake.

"Or maybe south," Dick said. "Some nice country there, too." He reached into the pan and broke off a piece of pancake, then popped it into his mouth. Using the spatula, I thwacked his fingers with mock sternness. The kids were ready with plates in hand, giving their daddy a beady-eyed stare. Katherine eyeballed the misshapen pancake on her plate. Then she sighed a big theatrical sigh and tapped her foot several times at Dick.

"You're being silently reprimanded," I told him and nodded toward Katherine.

"Just looking after your best interests," he told her, "that one had a bad spot on it."

"I s'pose mine did too, huh Dad?" Ricky said, looking accusingly at his own, less-than-perfect pancake. Dick was a slick one. I hadn't even seen him snitch that piece.

"Don't worry," I told them both, "there's more where those came from." I flipped a saucer-sized pancake onto Dick's plate. Immediately, as though rehearsed, both kids leaped up and each tore a piece of his pancake away, saying, "Oh, oh! Another bad piece!" laughing with glee at the surprised look on Dick's face. He had half of a pancake left. I couldn't help laughing with them as I dished out more blueberry goodies.

"Should break camp here then," Dick said between bites, "and look for land elsewhere." He finished sopping up the syrup on his plate with his last bite of pancake.

"We leaving here?" Ricky asked.

"Sooner the better, son."

"Darn." Ricky said. He and Katherine had grown accustomed to this camp spot and way of life. They didn't realize the work that lay ahead of us, whether or not we found land. To them, this was just a great vacation.

Katherine and Ricky were both assigned their own chores to help break camp. After repeated checks of "did we forget anything?" and after the kids had revisited their favorite spots near camp, we pulled out.

We were on the move again the next morning, rolling along, looking for our dream and hoping that soon we would find what we were looking for. Or at least something close to it. We drove the hundred miles between Tok and Delta first, stopping at Moon Lake to swim awhile. Soon we found ourselves refreshed and free of Taylor Highway dust.

"Let's stay here, Mom," Ricky said, looking wistfully at me.

"Can't live in a campground the rest of our lives, Ricky. This land isn't for sale. We can't buy it. We can't live on it. Have to push on and find our own place."

After two days and much searching, we came to the conclusion that searching west was also out. Next came south. Glennallen was as far south as we cared to go. It lay 137 miles south of Tok and, again, we came up empty-handed. I'll have to admit that Dick and I were getting discouraged.

I have always been the type of person, who, no matter what the odds, does not discourage easily. Friends would first describe me as stubborn, but would later change their terminology to determined. Dick and I shared that trait, although *stubborn* usually was the better word for Dick. If we were both faced with the same brick wall, he would almost always attempt to scale it as many times as it took to get over it. I, on the other hand, might try the same scaling method, but after a few futile attempts I would be the one finding a different way of reaching the other side. And, still using that same hypothetical wall, we would both reach the other side, but more often than not, I would be waiting for him on the other side when he finally successfully breached that wall. Neither of us had given up in our objective. We just reached them differently. *Discouraged* wasn't a word either of us succumbed to very often. But at that moment, we seemed to be standing in front of another brick wall.

When you live in a place as big as Alaska all of your life, it's hard to accept the possibility that there may not be a piece of that much-loved wilderness in your future, yet that's exactly what we were beginning to think.

We decided not to go past Glennallen, because it had became more populated than we wanted. We refused to go back to Anchorage, but where now? On our way back toward Tok from Glennallen, we stopped at Broken Bridge, so named because of the old bridge that crossed the Little Tok River. It was, in reality, broken in half. We fished and caught Arctic Grayling, a member of the trout family with a high dorsal fin and it was quite good eating. The kids waded in the cold mountain water and picked up rocks. In spite of the urgency we felt, we were still enjoying ourselves.

I cooked the grayling over a campfire that night and we decided to go on into Tok the next day and ask about land. Not land available in Tok, but perhaps someone who lived there might have other land for sale that would interest us. We didn't even pitch a tent that night. The weather was beautiful, the sky cloudless.

Katherine and Ricky unrolled our sleeping mats and down bags and arranged them in a row on the ground. After a summer of all-night sunlight, we began to notice that darkness was creeping up on us. It actually got dark now at night, even a little chilly, but once inside our fluffy bags, we were snug.

I lay there staring at the night sky for a long while. Finally, I shifted a little to move a stone that had been slowly drilling its way through my sleeping mat and into my shoulder.

"You awake, Mom?" Ricky whispered.

"Yes."

"Me, too," Katherine said quietly.

"Count me in." Dick was also still awake.

"Aren't they something?" Ricky continued, "Is it true what the sourdoughs say? If I whistle will they come closer?"

"Try it and see," I said. We were talking about the northern lights — the aurora borealis. They were so brilliant tonight, how could anyone sleep?

Alaska, the scientists say, because of the northern hemisphere's auroral oval being centered about the geomagnetic North Pole, is the best place in the world to view the northern lights. Scientific data leads several directions as to their origin and cause, but physicists tell us they are an interaction of particles streaming from the sun, especially during solar storms, the earth's magnetic field, and the gases high in earth's atmosphere that cause the phenomenon known as the aurora borealis. None of this scientific explanation impresses anyone who has ever seen the northern lights in action. The lights speak for themselves.

Colors flashed above us. Yellow, red, green, purple. Wave after wave they danced across the sky. In curtain-like ripples, long spears of light shot down from the heavens with breakneck speed, then gave way to waving curtains again.

"Ooh." I heard Katherine comment in a completely awed tone.

We had all seen the northern lights many times before, but never with so much fire. With fluid mobility, they swept back and forth.

Ricky began to whistle softly. As if in response, great shafts of green light appeared in the sky.

"I can do it, too," Katherine whispered, and began to whistle with Ricky. It's only an old sourdough's tale of the north, but I swear those lights seemed to rise in brilliance at each whistle. Great sheets of color danced in a silent, fanciful fantasia as the kids whistled them ever nearer.

Dick spoke, his voice subdued, "It's not hard to see why the Indians had so many superstitions about the lights, is it?"

Suddenly, the waving curtains stopped. All around the horizon, in a 360 degree unbroken circle, was a slim band of gently waving color. Then long, thin spears began pushing upward, pulsating from this ring, growing in length and magnitude with each second.

No one spoke. No one whistled. I knew what was going to happen. I'd seen it only once in my lifetime of watching the northern lights. I was seven years old at the time, and my parents woke me in the middle of the night, wrapped me in a warm blanket, and took me outside in mid-January to watch the most spectacular show in the sky. I had never forgotten that night. Now, here it was again, twenty six years later.

"Watch," I whispered to everyone. "You'll never forget what you're going to see next."

We barely breathed as the lights continued their upward climb, reaching higher and higher, to an invisible point in the center of the sky directly above our heads. The aurora borealis was forming a gigantic cone of light. It funneled still higher. Night became bright as day.

In seconds, the pinpoint of night sky overhead was gone, completely filled with pale green light. Nowhere in view was there any night sky.

It was like being inside a gigantic, glowing funnel. The feeling we all had was electrifying, completely awe-inspiring to think that something of this magnitude was going on all around and above us. The hair on my body stood erect.

I felt privileged to witness it once more, and at the same time, reinforced my feeling of being such a small speck in this enormous universe.

"It's especially for us, you know." Dick had scooted his sleeping bag over next to mine.

"I believe it. Maybe this is a sign of good luck tomorrow?"

"Could be," he said.

The kids were speechless. It was the first time I've ever seen them without comment. Suddenly, the cone began to dissipate. As swiftly as it had formed, it was fading. The northern lights are a fickle sort, changing within seconds from brilliant spectacle to just a hint of what had been.

"Are they tired now?" Katherine questioned.

"No," I told her, "they just know we need our sleep. If they keep it up, we'll stay awake all night watching them, won't we?"

"For sure," Ricky said.

Ten minutes later the sky was dark, completely devoid of the lights. In their place were twinkling stars. Seconds more and everyone was asleep.

The next day we set up camp at Tok River. This gave us a base point to come back to. We could go into Tok, scout around, check out leads on land and return to our camp.

Tok itself was a small community of around five hundred people including outlying areas. It had a small post office, a couple of bars, two small grocery stores, several gas stations, lodges, a school, the bare necessities needed for serving a tiny community, several Indian villages and people in the bush. Situated between the Tok and Tanana Rivers and between mountain ranges, with the Alaska Range lying to its southwest, the community was built in a large, flat valley.

It was not, by Alaskan standard, a place of spectacular view or importance. The area abounds in wildlife, though. It is not uncommon to see moose at your doorstep or an occasional black bear nearby. Caribou, sheep, wolf, lynx and other small game are readily abundant.

It had been nicknamed the *Dog Capital of Alaska* for good reason. Probably more dogs than people lived in Tok. Alaska's state sport is dog mushing and Tok is a major place for sled dog breeding, training and mushing. Ironically, Tok was named for a dog, years prior to its dog mushing activities.

Tok had its beginnings as a construction camp when the United States Army began building the Alaska Highway in 1942 during World War II. A dog accompanying the men laying out the course of the highway was named Tok. Making camp for the night, they were discussing the need to name this future junction while roasting a snowshoe hare over an open fire.

The dog, much-loved by the men, anxiously awaited dinner and began pacing in anticipation of eating. Suddenly one man, noticing the pacing dog asked, "What's wrong with Tok?" The other man, not realizing the former was referring to the dog, replied, "Nothing. Tok it is," and penned in *Tok* on the map.

Today, it is the first community on the highway inside Alaska, ninety-three miles west of the Yukon border — the junction for travelers going south to Anchorage or west and north to Fairbanks.

But Dick and I had never cared much for Tok, even as many times as we had been through the area on trips to the lower forty-eight states or Canada. We didn't care for its severely cold, long, dark winters, and we weren't dog mushers. That eliminated Tok. It just never seemed like our type of spot. We checked the likely places for land ads; bulletin boards in the few businesses, and the ads in the *Mukluk News*, Tok's newspaper that was printed only twice a month. We came up with zero.

Again, we were ready to pull up stakes and press on. The problem was, where? Dick and I decided at that point we'd have to compromise and search for land beyond Glennallen and closer to Anchorage, which we didn't want to do.

Then a man told us the *Mukluk News* people had land for sale. We didn't know where it was, but we found the owners and asked them. Their name was Jacobs, and they owned part of an old homestead which they were selling off. They seemed like very straitlaced types to be living in this part of the country. I wondered what brought them to Tok and why they had stayed. *Why would anyone want to stay in this little whistle-stop?*

George Jacobs taught school. Beth did a little of everything, including editing the newspaper. They had two young children and a great big house overflowing with various projects. After Dick and I talked with them, we found out the land was not actually in Tok, it was on the outskirts, which means anything between one mile and 25 miles from the junction. It was divided into different sized parcels and there was no road blazed into it yet. The Jacobs wanted cash.

Well, that was a blow to us, but we went out and looked at the land anyway, walked it and found a spot we liked.

"It's not far enough out in the bush," I said. "It is out, but I had in mind way out, and 50 acres, not five. And certainly not in, or near Tok, of all places."

"Well, I don't think we have to worry," Dick replied. "In the first place, they want cash. In the second, we don't have near enough of that. We could offer to give them a little down and a payment each month, but Mr. Jacobs said he wants cash."

"So what now? Glennallen and beyond?"

"I guess so. This is a nice piece of land, though. I'll go by and tell them we like it, but can't pay for it. Then we'll go back to camp and tomorrow pack up everything and go on to Glennallen. Okay?"

"Fine with me, I guess."

We stopped by the Jacobs' house long enough to tell them that we liked one particular piece of their land but could only give them a low down payment and small payments each month. We wanted them to know that we were sorry for taking up their time and that we'd be leaving for elsewhere tomorrow.

Dick and I broke the news to the kids that night and told them we'd be breaking camp the next day. As I drifted off to sleep, I wondered about the good luck I'd hoped for the night we all watched the northern lights.

Next morning, nobody could seem to get moving. We were all stuck in low gear and couldn't shift into anything faster, and were in no hurry to get on the road again. I was down at the river, getting a pan of water, when a green station wagon came bumping into camp in a cloud of dust. I couldn't hear what was happening.

It was the Jacobses. I hurried to see what was going on.

"You can have the land," George was saying as he got out of the car, "low down, low payments, it's yours. I thought it over and decided to go with it."

Dick was dumbfounded. He mumbled something and the Jacobses drove off. I set the pan of water down and almost apprehensively asked what that was all about. He told me. It was my turn to be dumbfounded.

"But...he said," I stammered.

"Yeah," Dick said.

"We don't..."

"I know," he nodded.

"Tok?" I said.

"Yup, Tok."

"But...not Tok!" I wailed.

"Looks like." He said. "It's this or nothing, you know."

"But, we don't even like Tok. We can't put our roots here. We don't ... we can't, I don't think ... " I trailed off, thinking.

For a while we were both silent, yet separately drawing our own conclusions. We had been knocking our heads against that proverbial wall all summer trying to find land. We had deliberately avoided Tok. We weren't impressed with Tok. The only land available in Tok was supposed to be a cash only sale and now the owner was so happy to take a low down payment, he had driven out to tell us.

It had to be our answer. It had been thrown right into our arms. Dick and I drove to the Jacobs' house, gave them the money I had saved to buy a treadle sewing machine as the down payment and signed the papers, still wondering why we were doing it.

Now we had our own land. We could start building, set roots, make a new home, bring up our kids away from city life. It all stacked up right.

But why did it have to be Tok?

CHAPTER THREE

Now The Work Begins

Now that we actually had land of our own, the real work would have to begin immediately. Our acreage was just that — acreage — land and trees. Nothing else. There was a small clearing where we pitched our small four-man tent as temporary housing. I cooked over an open pit in the clearing, and we set up housekeeping for the first time in our married lives on our own land.

Our own land. What a beautiful ring those words have. It felt right. At last we could build a permanent home for our family. We were never able to do that in Anchorage. It wasn't supposed to be.

Our first job was to walk the land and decide where to build the cabin. We found a natural clearing almost exactly in the center of the land. It had only a few small trees and shrubs, yet it seemed to be the right spot for our cabin. Then we wound our way from the clearing to our tent, marking the trees as we went. This trail would be our driveway, and before we could begin building, we'd have to clear it to have access to the building site. Since it was already getting late, just walking the land, setting up the small tent and fixing supper was all we could do our first day.

August 20th, 1977 — the first day of the rest of our lives: a new start, a new life. Our dream, come true. Dick and I were almost too excited to sleep that night in anticipation of beginning our clearing task the next day. The kids were excited, too. This was a new adventure for all of us.

We were up early the next morning, ate breakfast, and began clearing trees for the new driveway. Dick cut the trees and limbed them, then cut the bigger ones into lengths for firewood. Katherine and Ricky helped me stack them in a nice, neat woodpile. Several of the smaller, fairly straight trees were cut into long poles and saved for future tent poles. At the end of our driveway, and in front of the cabin site, we intended to set up a larger tent. The four-man was fine for camping, but not adequate for what we now would need.

Our plans included a big, 16' x 32' army tent that we'd brought with us. It would hold all of our personal belongings, everything we had boxed up and stored in Fairbanks, all of our building tools, stoves, etc. as well as house the four of us while we built our log cabin. It would be perfect. A little rough, but perfect. The tent was big, roomy and dry. Things would work out well, we thought. By erecting it in front of the building site, everything we needed would be handy. Then, when the cabin was finished, we could simply move everything from the tent into it, collapse the tent and use the space where it had been as a driveway turnaround. We would avoid cutting any more of our precious trees than we had to by making the driveway double as the tent site as well.

It took two days to clear the trees and brush enough to actually get to the site where the cabin would be built. During that time we not only cleared the driveway, but the tent site and cabin site as well.

The kids took many breaks and loved to go off in the woods and explore. They were cautioned not to go too far and risk getting lost or running into a wild animal — always to stay within shouting distance. Ricky found spot after spot that he enthusiastically described as *neat forts*. These were places with tall trees grown close together and eight inches of soft, green moss growing on the ground beneath.

Katherine loved the squirrels. There were so many in the trees causing a constant source of chatter. She could hold bread in her hand and the squirrels would come right to her and take it. Then they would dart away to their food caches, deposit the bread and come back for more. The squirrels dug holes in the moss beneath the spruce trees and stored spruce cones, bread, nuts, apple peels, anything they could find for the coming winter. Each one had many of these pantries and when one squirrel tried to borrow from another's stash, the resulting clamor could be heard over the sound of our chain saw.

It wasn't long before Katherine grew so friendly with the little critters that she could identify most of them and call them by name. She'd scold one for taking too much bread at a time and encourage another to take an extra piece. They were busy preparing for winter just as we were, but they had a head start.

Birch trees and cottonwoods were already turning from green to gold, the nights were nippy and there was the soft rustle of leaves under our feet as we worked. In Anchorage it was still summer, but in Tok, three hundred and fifty miles farther north, it was autumn. The length of the seasons was obviously much different here. It looked as though winter might come sooner than we had expected.

Dick was tugging at the huge bulk of folded tent, trying to move it to the end of the driveway. Folded, it was at least a four foot by four foot square, one foot deep and the weight of all that heavy army canvas was too much for one man. I called to the kids.

"Katherine! Ricky! Come help. We're going to put up the big tent." They came running and we each lifted a corner and carried it to the site. Katherine's corner dragged in the dirt, but she thought she was helping, and she was just as winded as the rest of us. We began unfolding and laying it out flat, lengthwise along the direction of the driveway. It looked huge, once unfolded. Sixteen by thirty-two feet hadn't quite been a reality to me until that moment. There was lots of canvas.

We had two spruce poles already cut to length for the main support poles in the tent. This was not a tent with one center pole. It had two, one at each end, and they needed to go up simultaneously. Each pole had a long spike driven halfway into one end which would be inserted into the proper hole in the top of the tent. Dick took his pole and ducked under one end of the canvas. I took mine and did the same, and then we both had an immediate problem. Compounding the weight of all that canvas on top of us, engulfing our every movement, was the dark. The canvas was stifling, pitch black. The air hung heavy, pressing in from all sides. There was no way to see what direction we were going in to find the proper holes and position the poles.

I called to Ricky, "Grab the flashlight in the truck and bring it in to us." He lost no time. This was his chance to get in on the action, the *fun* underneath a ton of canvas. He crawled under with the light.

"Take it to Daddy's end first. Then he can help me on this end." Five minutes later, Dick's pole was up where it belonged.

"Can I come in now, Mama?" Katherine called.

"No, Baby, wait a few more minutes."

Dick held up the canvas on my end while I worked the spike into the hole, then pushed the pole upright where it stood alone.

"Yippee!" I heard Katherine squeal from outside. In seconds she was inside with us. "Boy! Big tent!" She exclaimed.

So far, all we had up were the two main poles. Now we had about two dozen smaller poles to put up along the walls for support. Each was four feet long. Dick had cut them from the driveway clearing. It took us most of the morning to finish securing all the poles and getting the guy ropes stretched out and anchored.

By lunch time it looked like a real tent, the same kind the *M.A.S.H.* people had used on television. We hadn't spiked the canvas walls down to the ground yet. They still hung free and moved with the fall breeze, but I couldn't resist a little art work. Taking a can of white spray paint, I sprayed the letters M, A, S, and H on the front panel to the left of the door. To the right I painted 4 0 7 7.

Dick laughed, but challenged, "Okay, What's that stand for? We're sure not an army unit!"

I had to think for a minute. Then, "M-A-S-H—<u>M</u>any <u>A</u>laskan <u>S</u>ourdoughs <u>H</u>ere!"

"And the 4077?"

He thought I wouldn't have an answer for that one, but I did. "There are four of us and the year is 1977!"

"Couldn't say it better myself," he said and gave me a hug. We stood gazing at the tent. I had to agree with Katherine. This really was a big tent. For the moment, we would do no more to the tent. It was up and it was dry shelter in case of rain.

The more pressing item was the cabin, so after lunch we started smoothing out the area we had cleared for the cabin. By hand, we removed stumps and roots and leveled out the high spots. The clearing itself was about twenty feet by twenty feet. Dick and I had wanted to build a big log house, but with the fall already here and winter approaching, we decided the best thing to do was build a small log cabin for the winter, then either add on to it in the spring, or build and entirely new, bigger house later and use this cabin for storage. We agreed that a sixteen foot square cabin with a partial loft in the peak would suffice. That was the plan.

While Dick and I worked on the leveling, Katherine and Ricky carried our sleeping bags from the four-man tent and put them inside the big tent, along with some of the foodstuffs, pans and utensils. The children were having fun arranging things to suit themselves. Our cat, Denali, was still attached to her mailbox home. Ricky moved her close to the tent and gave her a longer lead so she'd have more freedom but not enough to get lost. In a few days, once she was aware that this would be home, we'd let her off the leash. But not yet.

One of my favorite things I'd brought with us was a big Christmas cactus. I had bought it when it was a small plant and planted it in a big, globular goldfish bowl. Now it quite large and beautiful, and since I couldn't bear to part with it, I had lugged it all the way to Tok, taking great care to keep it healthy and unbroken. It hung in a macramaed holder inside the car. The kids were preparing to hang it inside the tent when I stopped them.

"No, no. Hang it outside on a tree," I instructed. "Let's give it all the sunshine it can drink. There's a long, dark winter ahead."

They finished hauling everything else into the tent and found a good sturdy branch for the cactus.

Dick and I felt pretty good about things that night, satisfied with a good day's work and the progress we'd made. The kids were excited about spending the night in the big tent. They had carefully arranged all four sleeping bags inside on the soft tundra. When Dick and I finally turned in that night, Katherine and Ricky had already been in their sleeping bags for several hours. Not asleep, just inside the bags, playing pretend games and talking. All the while we had been busy working outside in the twilight, we could hear their happy laughter inside the tent. *Oh, yes,* I thought, *this is a big, fun, adventure to them. They love it!*

We snuggled into our bags nestled on the ground, almost lost in the soft moss. It was more comfortable than the most expensive bed. I watched Dick in his bag beside me. He was so big, his sleeping bag looked like a half-bag on him. His huge barrel chest and gigantic arms stuck out of the top of it. To fully cover himself, he used a blanket on his upper half. He moved closer to me, gave me a kiss and enveloped me in his arms. The kids were still giggling. Dick's breathing became heavier and heavier as he progressed further into sleep. Finally, he was snoring and the kids were quiet. I buried my face in his big chest as it gently rose and fell and I soon drifted peacefully off to sleep.

I awoke the next morning to the smell of musty tent and moist tundra, and cold.

"Boy, Mom," Ricky was joking, "someone turned off the heat!"

It was true. In spite of the bright sun streaming through the vent of the tent roof, it was cold.

I wiggled out of the bag and grabbed my clothes, then threw open the tent door. Overnight, the season had changed. It was no longer summer going into fall. Now, suddenly, it was fall going into winter. The ground, the grass, weeds wildflowers, a pan full of water, were all frozen hard. And my beautiful cactus was still beautiful, but shiny and hard. It looked as though it had been made of delicate green glass. I shook my head. As soon as the air warmed a little, it would thaw and wilt. It was already too late. If only I'd let the kids bring it inside. Ricky was as sad about it as I was. He liked plants and thought that one was especially neat.

"Well," I told him, "we'll have to get a new one when we finish the cabin. Okay? A new plant for our new home."

The next week was spent entirely on the cabin site, clearing and leveling and digging out the tundra. We were going to build the cabin on short pilings set in the ground, but the pilings had to rest on gravel, not earth, to prevent rot.

Because Tok is located in a valley, an ancient riverbed, the surface tundra and dirt is not very thick, a foot or two at the most. It's wonderful as a base for building and the area has excellent drainage.

We dug holes for the wooden pilings, put them in place and leveled them. Since we didn't want to use our own trees for the logs, we scouted the outlying areas for good log trees. Fifteen or 20 miles on the other side of Tok were some nice trees, tall and straight, just right for our cabin logs. They stood in a thick stand and we would consider them ours. So began our daily trips to cut trees for logs.

Dick always sized up a tree before beginning to cut. Was it straight? How big was its base? A tree too big in diameter meant that we couldn't handle it. Too small at the base meant an even skinnier tree at the top. It couldn't have too great a taper in it either. Did the top split? If so it was no good. Was it too far from the truck?

Once cut, Dick and I would have to lift this log to our shoulders and carry it to the truck. Did it have an over abundance of limbs? If so, we would waste time limbing it. Excess knots more than likely meant a crooked log once the bark was peeled away. Did it lean? If it did, the log would probably be twisted or bent dramatically. A twisted log is hard to use. He took all of these questions into consideration before cutting a tree. Obviously, not just any tree would do. If it measured up, he'd first notch it on the side we wanted it to fall on, then cut through from the opposite side.

As soon as the tree hit the ground, I started at its base with an ax. Walking on, and up the tree, I swung the ax with a deftness that surprised me every time I did it, limbing both sides of the tree as I went. Dick measured the length we needed and cut the tree into a log. We usually got two short logs from each tree. Most of our logs were six to eight inches thick. Anything less than that wasn't worthwhile. We didn't want skinny, thin walls. Anything larger was too hard to handle.

A six-to eight-inch log, twenty to fourteen feet long, doesn't look very heavy laying on the ground, but trying to lift is was another story. The full weight of that, just-a-few-minutes-ago living tree, suddenly becomes hard, heavy reality. These were green spruce trees and much heavier than a dead tree or a log that had been allowed to dry.

Dick always positioned himself on the bigger end of the logs and I took the other. We'd stand with it on our right sides, bend down and on the count of three, simultaneously lift the log to our waists. Then, one, two, and lift it onto our right shoulders, where it would rest while we carried it to the truck. There was always too much brush, moss or stumps around to drag our logs out. We had to shoulder them. And more often than not, at the very spot where it rested on our shoulders, there would be a big knot or piece of limb to dig into the bone. Dick was tough and had lots of padding, but my right shoulder was always black and blue and very sore.

The first round of logs we needed had to be very long and each had to be in one piece. We couldn't splice them because these were to be the bottom row. The very foundation of our cabin. They would rest on the pilings. Each log needed to be twenty five feet long to allow for the cabin size and notching. They were a little bigger, thicker, than the rest of the logs would be. The biggest ones would be used for the bottom. By the time Dick and I had shouldered and loaded two of them, we were too tired to cut and shoulder the other two, so we decided to cut them the next day. He finished cutting the tops of these first trees into firewood lengths and loaded them into the truck.

We never wasted a tree. Dick and I always figured that if our beloved Alaska was being good enough to supply us with the trees we needed, the very least we could do was not waste what she was giving us. What wasn't suitable for building logs became firewood.

It was slow driving home. Only ten feet of the logs were contained in the truck bed. The other 15 feet stuck out behind, and had a tendency to bounce out when going over a frost heave. The firewood helped to anchor them but it wasn't enough. I got out and rode in back, sitting on top of the logs and firewood and being careful not to let my fingers, toes, or hindquarters get pinched in the process.

Donna Blasor-Bernhardt

Once home, the base logs were pulled from the truck, one by one with log tongs. Dick and I each held a side of the tong handles and pulled hard. Then we lifted the first one into the log cradle.

The cradle stood waist high. Dick built it from scrap, rough-cut lumber and deliberately designed it with a few advantages in mind. It would hold, yet not interfere with the log while being peeled. It was low enough to lift a log onto without straining too hard, yet high enough to prevent excess bending or stooping while using a drawknife.

The drawknife was the tool we used to peel our logs. It was the most efficient tool for us. Once we got used to using it as a team, we could strip a log of its bark in no time. Usually I did most of the peeling, though. Dick spent his time pondering the next cut, or round of logs, sizing up what to do next, or using his ever-perfect *level eye* to make sure things were building on an even keel.

I didn't mind the peeling; in fact, I really enjoyed it. For me, it was the easiest thing involved with the building of the cabin and it gave me time to think quietly while working, or listen to the birds, or the kids, or just enjoy life. The logs were green and they peeled easily. I loved those logs. Each time I reached forward, sank in the drawknife and pulled it toward me, I got a fresh spray of pitch. Usually it went all over my shirt or down vest, which eventually looked as though it had been varnished. The smell of fresh pitch is wonderful. It is fresh, invigorating, and even the bittersweet flavor does not offend the tastebuds. More than once the kids and I picked a piece of the sweet, juicy inner bark and chewed it like gum.

Each log revealed its own character as it was peeled. Some had beautiful *cat faces* — places where, as a young tree, it had been injured and healed itself. One of the first logs we peeled had what looked like a perfect beaver's face. The grain of the logs revealed their history. We learned which ones had grown fast, which ones had not. Some were crowded on one side. Their rings were lopsided. Forest-fire scars were there to be seen, as well as old injuries where animals had chewed into them as saplings. Even the colors of the wood varied with its own lifestyle.

Knots were pretty, too. Some of them, once smoothed even with the surface of the log, took on human characteristics. They looked like a nose or an ear or a clown's face. One was a perfect silhouette of a mallard duck.

Each log was an individual, each with its own history to be shared with us. Dick, the kids and I became one with them. Our paths had crossed. We would share histories now. Katherine and Ricky had great fun using their imaginations with all the natural art work around them. Some real *whale* stories came out of those funny-looking knots.

After peeling the two base logs, we had to let them dry a little. They were quite wet, indeed slick, with their own juices oozing from them. The sun and wind helped to dry their surfaces quickly and soon we were able to work with them.

Dick had been busy checking the log pilings, making sure they were level, and pouring a mixture of oil and diesel fuel all over and around them, completely saturating their wood pores. This, in turn, would prevent them from rotting, at least in our lifetime.

We carried one base log, now much lighter because the weight of the bark was gone, and set it into place, then set the other in place. Dick spiked them down using three-eights inch by twelve inch spikes. He drove the spikes all the way through the logs and into the piling with a sledge hammer while I sat on the log, straddling it and holding it to prevent it from twisting or rolling. He continued pounding the spikes until each was driven and countersunk at least an inch. Because the logs were green, they would shrink as they dried. Countersinking would allow for this.

We stood back and viewed our handiwork in the twilight of the evening. The first two real logs were in place on our future home. We had the beginnings of an east and west wall.

CHAPTER FOUR

First Day Of School

The first day of school came too quickly. *Where had the summer gone?* Now it was time for school again. Ricky would be in fifth this year. And Katherine, our baby, was entering first grade.

Fall was upon us. Outside, I could hear the rustle of gold and brown cottonwood leaves. The tent was without heat, causing me to shiver a little when I woke the kids.

"School today! Rise and try to shine!" Their enthusiasm wasn't the greatest and I couldn't blame them. Just crawling out of a sleeping bag in a not-too-warm tent was a chore. For Ricky it meant a new school, new faces, making new friends. He hadn't yet met any of the other children living in Tok. Ricky was our loner. Never needing lots of friends, yet always having plenty. He was well liked and had made many friends in Anchorage without even trying, but he had misgivings. Always misgivings. Today would be hard for him.

Katherine rolled over, opened one eye while pushing blond hair from her soft face and studied me. Through the haze of a six year old's sleepy thinking, today was finally soaking in.

"School?" She questioned. "Ricky!" Suddenly coming alive, it had hit her. "Ricky!" Louder this time. "Get up! We get to go to school today!"

That was our girl. She had waited so long for this day, she could barely contain herself.

"Do I get to take a lunch, too, Mama?"

"Sure, you both do."

They scrubbed off the night's tent dust that had settled on their faces, dressed and were ready for breakfast. That took some doing for Ricky. He was not in a hurry to go anywhere.

"Do I hafta go?" He pleaded. "Just take her and I'll stay here." He thought for a minute. "I'll do anything you want. I'll even peel logs. They don't need me at school. You need me here to help you, right?"

"Wrong. Eat your eggs." While he hadn't yet stirred, and both eyes were still closed, Dick had quit snoring and I'd known for some time that he was awake and listening. He rolled over and eye-balled Ricky.

"You're going to school today and like it or not, make friends. It's easy. Just walk up to somebody, say, 'Hi, I'm Ricky. I live in a tent,' and Bingo, you've got a new friend. Case closed."

Was Archie Bunker living with us this morning? I wondered.

"Mama," Katherine said again, "I really don't want a man teacher. They're mean. Could I have a lady instead?"

Her big blue eyes were serious. I'd found out weeks before that the first-grade teacher was a man. Tok's school had one teacher for each grade. Some of the classes were quite small. All grades were in the one building, right up through high school. First grade was a big class though.

"What makes you think men teachers are mean?" I asked her.

"Ricky says!" Katherine answered without blinking.

I shot Ricky a glance. He was too busy snickering to see it.

"I was just kidding," he said, still laughing. "They're not too bad. They don't spank the girls, just the boys."

Katherine breathed an audible sigh of relief.

He went on, "They just lock the girls in a closet all day!"

"Mama!"

"Knock it off, Ricky," we heard from Dick's corner. "How would you know? You've never had a man teacher." He looked at

Katherine. "Just never mind what he says, honey. Listen to your mama."

"Can I come home if he's mean, Mama?"

"Sure, but he won't be, you'll see."

They finished eating and I decided to take their pictures outside the tent before we left. I had to record this great event in their lives. With sack lunches in hand, they stood in front of the tent while I told them to smile. Ricky looked like such a big little man. *Katherine was just a baby*, I *thought, now she's standing here in her granny dress ready for school.*

"Do I get any last requests before sentencing?" Ricky asked.

"Ricky!" His daddy warned.

"Just joking, Dad. Honest."

The truck was strangely quiet as we drove to town. Neither of the kids had much to say. We pulled in front of the school building. Other children were getting off buses, laughing and talking. We walked into the school, found the office and I registered them. Ricky rolled and re-rolled his sack lunch a hundred times. Katherine sat with her legs dangling, neck stretched, trying to see into the room across the hall.

The office lady spoke, "Erik..."

I broke in, "We've never called him Erik, though it is his real name. He goes by Ricky."

"Ricky will have Miss Culver, right down there on the right." She continued, "Kathy..."

"My name is Kath-er-ine," Katherine pointedly corrected her.

I explained that we had never nicknamed her Kathy, but always called her by her real name.

"Katherine's teacher will be Mr. Wothke. His room is right over there. The one with the animals in it."

"Oh, boy! Animals!" Then, silence. "Mama, it *is* a man teacher."

The lady spoke again, "Oh you'll like him. All the children love him."

Katherine looked doubtful. "Look," I said to her, "if you don't like him after you meet him, you come to this office and the lady will telephone me. I'll come pick you up. Okay?"

"Okay."

We walked Ricky to his new room and met his teacher. She was nice. Ricky took an instant liking to her and even seemed pleased with himself.

He told Katherine, "Now you know where my room is. Meet me here after school and we'll get on the bus together. Don't go anywhere else. Just come straight here. Got it?" This was certainly not the same impish Ricky I had seen bugging his little sister in the tent. Now he was protective.

He watched as I walked with Katherine to her classroom. It was already full of kids. This was a big class. I counted twenty-eight, Katherine would make twenty-nine. Mr. Wothke came to the door and we introduced ourselves.

"Do you like animals?" He spoke gently to Katherine, then taking her by the hand, he led her into the classroom while I stood and watched.

"Class," he spoke softly, but with conviction, "this is Katherine Bernhardt. She's new in Tok and we'd like to be her friend."

She looked at me and blew a kiss. It never occurred to her that because we were living in the tent that we didn't have a telephone.

I cried all the way home.

CHAPTER FIVE

Just An Ordinary September

Dick had the chain saw and logging tape ready and waiting when I got home. We went back to our logging operations.

"This one looks real good," he said, more to himself than to me. He notched and felled the tree. This tree was to provide the third base log of our cabin. While I limbed it, he selected another tree for the fourth log.

"Timber! Heads up!" He yelled at me. I stood, ax in hand, watching it fall. The trees always went exactly where Dick wanted them to fall. I finished limbing and moved to the newly fallen tree while Dick began measuring and cutting the third log to length.

"These look a little bigger than the first two," I commented. "Heavier."

"Yeah, I need them to be big for the other two walls." He finished the logs and cut the tree tops into firewood which I stacked in the truck.

"Well, let's do it. Ready?"

I nodded. My shoulder was black and blue from the day before. I wondered how it would look after today. One, two, we heaved the log to our shoulder and carried it to the truck.

"Just between us, "I said, panting, "that's about the maximum I can shoulder."

"Piece of cake," he said sweating. We returned for the other log, got ready to position ourselves.

"Time out," I said, "Mother Nature calls. I'll be back in a jif."

I returned just in time to see Dick hoist the last base log to his shoulder, alone, and crumple under its weight. He went right to his knees with the log still on his shoulder. Pain crossed his face. I shouted, afraid for whatever part of him was hurt.

"Back," he said, "my back."

Then rage began to grow inside me. "Can't turn my back on you long enough to go to the bathroom, can I? That was dumb. Just plain stupid! Who do you think you are? King Kong? What made you try something like that? Don't you know better?" I was almost crying in both rage and fear for him.

He was still on his knees. "Thought I could manage it. Save you from lifting it. Oohhh," he moaned.

Anger left me. Concern crept in.

"Help me get back up."

I began to roll the big log off his shoulder. "No!" He shouted. "Can't. Can't pick it up again. Get under it and help me get back on my feet. Got to load it in the truck." I knew better than to argue. His bull-headedness was showing again. We managed to load it in the truck bed. I knew he was hurting, but he wouldn't admit it. The grimace on his face all the way back to the tent was evidence enough.

Dick decided he'd had enough for that day. I was glad. I knew he'd had enough. Unceremoniously, we dumped the logs out of the truck and he spent the rest of the day taking it easy. I didn't have to talk hard to make him lie down and relax.

The next day, he insisted that he felt better. We peeled and spiked the remaining base logs. Now we had one round on all four walls. I could tell Dick wasn't completely all right, though he never said anything. We used the next couple of days for other projects.

"Got to have an outhouse," Dick said. We decided on a *quickie*. Something to get us through the winter; a more elaborate establishment could be built next summer. I dug as far down as I could with a shovel and just wide enough to slide a 55-gallon barrel into the hole. Dick had cut both ends out of the barrel. This was the casing for the hole. After I reached on barrel's depth, the kids took over. I no longer had room to bend over and maneuver in the hole, so the kids used a gallon can, handing it out of the hole for us to dump. They dug down one more barrel's depth.

"Hi, ho! Hi, ho! It's digging down we go," Ricky sang from the bottom of the hole. "Look at all the pretty rocks down here!"

"Cold, Mama," came Katherine's voice from inside the hole. She was *helping* mostly by getting in Ricky's way. He lifted her out to me.

"Yes, of course it's cold," I explained. "It's always cold in a hole, especially in this country. Makes a good refrigerator, though. We'll have to remember that, won't we?"

Dick welded the two barrels end-to-end and we lowered the culvert into the ground. He had been busy fashioning a platform to go over it and had already attached the *throne*.

Indeed, that's just what we christened it. A metal stool sitting on a wooden platform, in the bushes, with no house over it. No more appropriate name could exist. There would be no time wasted on the *house* part of our outhouse. It would sit, or rather *we* would sit, exposed to the elements, at least until next summer. We had what was necessary. I wondered about that metal seat, though. It was going to be mighty uncomfortable in cold weather.

There are always days when everything seems to go wrong. The next day was one of those. Denali was still on her leash attached to the mailbox. I figured a couple more days and we would let her loose. By then, she should know this was home, be accustomed to the sound of the chain saw and not run away.

I was less than 100 feet away from her and the mailbox when I turned and noticed two big, strange dogs approaching. One she might be able to handle, but not two. They were smart. The first dog, the one she could see, was approaching from the front. But the other was sneaking in to attack from behind.

I grabbed a shovel and my feet flew into motion, screaming as I ran. Too late. With her attention drawn to the first dog, she never saw the second one.

The dog leaped over her mailbox and sank his teeth deep into Denali's back, giving her one vicious, hard shake before I split his skull with the back of the shovel.

Dick had already grabbed his rifle and quickly finished both dogs. I swept Denali up in my arms. Her eyes were wide and black with fear. She hissed at me.

"Denali," I spoke softly to her. Recognition came through her fear. She relaxed in my arms. She was bleeding very badly. Her heart was racing. The worst part was, she lay paralyzed. The dog had either broken her back or neck. She looked like she was in horrible pain. The kids were staring in shock.

Denali looked at me pathetically. Knowing she was safe, she attempted to purr. Only a soft gurgle emitted from her bloody mouth. Mercifully, she took one last breath and died in my arms. I cried. Everyone cried. Even Dick.

Katherine and Ricky put Denali in a shoe box. "We're gonna bury her, Mom," Ricky informed me.

"That's good. We'll find a good spot," I sniffed.

"With lots of flowers," Katherine said sadly.

"Lots."

After finding just the right place for Denali, we buried her, mounding the dirt high. The kids piled rocks on the dirt. Special, hand-picked rocks. Ordinary ones wouldn't do. Denali wasn't an ordinary cat. She was a gentle, loving creature, a calico the color of the sun setting on Mt. McKinley. The kids had done a fine job. Afterward, we transplanted wildflowers between the rocks.

To break up our sadness, which seemed to hang over all four of us, Dick announced we would be going to Fairbanks the next day. "Gotta go, might as well do it and get it over with. Need to get our wood stove, tools and stuff stored there."

"Okay," I said, not too enthusiastically. We really needed our wood stove, but we figured it would take four trips to Fairbanks to haul home all of our things that were stored there. Not exactly an exciting prospect; four trips to Fairbanks, I mused. I couldn't have been more wrong.

One trip took a lot of hassling and money. We discovered that the storage company personnel were experienced rip-off artists. Everything had been prepaid when it left Anchorage. Freight, storage for the duration, everything. But on our fourth and last trip, we were hit with another bill. They said there had been a mistake. We had not been charged enough to begin with.

"Not charged enough!" Dick was blowing his cork.

"I'm sorry, sir, but until we have eight hundred more, nothing else leaves the storage area," the wimp behind the counter said.

"I oughta break you in half," Dick was fuming. "I wanta' see the manager."

"I *am* the manager."

"Then I'll see the owner. I'll straighten him out."

"Sorry, sir, the owner is in Hawaii, on vacation for a couple of months."

"Probably spending some other poor bastard's money he's ripped off," Dick spewed.

I was afraid he might pull the man across the counter.

"We got to have our wood stove. We're living in a tent. My family needs heat!" Dick's eyes merged into one. It was a strange metamorphosis that always took place when he was really angry. He looked like a giant, hulking cyclops.

"Not 'til I see eight hundred dollars."

"I'll stick it up your..."

Just then the telephone rang. The little man reached for it. Dick turned to me, trying to resume some portion of calm. "We're up a creek. How much we got left in the bank?"

"Six something," I did some mental figuring.

"It'll have to do."

The little man returned to the counter.

"I've got six hundred. You either take it and like it or I'll wipe you all over the floor," Dick threatened. Dick was not a small man and could very well have done it.

"Sounds reasonable," the little man croaked. "Just make the check out to me."

Dick and I looked at each other. This rotten little man had quite a racket going on here.

"On second thought, honey, we're not paying *Mr. Cool*, here, anything."

"Oh dear, Mr. Bernhardt," Mr. Cool said, simpering, "I think we might have misplaced your stove. It could take months to find."

"It's insured," Dick bellowed, almost gleefully. "If you lose it, you pay for it!"

"Well, that may be true, but we may be looking at months of paperwork." The scam man was enjoying the situation. He had us right where he wanted us.

Dick slammed his fist on the counter, holding the crumpled check. A tray of papers vibrated off the end and scattered on the floor. "Here's your dirty money, scum bag. Choke on it." He whirled and marched out the door.

Scumbag was waiting at the warehouse. Dick pushed him aside saying, "Get in my way and it'll be the last time. Got it? You got me mad now. Don't push it." He shoved him against the wall, then let him drop. "You're just one of the reasons we left the city. Don't mess with me." His cyclops face emerged once again.

"Get him, Dad!" Ricky was shouting from the truck. I shot him an *or else* look. He rolled up the window.

The stove weighed four hundred pounds. Dick headed toward the forklift sitting on the floor.

"Cost ya fifty more bucks." The worm was getting real stupid and greedy. I wondered how much longer Dick's patience would last.

I was afraid he might end up spending the night in the Fairbanks jail at that point, but Dick swaggered up to him, both thumbs curled under his suspenders. "Tell ya what, Creep. I'm gonna use that forklift to load my stove for free. If you as much as whimper, I'm gonna give you fifty days in the hospital, if you're lucky." It looked as if smoke might be coming out of his ears.

The creep must have known he'd pushed Dick enough and was risking a great deal. He never said another word. Dick loaded the stove with no more trouble and we left, with me letting out a big sigh of relief, Dick grumbling in his beard and Ricky pouting because there hadn't been a fight.

Our last stop before leaving was to McDonald's. There we treated the kids to burgers and french fries, a luxury they hadn't had for months.

It was refreshing getting back onto the highway, heading home to sanity. All the way home we watched flock after flock of geese, ducks and swans flying south for the winter.

Once home, we unloaded everything, including the stove. It was not easy manhandling it out of the truck and into the tent. It was about all Dick and I could manage. Once inside, we quickly put up the chimney, threw some wood into it and tried it out, making sure everything worked properly before nightfall. That night it was nice and cozy in the tent for the first time.

The next few days were spent shuffling back and forth to the local sawmill, picking out rough-cut lumber for the cabin floor. It wasn't cut to any standard lengths and each plank tapered badly on the ends, so we spent a lot of time trimming and cutting each board to a usable length.

Dick and I were busy nailing the floor framework together and fitting it inside the four base logs when the commotion began. Great squawks were issuing from the sky directly overhead.

"Mama! Daddy!" the kids were shouting, "Look at them!"

Directly over the cabin were large flocks of geese. They weren't flying their regular V formation. Instead, each separate flock was circling at different altitudes and making a great deal of noise. We watched as they seemed to be giving each other instructions, shouting and calling. Soon, in the distance, we heard another flock moving our way, and another and another.

Katherine and Ricky were dumbstruck. "Are they lost, Mama?" Katherine questioned.

"No, just regrouping. See the storm clouds they just came through? Must have been bad enough to separate some of their groups. These above us are flying in circles, waiting for the others to catch up." For more than half an hour, hundreds of geese circled above us. It was quite a sight. Finally, they regrouped into big flying "V's," and headed south, leaving us all with a sense of urgency.

Winter was on its way. I've often heard people talk of the quiet wilderness. Ours has never been quiet. The squirrels chattered day in and day out, busily gathering winter supplies. A woodpecker was forever hammering his beak against dead trees. He became a regular visitor to our log pile, searching out bugs and bark beetles and living in a big, dead snag not far from the tent. At night, our friend the owl hooted the darkness away. No, I've never been in a quiet wilderness. It has noises of its own.

Dick interrupted my thoughts. "I think I've about had it for today," he said.

I looked at him. He didn't look too good. "Feel all right?"

"Naw. Guess I'm just tired. Feel sort of sapped out."

I called the kids and set them to gathering kindling. Dick spent that evening just doing some mental figuring and building inside his head. I could see he didn't feel well.

By morning, the storm clouds had moved in on us. Rain was beating down on the tent roof. I was thankful we had a roof. It was miserable outside. Dick was miserable inside. He had the flu and was very sick After the kids went to school, I straightened up inside the tent a bit. Dick was too sick to work efficiently, so I talked him into staying in his sleeping bag and try to regain his strength.

Then the wind started. Blowing rain. Cold, blowing rain. I stoked the wood stove. The wind and rain increased and began blowing into the tent. We hadn't yet anchored the canvas walls to the ground. They hung free and now the rain was literally being hurled into the tent while the walls flapped. Everything in his bag, including Dick, would be wet if it continued. One look at the sky assured us that we were in for the duration of the storm. There was only one thing to do; go outside and anchor the walls.

I pulled on my jacket, grabbed a handful of spikes and the hand maul and glumly stepped out the door. Wind swept my long hair across my face. I wiped it back. Systematically, I spiked down the first flap, then the second, and next the third, as rain needles drove into the back of my neck. I was already soaked to the skin. The temperature was dropping. My fingers were stiffening. Now the rain was freezing on everything it touched. I shivered, rubbed my hands together and spiked the fourth flap. I wiped my face. Rain was dripping off my bangs, freezing on my eyelashes. A gust of wind caught the next flap, whipping it into my cold cheek with a loud snap. "Damn, that hurt!" I cursed.

"Nasty bit of weather, hey?"

I jumped, startled by the voice. Looking up through rain-bleary eyes I saw a figure. I stood up, my knees muddy from kneeling on the ground.

"Huh?"

"Nasty weather, I said."

"Yeah." I wasn't particularly happy to see him. He was a preacher from one of the churches in Tok. On several occasions he had come out, trying to get us to go to his church, and we had, twice. But we needed to get our cabin finished and his church didn't seem right for us. Still, he kept trying.

I grabbed another spike and pounded it into the wet ground.

"Where's Dick?"

As if in answer, I could hear him throwing up inside the tent.

"Sick, got the flu. Really sick. High fever, chills, miserable," I said, involuntarily shivering. "Go on in and see him."

The preacher stood there a minute, weighing my words. "Think I'll pass. Don't want to get sick myself!"

I went ahead pounding spikes. My fingers felt like clubs in the wet cold. The preacher shifted a little, then stepped up onto a log just as I swung at yet another spike and missed. I was watching him and not what I was doing. Missing the spike, I hit and mashed my index finger.

"Yeeoww!" I howled, grabbing the injured finger. I was injured and mad. What made me even madder was the fact that he was standing on a newly peeled log with his muddy boots. That log was our future wall and he was getting it muddy. And I told him so.

"Oh, just trying to keep my feet dry," he replied.

"Look," I said, "I've gotta go in and warm up. I'm freezing."

"Well, I just wanted to invite you to church next Sunday and salvage your soul. See you later."

I tromped inside and stuck another log in the stove, warming my hands inside the firebox as I did so. Dick turned over in his bag. His eyes had dark circles under them. "Who was that?"

"Stupid preacher, again."

"What did he want?"

"Same thing," I replied, exasperated.

"You're wet. What have you been doing?" I told him I had half the tent walls spiked. Still had half to go. "Did he offer to help you?"

"Nope."

"City slicker. And he calls himself a Christian. Preacher at that! Did he know I'm sick?"

"Yep. He didn't want to catch your bug."

"Figures," Dick said sarcastically.

"Well," I pointed out, "we started into this ourselves. Never figured on anyone helping us, did we?"

"No, by god, and it looks like no matter what, that's the way it's gonna be."

I figured he was probably right. We were loners anyway.

CHAPTER SIX

Two New Bernhardt's

Fitting all those different boards together for a good, usable surface was tedious piecework. Dick and I were working on the cabin floor. We'd lay a row of planks that fit right, mix-or-match fashion. He would hammer one or two nails into each one and go on to sorting out boards for the next row while I finished nailing down the previous row. It was a good, efficient system.

The only problem we were having was snow. Overnight, the freezing rain turned to the white stuff, making it difficult to lay a floor with several inches of snow all over everything. We kept at it diligently, and in one long day, completed the cabin floor. Now this was progress. Even Katherine and Ricky thought it was great and joined in the festivities that night at supper. We toasted each other with paper cups of Kool-Aid.

"Boy," Ricky praised, "before long we'll have a cabin!"

"Thought you liked this tent," I said dramatically, sweeping my arms from side to side.

"Oh, it's neat for a fort, Mama!"

I winked at Dick when he replied, "Guess we're living in a fort!"

Sun was shining through the ceiling vent early the next morning. Not much warmth, but it was cheerful anyway. The snow had all but disappeared.

Everyone was awake, but no one had crawled out of the sleeping bags yet. I wriggled out of mine and threw a log in the stove. It felt like a beautiful morning. Things had to go right today. It just felt good. I stretched, limbering up some sore muscles, and walked over to the door, threw it open to let in more sunlight, then stood in amazement.

Sitting in front of the door was the most beautiful Siamese cat I'd ever seen. She had the biggest blue eyes. She just sat there, blinking at me, her head tilted to one side.

"Well, good morning," I said to her. She blinked at me again. "Where did you come from?"

"Where did 'who' come from?" Dick asked.

"A beautiful Siamese cat, just sitting here politely almost like she's waiting to be invited inside."

Now the kids were up. Mention an animal and they're all ears.

"She's blind!" Katherine wailed.

"No, just cross-eyed. They're supposed to be that way."

"How can she see? I can't," Katherine said, crossing her own eyes.

"They're gonna get stuck that way," Ricky teased. "See what happened to that cat when she did it?"

"Okay, okay," I warned.

The cat swished her tail. "Well, do come in," I said to her. She stood up proudly and walked inside as though that's just what she had been waiting to hear.

"Well, that beats all," Dick said, leaning out of his bag.

She inspected the inside of the tent, then settled on Dick's sleeping bag.

"Oh, boy!" the kids said in unison. "We've got us another cat!"

"The Lord taketh away and then He giveth," I thought to myself.

Our new resident was, of course, the center of attention for the rest of the day. She was also quite comical. Obviously, she was a city cat and until now had never walked in tundra. With every step she took, she would shake each paw, giving her the appearance of having some strange affliction. And she was grossly overweight. We discovered she didn't know the first thing about hunting. The squirrels scared her at first, and she couldn't climb a tree. She tried, but was a complete klutz until she got the hang of it.

We conjectured that she must have gotten lost from a camper on the Alaska Highway and found her way to our tent. Maybe she had spent her life in a penthouse apartment. She wouldn't touch cat food. No, that was definitely not her style. Fried chicken was her specialty.

The kids named her Criss-Cross, which we shortened to Chris. Dick just referred to her affectionately as the Jerk because, as he pointed out, it fit her better. We set out a bowl of dry cat food and milk for her, but it was weeks before she *lowered* herself and began eating it. And she lost plenty of weight, too. I'm surprised she stayed with us, but, stay she did, and she became an excellent mouser.

Within a week another four-legged animal became a member of the Bernhardt household. It happened one evening while Dick and I were grocery shopping in one of Tok's two small stores.

The owner, Mike Crozier, was one of the first friends we had made in Tok. He and I had known each other prior to Tok, sort of. Having recently purchased the store, he too, had moved from Anchorage. Upon comparing notes, I learned that he had been a swimmer at the same pool where I had worked. He remembered seeing me there. I didn't remember Mike, but I had graduated from high school in the same class with his sister.

I had just placed a gallon of milk and a loaf of bread on the check-out counter while Dick was fumbling for change.

"What you guys need is a dog," Mike was saying.

"That's just what we don't need," I heard Dick answer.

"What? What don't we need?" I asked, slowly coming out of my own thoughts.

"A dog. Mike says we need a dog."

"No," I found myself answering almost too quickly, "we do not need a dog."

Mike continued, "Not just any dog, the right dog."

"There isn't a right dog," Dick said. "We just plain don't need a dog. Got enough problems without asking for more."

"But, the right dog would be great protection for the tent, and the kids would love it. Kids really do need a dog. What is the big deal about a dog all of a sudden, Mike?" I shouldn't have asked.

"Well, uh ..come here a minute..." Mike's words trailed behind him as he left the counter and headed to the back room. Dick and I gave each other a questioning look and followed.

Mike took us through the back door and outside. A huge bear-like ball of fur was curled up near a trash can. In an instant the fur ball was happily wiggling its body around our feet, making little puppy noises and melting my heart. I bent down. Kneeling, my face was on the same level as the puppy's. A warm, wet tongue licked my cheek.

"Oh, no," I heard Dick groan.

"God," I heard a strange voice that sounded a lot like mine say, "he's so cute!"

"Oh, great..." Dick again.

"Oh, just look at him! He's all fur, and he's so big. He's just a pup, but he's enormous. And look at the size of those feet! Isn't he great?" The pup and I were already friends. I looked up at Dick.

"Don't look at me with those big baby blues. You just said yourself we don't need a dog." I could see in Dick's face that he liked the pup but wanted me to talk us both out of it. Then he bent down. The big hairy puppy gave Dick a loving slurp. Nothing else could have, so instantly, caught both our hearts that moment.

"Whose is he?" I asked Mike.

Mike was already grinning from ear-to-ear. He'd thrown out a line. We were nibbling at the bait. "Yours," he said with conviction.

"Uh, uh, and no thanks, Mike," Dick said.

"Just look at him." Mike replied. "He likes you guys, and he fits you. You need a big dog. He's gonna be a big one. MacKenzie River Husky. He'll be a good dog."

"Mike," I asked, "where did you get him?"

"Awww, that's the sad part," he said, sinking the hook. "He's a stray. Been hanging around the store for a week. He's hungry, so I've been feeding him. He stays around; sleeps out here at night. I figure somebody discovered they didn't have the right paperwork to take him through Canadian customs on their way outside, so they brought him back to Tok and dumped him."

"Poor little fellah," Dick said softly.

Mike started reeling us in, "Sorry a lot of people do that, but it happens. He sure does need a good home."

"Yeah, he does," I rubbed the pup's furry back.

"Mike, we need a dog like I need a hole in my head," Dick was weakly protesting. Then, "Besides, we'd have to feed him. I can't afford that. We're gonna have a hard enough time as it is. He's sure a great-looking dog, though." Dick was definitely softening.

The line had been baited and cast, the hook securely set, the reeling almost completed.

"Take him home and I'll supply you with free dog food for the winter." Mike had just landed us.

We returned to the tent with a gallon of milk, a loaf of bread, one happy pup and two one-hundred pound bags of dog food.

The kids were ecstatic. Within hours he had been christened Yukon Von Hairy. He sniffed out the tent, then found a spot outside and curled up for the night.

I could hear both Dick and the pup snoring as I turned out the lamp and crawled into my sleeping bag. Double snores, the kids softly breathing, Chris purring on Dick's cot. I snuggled warmly into the down of the bag and relaxed, staring into the dark. What more could anyone want?

CHAPTER SEVEN

Winter ... Too Early

Dick's birthday, October 2, was one of preparation and pre-planning for more logging.

"We've done everything we can do without logs." Dick was sitting on his cot sharpening the chain saw. He continued talking while sharpening. "And we've sure wasted enough time with me being sick! Time is getting drastically short. There's a first snow on the ground. We're at a standstill without logs. Time's a-wasting, my Lady!" He pulled me down on his cot and kissed me.

"Happy birthday, my Love," I said giving him an extra big birthday hug, "but no logs today, all right? Give yourself an extra day. Ease into it. Call it a birthday present, Okay? We can just go out and cut up firewood."

I sat there gazing at my big mountain of a man. I loved him more every year, every day. "My gosh," I thought to myself, "by the time we're both in our 90's I'll love him three times as much as I do now. How is that even possible?"

I must have had a dopey look on my face. "Penny for your thoughts," he said. It was a game we played. Whenever either of us said it, the other had to say exactly what they were thinking. We had practically founded our marriage on it. I told him my thoughts.

"Yeah, I know exactly what you're saying. I feel that way, too. Before I met you, I'd never have believed that was possible. Never could understand how people stay married for 50 years and stay in love. Now I do..." He let his words trail off, then, "I love you with all my heart.."

"Do you want your birthday present now?" I interrupted.

"You didn't need to buy me anything."

"I didn't."

"Then what...?"

I gave him another kiss, then began unbuttoning his wool coat.

Hours later we finally went out for that load of firewood.

The next day Dick and I brought back two loads of logs, peeled and spiked them. Each day we worked feverishly, cutting more trees, shouldering the logs and bringing them back to the cabin site. More often than not, the days were dismal gray. We worked in freezing rain, cold wind or blowing snow, or a combination of the three.

We were always careful to stay warm and dry. Hypothermia is a high possibility under those conditions and it can sneak up without warning. The body gradually loses its ability to keep warm, requiring an outside source of heat to maintain it. The mind begins to do funny things, slowing down and dulling. A person eventually becomes sleepy, may even feel warm, and death follows if the person is not helped. It was always on our mind, which is probably why we were never afflicted with it.

Dick removed a wet outer jacket, placed it in the truck and put on a dry one. We were logging in miserably cold, drizzling rain. "Good idea," I commented, and did the same.

"You know, I've been thinking..." he paused for a moment. "We should make use of the roof peak. You know, on the inside of the cabin; no reason for it to be dead space just taking up heat." He wiped rain water from his mustache.

"How about a small loft," I ventured. "We could put the kids up there. It could be their sleeping loft."

"Just what I was thinking." He cut off a piece of beef jerky with his knife while we sat resting on a log under a tree. The tree offered little protection from the rain, but we needed the break. He handed me a piece, then cut another and popped it into his mouth. I gazed at the knife, mesmerized. Dick had made it himself. It was a short hunting knife with a fat blade, modeled after a modified ulu, an Eskimo skinning knife, that made it perfect for skinning or cutting. He carried it in a sheath on his belt. Perfectly balanced, it sat just right in his big, bearpaw-like hands.

He brought me back to our original conversation with, "Means gathering some more long, big logs though, to support a floor for the loft."

I sighed. *More big, heavy logs. It only made sense, though, and a loft would give us much more space.*

Dick scratched out a blueprint in the dirt with a stick, showing me what would need to be done to build a loft.

"Let's do it." I agreed.

Three logs were needed. We cut and carried them out in the next two days, along with some smaller wall logs. The first two logs were peeled and laid across the walls, spanning the cabin. With each round of wall logs that went up, we'd move the loft logs up a little higher, step fashion. When the walls were high enough, the loft logs would already be in position.

The third and last loft log was a problem. *Why is it, the last one of anything is always the one to give you trouble?* The day, again, was dreary. Freezing rain chilled us to the bone. We cut the proper tree and Dick cut it to length, twenty-five feet long with an eight-inch butt and six-inch top.

"One, two, lift!" We shouldered the monster log. *Lord, it was heavy and my fingers ached from the cold.* I groaned.

"Ready?"

"Ready as ever!"

"O.K., one, two, right step, forward." Sounded like some crazy dance step. Maybe it was, the *Waltz of the Logs.* We were synchronizing our steps, the best and only way to stay together and carry out the timbers.

We had walked about one-hundred feet with the log when Dick, in the lead, slipped on an icy stump and fell forward. The log ground hard into my left shoulder. Tears of pain welled in my eyes as I tried to keep some of the weight off Dick. He laid there face down, sprawled out with his end of the log still across his back.

"You Okay?" I grimaced. I knew he wasn't, but I couldn't help him and still support my end of the log.

"Sure, what ya think?" He bellowed like a bull moose. "Feel fine. Just like Christ falling with the cross." He was on his knees now, trying to regain his composure. The log still balanced on my shoulder and his back. Finally, with much effort, he stood. We marched carefully out of the woods with it. Dick was quiet all the way home again.

The next morning we stopped at the grocery store before heading out to cut logs. Dick overheard a conversation concerning the need for jail guards at the Tok jail. He immediately went to the troopers station and applied for the job. They told him they'd be glad to call on him, that the work was pretty simple, but it would only be on an occasional basis because there weren't a lot of arrests made in the tiny community. Dick was glad to know there was even a small amount of work available. He thanked the troopers and left.

We continued cutting logs for a couple of weeks, peeling them, spiking them in place. The weather was much worse. Snow was everywhere now and the cold was settling in for winter. Work was very slow. Still, we were up to the windows with our log walls. It looked good in spite of the weather.

Colder and colder. Finally, we needed to cut firewood as much as we needed to cut logs. And because of the cold, we were having trouble with our logs splitting as Dick tried to spike them into place.

Toward the end of the third week in October, we were forced to stop work on the cabin and resign ourselves to cutting firewood for the tent stove. That's what we were doing on our thirteenth anniversary, October 29. Superstition places bad luck on the number thirteen. I never held much to that, but it did turn out to be a bad day for Dick.

We were almost finished loading the truck with firewood when Dick picked up a large piece to throw in with the rest. It wasn't any bigger than the others, so he must have picked it up wrong, or twisted or something. Instantly, he felt severe pain in his back, and there was no covering up this pain. "Can't bend," he panted. And he could barely move his neck. I helped him into the truck and drove him and the firewood home.

I helped Dick to his cot and made him lie down. His pain was obvious. Throwing a thick towel on top of the wood stove, I let it heat, then placed it on his injured back as an improvised heating pad. Then I went out and unloaded the firewood.

His pain, in spite of the warmed towels and aspirin, was almost unbearable. I felt his back. The muscles were knotted into spasms. By early evening it was obvious that he needed help and I couldn't do it. The nearest doctor was two-hundred miles away in Fairbanks, but there was a physician's assistant in Tok, maybe he could do something. The kids and I loaded Dick into the truck to seek medical help.

Though it was after normal hours, the P.A. was still there. After a brief explanation of what Dick had done to hurt himself, we helped him out of the truck. *Doc* took him inside while I stayed with the kids in the truck. We left the truck running, as it was getting colder by the minute.

After a very short while, I was surprised to see the P.A. helping Dick out of the building. I ran to help.

"He'll be Okay?" the P.A. was puffing. Dick was leaning heavily on him with his arm around his shoulders. "Needs rest and a heating pad on his back. He's pulled some muscles is all. I gave him something for pain. He'll also sleep. Take him right home and put him to bed."

Home? Doc obviously didn't know we were the *tent people*. We loaded Dick into the truck. On the way home, Dick began to giggle a little and got a glazed look in his eyes. Katherine and Ricky eyed him suspiciously.

Back in our driveway, I told the kids to stay in the truck with their daddy until I could get a lamp lit. Groping around in the dark of the tent, I heard the truck door slam.

"Great," I thought. *One of the kids has disobeyed me.* Exasperated, I lit the lamp. Suddenly, both kids began hollering outside. "Mama!" Ricky called. There was an earnestness in his voice. I sped out the tent door into the bright moonlight.

"Daddy's drunk!" he shouted.

"Funny Daddy, fun-n-n-ny," Katherine laughed.

Dick wasn't in the truck. He was the *kid* who had disobeyed. "Where is he?" I demanded.

"Out there, Mama!" They pointed into the woods. I could hear Dick thrashing through the trees. I could barely make out a large form in the night as I tramped out to get him. Thrashing, crashing. Was that really Dick? Or was it a bear? What if it was a bear? The rifle, if I needed it, lay too far away in the truck. What would I do?

CRASH! My heart pounded. Surely that wasn't Dick. He couldn't possibly make that much noise. But what about Dick? Was he wandering around out there, about to come face-to-face with a bear? The thought sickened me. I turned back to get the rifle just in case.

Snap! CR-R-A-SH! Right behind me. Adrenaline pumping, heart racing, I spun around to meet my aggressor.

"Dick!" I yelped in relief. "Dick, what...the...?" His broad, hairy chest reflected moonlight. For reasons only he will ever know, he had taken off his coat and shirt. Here he was, bare-chested at twenty-five below zero, and obviously feeling no pain.

"Come to the tent with me," I pleaded, "inside where it's nice and warm."

"Fine here," he mumbled, stretching his arms wide. One bare arm connected with the dead limbs of a cottonwood nearby, breaking them with a familiar snap.

"Come on, you've got to get inside," I tugged at him.

He turned away. "Oh, hello, pretty tree." He patted a small skinny spruce. Snow tumbled off its branches and cascaded onto his arms.

"Little devil. Lookee, the pretty tree peed on me! Naughty, naughty tree!" He shook his forefinger at the little tree.

I took his wet arm in an attempt to guide him.

"Wanna dance?" he said.

"Yes, inside the tent. Come on."

"Gimme kiss." I kissed him.

"Hug, too," And a hug.

"Rub noses!" We rubbed noses.

"How 'bout a little...?"

"Later!" I broke in, "inside the tent."

He began moving toward the tent with me. He moved so slowly, lumbering, stumbling. My fingers were ungloved, wet and cold. He had to be freezing, he just didn't know it.

We reached the tent. I led him to his cot, coerced him into lying down and covered him with a blanket. The kids followed.

"Stay put," I instructed, "I've got to split some kindling. The fire is out." Grabbing a log and the splitting maul, I headed out the tent door.

It didn't take more than a few minutes to split the log into small sticks. The minus temperatures were a real blessing when it came to wood splitting. The colder it was, the more brittle the layers of wood. Sub-zero temperatures required little more than a good tap of the maul to break a large chunk of firewood in half.

Gathering up an armload, I stepped into the tent.

I got a glimpse of Dick kneeling in front of the stove door, poised to strike a match. The full realization of what he was about to do hit me. I opened my mouth to shout "NO!" But it was too late. The next instant he struck the match and tossed it into the stove.

The following seconds unfolded almost in slow motion.

My feet were already moving toward him as the stove belched a great explosion. Flame spewed out the door, engulfing Dick. The force of it knocked him backward, somersaulting past the now empty gas can, and into the dirt. Great clouds of noxious black smoke issued from the stove and filled the tent. When I reached Dick, he lay sprawled, like a grizzly that had just been backhanded by King Kong. His chest and face were black; his hair, beard and eyebrows singed and still smoking.

"No need for kindling," he was half-bellowing. "I got a *real* fire going!" In his drugged state the enormity of what he'd done didn't dawn on him.

The fire was out. A haze hung in the air. I gazed at the single, round log inside the stove. The log was so big, I couldn't imagine how he'd even gotten it through the stove door opening. And then he had dowsed it with gasoline!

Katherine and Ricky were sitting on their beds, silent and wide-eyed. They never said a word as I helped Dick back to his cot and undressed him. He was getting sleepy now and if I didn't get him down where he belonged, he might end up sleeping in the dirt because I'd never be able to move him. As I zipped his bag around him and covered him, he fell fast asleep.

Turning to the stove, I removed the big blackened log and started the fire the proper way.

Though he was still awfully sore the next morning, there was marked improvement. I wondered, though, what the *something for pain* was that the P.A had given Dick.

CHAPTER EIGHT

Settling In For Survival

The kids prepared to celebrate Halloween by making monster masks with paper shopping bags. Once they sufficiently *gruesomed up* the masks to their satisfaction, I loaded them into the truck and we headed for town. They were excited as they returned from each house or cabin, comparing their loot. Tok's businesses were also in the spirit. Grocery store or gas station, it made no difference. The owners had seen to it that no one left with an empty bag.

Katherine and Ricky were bundled up warmly. Costumes either were nonexistent or covered by layers of warm clothing. Halloween in Tok was certainly different from Halloween in Anchorage. There was plenty of snow here and sub-zero temperatures.

As we drove home, I realized the old saying about there being several different Alaskas was correct. The most obvious difference, to us, was the weather and length of seasons. Tok had much earlier, much colder winters than did Anchorage.

Von Hairy greeted us happily in the driveway. It was apparent that even he was preparing for a cold winter. His hair was growing longer and thicker. Daily, he seemed to increase in bulk; a good portion of it hair. Indeed, our gigantic MacKenzie River Husky was beginning to look more like a bear than a dog. But he was still a Husky at heart. He never slept in his doghouse. He slept on top of it, and the colder the weather, the better he liked it. Von Hairy was definitely suited to Tok!

The day after Halloween was Ricky's birthday. This would be his eleventh, and the first one he'd ever spent in a tent.

"Can I open it now, Mom?" Ricky begged. "Can I?" The small yellow package with the giant yellow bow sat mysteriously on his bed.

I looked at Dick. He nodded.

"Okay, go for it," I said, removing Ricky's birthday cake from the oven and placing it on top the wood stove. He grabbed his present and ripped the yellow wrappings with great enthusiasm.

"Oh, boy! All right!" He was holding up his treasure, examining it carefully. "Now I can be like Dad!"

"Lemme see," Katherine clamored. Proudly, Ricky showed her his brand new folding knife, complete with a leather sheath.

"Oooh," she admired it. "Even got a envelope to mail it!"

"Dummy!"

I eyeballed him good for that remark. He continued on a less superior note. "It's a sheath, so I can carry it on my belt. All us men do that."

"Gosh, Mama, is Ricky a man now?"

Dick spoke up. "Yes he is. A young man, but still a man. Just like you are a young lady. And he's going to have to be extra tough and extra good from now on. So are you."

They could tell from the tone of his voice something was up. Both kids listened intently.

"Your Mama and I can't get the cabin finished. We're going to have to make the best of what we've got, so I'm afraid we're going to have to live in this tent all winter. This is home." He waited for their reaction.

"I knew it already, " Katherine said, matter-of-factly.

"Oh, sure you did," Ricky replied sarcastically.

"Did!"

"Baloney!"

"Okay, okay, " Dick broke in, "so how did you know already?"

"Mama told me so," she answered smugly, looking my way.

"She did?"

"Yep. But I wasn't s'posed to tell. She said to keep it a secret and I shouldn't cry or be bad. And I didn't, either, 'cause I'm a big girl!"

"Well, you certainly are." he praised. "And Rick's a big boy..."

"Man," Ricky corrected.

"...man." Dick went on, "And we can do this, but it won't be easy for any of us. It's going to be hard work even for you two. Still with us?"

"Yeah!" They both fairly rung with spirit.

"How 'bout some cake and ice cream to celebrate Ricky's birthday and our new tent home?" I didn't need to ask a second time. We all sang *Happy Birthday* and enjoyed eating warm cake and cold ice cream.

I wondered what the winter had in store for us.

In addition to our normal routine of cutting firewood, the next few days also involved rearranging the interior of the tent. This had to be done for maximum warmth and efficiency since it no longer was just a temporary shelter.

The kids helped us lug all our storage boxes to the north side of the tent. These we stacked clear to the ceiling and probably two-thirds the length of that wall. They would help insulate against the cold and act as a buffer to the north wind. Along the remainder of the north side and half of the east end was our kitchen area. Utensils, food supplies, etc., went there, handy to the stove.

That left almost the entire south wall for sleeping. We put Dick's cot along that wall, opposite the stove for maximum warmth, because of his poor sleeping bag. My cot was next in line opposite the table. Then came Katherine's bed and finally Ricky's bed, on the west end of the tent. Though the kids were farther from the stove, they actually slept warmer than we did. They were on real beds, complete with mattresses. Dick and I placed wood blocks under the bed legs, elevating them another foot, allowing both Katherine and Ricky to sleep in a much warmer layer of air. All Dick and I had were our low-to-the-ground army cots. They would prove to be miserable.

Each day after the kids left for school, Dick and I would cut firewood. We found that, at least in this early part of winter, we could cut enough firewood and return to the tent before the kids got home from school. Usually I would have supper started by the time their excited faces popped through the door.

"Know what?" Katherine queried one evening.

"No, what?"

"My best friend says her mama and daddy says no one can live in a tent all winter in Tok. Her daddy says we'll be gone before Christmas. Will we, Mama?"

Dick spoke, "Not unless you want us to, Baby."

"Tell her daddy to eat spiders!" Ricky retorted. "Tell her your daddy said so! It's true though, Dad. Everybody says we're crazy and won't stay. Somebody even said you're just too lazy to build a cabin and that's why we're living in the tent."

"I've heard the rumors, too," I said. "Guess as long as we know the truth, we'll just have to show them, huh?"

The next morning neither Dick nor I felt very well. Still, we went out and cut firewood. By the following morning, we were both very sick with flu-like symptoms. Indeed, it was all either of us could do to get out of bed. Once the kids were off to school, I felt like collapsing, but of course I couldn't do that. There was wood to cut.

"Drag out the first-aid kit." Dick mumbled. Our doctor friend had included in our super kit all practical applications possible for a layman to administer, even sutures and instructions on how to use them. There were remedies for a variety of things — real cures, not over-the-counter junk. We had ointments, diarrhea pills, Benadryl for insect bites and itching and penicillin. I withdrew one bottle of this and two disposable syringes. We filled one syringe with the proper amount of penicillin and Dick dropped his pants.

"No, me first," I said, "I've never done this before. I don't know how to give a shot."

"Watch and learn then," he said. "Drop 'em." Brandishing the syringe, he explained the *how-to's* to me while I paid strict attention.

Then it was my turn to give him his shot. I wished I could practice first, on an orange or something. I didn't like having to use him as my guinea pig and I was afraid of hurting him. Visions of breaking the needle in him flew through my head.

"Dick..."

As though on the same mind frequency he broke in, "Just do it, you're not gonna hurt me."

Taking a deep breath, I plunged the needle into his buttock and found it wasn't as hard an ordeal as I'd thought. In fact, it was simple. I was a success.

"See?" He grinned, "Wasn't so hard, was it?"

"Piece of cake," I laughed, rubbing my own rump. Those injections were the only thing that kept us on our feet and cutting wood for the next several days. We were still pretty sick, but the shots allowed us to keep working and still recover. Not that it was easy. And recover, we did, simultaneously.

Soon we decided to set a small trapline. Since we had to be out everyday for wood cutting, it only made sense to check out a trapline at the same time. Who knows? Maybe we'd get something, even though the area we were cutting in wasn't particularly good for fur-bearing animals. The sale of pelts would be nice for extra money and we could use them, too. Dick kept kidding me about the exotic love we could make on a fur rug! Not that there wasn't plenty of it without the fur.

As part of our winter preparations, we also invested in two fifty gallon barrels, one each of kerosene and gasoline. While neither would last forever, it would be a step ahead.

And we set snares on our own property, away from the tent. We'd look for a deadfall of trees surrounded by telltale rabbit tracks, then set a snare on a well-beaten game trail. I checked those snares each morning before we left to cut wood and occasionally we'd have rabbit stew or fried rabbit for dinner.

Each day we went for wood seemed a little colder than the day before. I always snuggled close to Dick in the truck while on our way down the road. It was part of our private time without the kids. More than once we were well *heated up* when we arrived at our woodcutting place and the truck became a temporary bedroom. Sometimes we felt like kids ourselves.

With the increasing cold, it soon was obvious that our *city boots* weren't efficient enough to keep our feet warm in the now thirty below zero temperature. Everyone in the area wore white bunny boots to keep their feet warm. Bunny boots are large, rubber, double-walled boots developed by the military especially for Arctic conditions. On the side of each is an air valve, allowing for inflation to obtain maximum insulation or deflation while flying. Even totally wet, feet remain warm inside those boots, but they also cost around one hundred dollars a pair and we couldn't afford that.

So we did the next best thing. I decided to make mukluks for all of us. Since Dick was the one most often outside, his would be first. We already had several tanned moosehides. What I lacked was a sewing machine, because we had spent my sewing machine savings on the down payment for our land. I set about the business of mukluk making every evening after supper.

First a pattern was made by drawing around our feet. A second pattern, for each top was developed by measuring up from the ankle to just below the knee, as our mukluks would be knee-high. Around the calf they would be roomy and warm. Too tight meant cold legs and feet.

Gradually, Dick's mukluks began to look like real mukluks. I stitched diligently, using a leather needle, waxed dental floss for thread, a thimble and pliers. Moosehide, unsplit, is very thick and durable. It is also very hard to sew by hand. I could push the needle through one layer of hide with no problem, but going through two layers was impossible without the aid of the pliers to pull the needle all the way through. I broke many needles in the process. It was tedious work and progress was slow. My fingers ached each night after wrestling with the hide. At times, Dick would try to spell me. His fingers were a lot stronger than mine, but he was certainly no seamstress. His heart was in the right place, but I always ended up reworking what he had done. It took about ten days to finish his mukluks.

"What do you think?" I asked. He wiggled his toes inside the new mukluks.

"Nice. Real nice. If it weren't midnight, I'd go out now and cut wood just to try them out!" He looked proud and they did look good on him. On the outside of each calf was a silver-dollar-sized, hand-beaded medallion that I had added as an extra touch of class. They looked nice, if I did say so myself. Dick strutted around the tent modeling them for the kids.

"Can you make us some, Mama?" the kids asked.

"Yes, we're all going to have a pair. No more cold feet!" Within a month, I had constructed all four pair. I made Ricky's, then Katherine's. Both pair had moosehide soles, but the tops were made from heavy white canvas and finished with decorative borders. Because the kids were going to grow out of their mukluks, it made no sense to waste valuable moosehide on the uppers when canvas would work as well.

My mukluks were last and identical to Dick's, all full moosehide, but instead of a medallion, I hand-beaded pink, dogwood flowers on mine. We all had heavy felt insoles inside our mukluks. With two pair of wool socks worn inside them, we never had cold feet again. Not even at 70 below zero. The Eskimos certainly knew what they were doing when they invented mukluks.

Now that Dick and I had proper footgear, we could stay outside longer, and that was good because we were to the point of needing an income. Our money was dwindling fast and we would have to keep it replenished. Since we were out cutting our own firewood, we figured we'd cut extra and see if we could sell it in town. Many people used wood for heat, even those who didn't live in a tent.

Because there is no formal form of government, and Tok is an unincorporated community within an unorganized borough, residents enjoy a loose, fairly unstructured, lifestyle. A fierce sense of independence is jealously guarded by those who live in the area and residents can live however basic they'd like. There are no building codes or restrictions, no taxes. There are also no sidewalks, city water or sewage system. That being the case, many "Tokites" had outhouses, though I doubt they had a problem with theirs as annoying as ours. In sub-zero weather, that seat was awfully cold. Indeed, a small amount of moisture on it can be downright dangerous. We all had visions of being stuck to the *throne* until spring came to thaw us out. Our hard, cold, frost-biting metal seat was doubly dangerous.

We tried several remedies, none of them satisfactory. First was the cardboard cut-out. All it did was slip all over the seat, as Ricky found out. One evening he left the tent with the cut-out and within minutes he was howling. We all dashed outside.

"What's wrong?" I yelled into the night. Dick swept the flashlight from side to side until Ricky was in the spotlight. He wasn't perched on the throne as we had expected. Instead, he was ungracefully draped over a small spruce sticking out of the snowbank. I couldn't help it, neither could Dick. We both started to laugh.

Ricky ruffled. "It's not funny!"

We laughed harder when he stood up, brushing snow from his clothing. "Just skated right off the thing! I was just sitting here looking at all the stars, and there was a shooting star, and then all of a sudden — who-o-sh!" He made a broad gesture toward the small spruce where he had landed. I envisioned the stars suddenly going topsy-turvy as Ricky made the wrong move, quickly going head over bucket off the throne. Inside the tent we discussed the problem at length, amid giggles and cursory glances from Ricky. As he embellished on the story, he began to laugh. Soon he was laughing harder than we were.

One has to have a sense of humor to survive tent life and an *out* with no *house*! The next day we tried a Styrofoam cut-out. Many *outhousers* use Styrofoam over their wooden seats in the winter. It's warm, doesn't slide and won't stick to bare skin.

But it does split and break. And it was Dick who made that discovery. The next evening he smartly grabbed up the new Styrofoam seat and headed out back. Sure enough, within minutes there was an awful lot of growling and cussing going on back there.

"Should we go see, Mama?" Ricky asked.

"Better we should wait," I replied. The growling worsened. Sounded like a moose thrashing around out there.

"Daddy's not very happy..." Katherine had just uttered the understatement of the century. Right then, Dick popped through the tent door.

"Worked great, huh?" I teased. "I can tell by the scowl on your face and the great reviews you gave it. Must be some new brand of Arctic humor."

"Damned thing split right in two as soon as I sat on it," he sputtered.

I howled with laughter, doubling over in an uncontrollable belly laugh. Mumbling something else, he stalked over to his cot, warming his rear near the stove on his way.

"Wha...What's that? I couldn't quite make it out," I goaded him between guffaws.

He stared at me with a *you-should-feel-sorry-for-me-and-not-laugh-at-me* look. It only made me laugh all the harder. By now the kids had also joined in the merriment.

"I said," he paused for greater dramatic effect, "that wasn't bad enough. When it split, it shot right out from under me. Dropped me like a hot coal right onto the cold metal."

That did it. I could not quit laughing. Reduced to tears, trying to squelch the laughter, I chanced a look at the kids. Ricky looked at me and we both broke into gigantic wails again. It was a long time before we regained our composure, and every time any of us looked each other, we broke up again. It was contagious. Dick was the topic of the evening. Tomorrow, I promised myself, I'll have a solution to this *ticklish* problem.

By the next evening, I had finished another cut-out. Only this one was cut from a piece of indoor-outdoor carpet. This, I reasoned, would be warm, wouldn't split and shouldn't slide. Katherine was the guinea pig for the carpet cut-out. She disappeared outside with it in one hand, the flashlight in the other. We waited and listened. The minutes ticked by. Nothing. *Was I a success?*

Not hardly.

Suddenly there was the sound of metal hitting metal, followed closely by Katherine's shrieking. We rushed into the darkness.

"Where are you, Baby?" No moon, no light at all. Just pitch black enveloping all of us. At least our kids weren't afraid of the dark. "Where's your flashlight?"

Only her wails returned to us. I stumbled over a tent guy rope on my way back inside, but Dick beat me to it. He emerged with a lantern. We could see Katherine standing at the toilet's edge, peering into its depth, sobbing.

"Oh, no..." I muttered.

"Oh, yes..." Dick mumbled.

The carpet cut-out had worked fine. But as Katherine stood up from it, she let go of it and it slid right down the nearest hole. In her haste to grab for it, she had also dropped the flashlight down that same hole! Ricky peered down into its depth.

"Boy, just scarfed it right down!" He shot a glance at his little sister, "Lucky <u>you</u> didn't fall down there, too," he tried to control a smirk. "You'd be down there the rest of your life!"

"Mama!"

"Ricky!" I admonished, concealing a smile. So Katherine's misadventure gave us another evening's entertainment.

But what to do about that seat?

I thought about it over the next few days, then began fashioning a new seat cover. This one was made of fur. I measured, re-measured, cut, re-cut, sewed and kept trying it for size. It took several evenings before this one was finished. It had to work. It just had to. I disappeared outside to try it myself.

"We'll wait for you to holler," they all said, already full of mirth and anticipation. Carefully, I fitted it to the seat. It was beautiful. Contoured exactly to the metal, it wouldn't slip because I had sewn elastic into a gathered band, then stretched it over the seat. Beautiful! And warm. And soft.

As time went by, everyone must have become concerned for me. One by one I heard them call. I stayed silent.

"Honey, you Okay?" Dick was on the move. He had come to rescue me from my fate. I just sat there, smugly. Soon I had an audience.

"Mom?"

"Lovely evening, isn't it?" I tried to be nonchalant.

"Honey? What happened?"

"Nothing, absolutely nothing! It works great!" So that evening I was praised highly as each one went to try out the new fur potty seat.

Ah, the satisfaction that comes with winning a small battle with Mother Nature!

CHAPTER NINE

Thanksgiving In Whitehorse

Thanksgiving would be here in a few days. Dick and I were discussing the possibility of combining some Thanksgiving pleasure with business.

"We could finance the trip with our woodcutting and what money we have left," Dick speculated. "I've heard more than once about some good jobs in Whitehorse. Short-term, high-paying jobs and there aren't any takers. There's only been a couple of nights of jail guarding in Tok and even that seems to be dwindling. I've gotta get work or we won't be able to buy groceries." He looked intensely at me, the first of many times I would see that same look of extreme concern for me and the kids. "And if I could get a job, we would be set come spring. Finish the cabin and live in style," he added.

"Yeah. Sounds Okay." I answered, "we could all use a break from the tent anyway."

Ricky asked if we could take Chris with us. "No, I'm sorry, we can't. Whitehorse is in Canada. Even though it's nearby, it's still a foreign country. They won't let us take her without the proper border-crossing papers, which we don't have."

"Then how will she live?" Ricky was always concerned with animals. Both kids were. I was glad they shared that trait.

"Well," I said, "you know she's very pregnant and wouldn't be able to travel very well anyway." It had become obvious to us that the reason Chris had been lost from her original owner in the first place was because she had been in heat. She probably got loose, went looking for a mate and got lost. Now she was about to increase our family size again.

I continued, "We'll leave a five-pound sack of cat food open for her. She can eat as much as she wants, whenever she wants to. The water is a problem, though. It will freeze. Cats do not eat snow, as dogs do. If they don't have water or liquid in some form, such as the blood and juices in raw meat, they will dehydrate."

Dick was deep in thought. "We'll leave the little kerosene heater on and put a big bucket of water right next to it, so it won't freeze." Chris lay on his cot, purring softly. He gently rubbed her head. "We'll be back here before she runs out of food or water."

"Can we make her a bed for her kittens too, if she has them?" Katherine asked.

"Oh, yes. We'll have to, because we'll roll up our sleeping bags so she won't get into them. It would ruin a sleeping bag if she had her babies on them. You and Ricky can have the job of making her a nice warm bed by the heater. Make it fluffy and comfortable."

Everything completed, we were off for what we hoped would be a fun and successful adventure. It took a day and a half of driving to reach Whitehorse, the first town of size, four hundred miles southeast of Tok.

We enjoyed the freedom of being on the road once again. Katherine and Ricky counted moose and caribou along the way, trying to outdo each other by being the first to spot an animal. They lost count of rabbits, there were so many hopping across the frozen surface of the Alaska Highway. We sang, told stories and cracked jokes.

It was a trip down Memory Lane, reminding me of my first trip up the highway as a child in 1951. Now here I was again, only this time I was the mother with my own children. *Where had the time gone?* I wondered. *Time must be relative*, I mused. *If life is good, it speeds by, if not it probably drags on.* My life was wonderful, even living in a tent.

We crossed the border into Canada, the Yukon, especially a vast and unpopulated place. Like sisters, Alaska and the Yukon share the same characteristics: beautiful scenery, great expanses, snow-covered mountain ranges, gold rush history, abundant wildlife, hardy pioneers.

Once in Whitehorse, we rented a suite right downtown for thirty dollars a day. It was spacious, with two queen-sized beds, a huge color television and indoor plumbing. The kids hadn't watched a television in so long, it was like something new and exciting to them. Dick's bliss centered around the toilet. He reveled in the leisurely warmth of its *no drafts* seat. And my big pleasure was the extravagance of plenty of hot, running water. I found myself soaking in the bathtub several hours at a time.

Of course we all took in the Whitehorse sights. The main street looked about the same way as I remembered it. There had been more buildings added, but the Whitehorse Inn, where I had stayed overnight as a child with my parents, was still there. Anything interesting, we stopped and investigated.

And Dick went to check on the job situation. He looked into several leads. Unfortunately, we found that all the job rumors we had heard were just that, rumors. There were no jobs, no big money. At this news we were, admittedly, downhearted, but not defeated. We were thankful for being able to be where we were and enjoy ourselves a little. Besides, we tried to console ourselves, maybe his jail guarding would pick up. But Dick looked doubtful.

Thanksgiving Day. Dick decided to make it memorable. Although Canada was not celebrating, we were. Dick ordered Thanksgiving dinner and had the hotel bring it to our room. Such style! The kids were quite impressed. It was served on silver trays with real linen napkins. Every morsel looked so good: heaps of king crab, lobster, shrimp and steak. And a complimentary bottle of champagne. Not your traditional Thanksgiving meal, but nothing about the Bernhardt family seemed to be traditional this year. Dick tipped the waiter handsomely as he left the room.

"He'd just die if he knew we lived in a tent." Ricky said, laughing. "Probably thinks we're rich." And he plopped a handful of french fries in his mouth.

"We are rich," I said, turning to Dick and looking him straight in the eye. "We are very rich." He nodded a wise, old *I-know-that-from-the-bottom-of-my-heart* nod, saying nothing and everything in that one gesture.

The meal was scrumptious. Later we walked down the main street, window shopping, finally stopping at Simpson-Sears, a big department store full of everything imaginable. I found the perfect sleeping bag for Dick, called a Canadian Sleeping Robe. It was very roomy, long, filled with down and had a wool liner for extra warmth next to the skin. It also had a not-so-perfect price tag on it. There was no way I had that much money, but I knew how badly Dick needed it, so...

After returning to our room once more, I excused myself and went back to Simpson-Sears, found the manager and cornered him in his office. Knowing I didn't stand a chance, I still found myself pouring out our story to him. He sat fairly quiet, but attentive, while I talked.

"So you see," I finished, "why we need that sleeping bag." I paused to take a breath. All the time he was eyeing me, as though sizing me up.

Then he spoke. "How long have you lived in Alaska?"

"Almost 30 years, sir."

"Folks still there?"

"No sir. Just us."

"And you pulled up stakes in Anchorage to live in a tent in Tok?"

"Yes, that's about what it comes down to." It seemed hopeless when I really thought about it. Fortunately, he didn't allow much time for thinking.

He stood up, suddenly looking very much older to me, and wiser. Putting his hand on my shoulder he said, "You're going to make it, too. I would never give an ordinary person credit under these same circumstances. In fact, I don't give much credit. But the few accounts I do still carry are all old-time Alaskans and I've never been sorry. Their word is as good as gold. You and your husband may be young, but you fit my old-time Alaskan category, and

I'm going to let you take the sleeping bag with nothing down. Just pay it off in three equal payments in three months."

I was astounded. This wonderful man was one of a kind. I thanked him gratefully.

"I won't let you down," I told him.

"I know you won't. I've never been wrong about someone yet."

He gave me a card to mail in with the payments and walked me downstairs. As he lifted the sleeping bag down from the shelf, he said, "I'd like to see more young people like you and your husband. Give him my regards."

Naturally, when I returned to our hotel room, Dick couldn't believe his eyes.

"How'd you manage that?"

"Just turned on the old charm," I lied. Then I told him what had transpired in the last half-hour.

"Do you know that you've just dealt with a one-in-a-million type of man?" he asked me.

"Funny, I had the feeling, he was thinking the same thing. The man has a soft spot for *old* Alaskans. He's a saint."

Dick squinted his eyes at me, "You know, of course, it means we have to sell more firewood to pay for this. We can't let him down."

"I know. We won't." And we didn't, either. We broke our backs to make sure each payment was prompt. It would have been sacrilege to miss even one.

Late that night, Dick rolled over in our big queen-sized bed and hugged me hard. "What's that for?" I whispered, "It felt pretty special."

"For being you and for the sleeping bag. Come here, my red-headed vamp." And we made some very passionate love in Whitehorse, with Dick promising it was just an appetizer. We'd be doing a lot more of it in the new sleeping bag once we were home in the tent. "Just like it was a new bear rug," he teased.

Alaskan tradition requires *breaking in* a bear rug, any bear rug, the proper way!

Even though it was Thanksgiving, the streets and stores of Whitehorse were already beautifully decorated for Christmas. Katherine and Ricky were elated each evening with the colored lights. The trip to Whitehorse had not been work productive, but it certainly proved to be a terrific morale booster.

The time went too fast and soon we were on our way back to Tok. Four of us in Arctic gear, crammed into the cab of our truck, it was cozy, not cramped. We were getting used to close quarters. It was twenty below zero when we pulled out of Whitehorse, broke, but happy and rested.

"Fifty-two below!" Dick announced. It was well past midnight when we pulled into our own driveway. The truck lights shone on the thermometer hanging from a guy rope. Dick left the lights on so we could see to enter the tent. The canvas had a brittle quality to it. Von Hairy barked his welcome and Chris greeted us at the door, much skinnier.

"Oh, boy!" The kids were clamoring, "Chris had her babies!"

I put a quick squelch on aimless moving about the tent to avoid anyone stepping on a kitten in the dark, just in case. Then I lit the lantern, and almost as quickly noticed my sleeping bag unrolled on my cot. A fast inspection revealed a fine mess: five frozen kittens inside my bag.

I was mad and sad as Dick and I got the wood stove lit. Our breaths hung thickly in the extreme cold air. Mad because my bag was a total mess of frozen blood and kittens. It couldn't be used. Sad for the dead babies. If we had just been here, I thought. Chris must have had a terrible time. The tent felt colder inside than the air outside.

"M-e-w."

"Listen! Quiet everyone!"

"M-e-w..."

There it was again. Just a faint mew, a kitten barely able to make a sound. I jumped to my sleeping bag, picking up each lifeless form and holding it for a moment. Four little forms, all frozen hard. The fifth one was stiff but not hard. As I held it, a weak mew came from somewhere inside its throat. By outer appearances, this kitten was dead, so weak and stiff that it could not move, still it held a spark of life. There was no body heat coming from it.

"Is it alive?" Ricky asked, his eyes big with wonder.

Quickly, I shoved the little grey kitten under my parka and shirt, placing it directly on my warm stomach. "Barely. It's probably not going to make it."

Chris was at my feet, watching intently. I held the kitten against my warm skin until the tent had warmed. Slowly, a miracle was taking place. As the little kitten drew in my body heat, it began to move its stiff, tiny limbs. I snuggled it into Chris's fur belly so that it could nurse. She picked it up and dropped it back into my lap. We repeated this action several times. She would not keep the kitten.

"Dumb mother," Katherine cried, "doesn't want her own baby."

"It's not that," I said. "It's something else. She's giving me her baby."

"But why, Mom?" Ricky asked.

"Here's why," Dick held up her water bowl.

It was frozen solid. "She's had no water. The heater is out. Water's frozen. Bet she's got no milk to give that baby."

He was right. She was dry. We melted some snow and she drank her fill. Then we mixed up some powdered milk and I tried feeding the kitten with an eye dropper. It was weak, but ravenous. There was no problem getting it to nurse from the dropper. That night, the kitten slept inside Dick's old sleeping bag with me. What a strange turn of events. This was Dick's first night with his new bag and my first night borrowing his old bag. Not to mention my new sleeping partner. It wasn't quite what Dick and I had envisioned for our first night back in the tent.

The little kitten survived the night and as I continued feeding him around the clock for days, he prospered. During the day he rode inside my upper shirt pocket for warmth, so we called him Pocket Puss. As the days turned into weeks, he grew too big for my pocket, so we made him and Chris a nest fashioned from an old fur parka. Thus his name evolved to Parka Puss.

When Chris felt it was feeding time, she'd bring him to me to feed. At night, as I lay sleeping, she would drop him on my chest and then stand there expectantly, making sure I did the job properly.

We finally called him *Perk* for short because he was a perky little thing. But his name really didn't matter. To us, he was a little miracle, in an otherwise cold and hostile environment.

CHAPTER TEN

Swallowing Our Pride

Thanksgiving cold moved into December. The mercury never seemed to rise above 50 below. Cold air pounded at the tent walls. It rolled inside in an icy fog whenever we opened the door. Dick and I were very busy just keeping up with our own wood supply. We couldn't seem to get ahead. With Christmas soon to come, townspeople were saving their money and we were selling less and less firewood.

The entire town was quiet. Not even the jail was busy. Dick had not been called to jail guard in weeks. His face began to show his desperation, especially whenever I mentioned groceries or money, so I avoided the subject as much as possible. I knew Dick was doing all he could do.

One day we were fortunate to find a customer wanting two cords, which we supplied over the course of two days. Upon receiving payment after delivery of the second cord, and knowing it might be a while before we sold another, we spent the money wisely. Both gas tanks on the truck were filled, as was the chain saw jug. Then we went to the grocery store and bought a few staples, including a small ham, two pounds of bacon, lunch meat, two beef roasts and ham hocks. Enough meat to supply us for several weeks in case the money situation got worse. After stashing the meat in our Blazo box cupboards, Dick and I gathered up the kids and splurged on a real shower at the public showers in Tok.

We had a real jolt coming once we returned to the tent, however. The truck lights shone on the tent door. The flaps were pushed open. Obviously we'd had an intruder. Was he still inside?

Dick grabbed his pistol and bolted out the truck door. "Who's there?" he shouted.

No answer.

"Come out or I'm coming in!"

Nothing but stillness. I was aware of my own heart beating, the kids holding their breaths beside me.

Dick cautiously threw back the tent flap exposing the tent's interior. "Damn!" he cursed. There was no one there, but we'd had visitors all right. The four-legged kind. Dogs.

No. One dog. Our dog. He peered sheepishly around the wood stove, then made a break for the door, charging right between Dick and me. Every piece of newly purchased meat had either been eaten or dragged away. There was nothing salvageable left, just some tooth-marked tin foil. We were all depressed. It was back to peanut butter sandwiches.

Dick was irate. He waited quietly by the tent door most of the night, waiting for the criminal to return to the scene of the crime. Just as the tent flap began to move, he picked up a broken ax handle and THWACK! he connected with Von Hairy's head on the other side of the canvas.

Dead silence. No movement. Not a sound. I was afraid Dick had killed the dog. It looked like the tent flap had received the brunt of the blow, but...

"Is he dead?" I finally dared to ask.

"Son of a bitch ought to be," Dick ranted. Then he began to get worried. Nothing was happening outside. Surely, he reasoned, we would have heard a whine, a footstep, something by now. He was clearly worried. Softening, Dick peered out the door. Von Hairy was lying in the snow, still looking guilty, but none the worse for what had just happened. He knew he'd done wrong.

The next day, as we prepared to go out once again for firewood, we had another unpleasant surprise awaiting us. Dick had just started the truck after messing with it for several hours, when he discovered the power-steering pump was broken. Weeks of minus temperatures had caused the oil inside it to thicken like tar. When the oil congealed, the impeller shaft sheered off, then the pump hoses bulged and split.

Dick removed the pump. "Should have been aviation hydraulic oil in it," he told me. "I should have known that. Normal power steering oil is too thick in this severe cold."

"We can't replace it. What do we do now?" I asked.

"Drive without it. Gonna be a bitch, I'll tell you. Four-wheel drive, oversize tires, off the road, in deep snow with a load of firewood. Ought to be a real picnic. Just have to manhandle it 'til we get some money."

He wasn't happy and I couldn't blame him.

Wood sales became fewer and further apart. We not only couldn't replace the pump, now we were having difficulty eating. He and I had already cut ourselves to a snack in the morning and then dinner at night to conserve on money and food. The kids were eating regular meals, but we were not. The situation was becoming increasingly worse. And Christmas was coming. What about Christmas?

Dick and I decided to do something we'd never done before; swallow our pride and apply for welfare.

"It's all we can do, Honey," Dick told me. "I've tried real hard to get a job. You know that. There just aren't any. This is our only hope right now." His face wore that familiar look of desperation on it.

"It's not your fault," I said, trying to ease his mind. "I guess that's what welfare is there for."

All we needed was to sell a cord of firewood to finance the trip. The very day we sold the next cord, all four of us headed for Fairbanks where the welfare office was located. After finding the office and making an appointment, we waited in line for hours. It gave us an opportunity to observe the hordes of people in other lines.

"Look at that one," Dick nudged me. We were standing beside a window overlooking the street. An expensive new car drove up.

A woman got out, took off her good coat, removed her rings and jewelry and stepped onto the sidewalk. "Bet she comes through this door!" Sure enough, within minutes she was standing in one of the lines. We watched it happen over and over, and we saw some of them leave the office with a fistful of foodstamps.

"If they can get it, we should have no problem," Dick whispered to me in a relieved tone.

Finally, it was our turn. They gave us pages of paperwork to fill out. I set about filling in all the blanks. Then the lady at the desk asked us for a rent receipt. "Don't have a receipt," Dick replied. "We're living in a tent and we own it."

"How about a receipt for utilities?"

"We live in a tent. No electricity, no phone. No receipts," he said.

"Well then, how about heat? How do you heat your tent?"

"With wood," I answered.

"How much does it cost to buy it? Do you have a receipt for that?"

I could feel my skin begin to crawl. Something did not feel right here. "No, ma'am, we cut it ourselves."

She looked sternly at Dick, "Do you work?"

"You bet," he replied, excitedly, "both of us work our tails off just to survive."

"Where?"

"Cutting wood to heat the tent we live in. It takes a lot of wood and a lot of work, and I've worked off and on in Tok as a jail guard. I'd gladly do *any* kind of work to feed my family. There just isn't anything available right now. That's why we're living in a tent." He began to bristle.

She laid down her pencil and folded her hands in front of her ample belly. "Well, according to what you've told me," she paused, then continued with an air of authority, "you don't qualify for foodstamps. Since you have no receipts or the right bills, you don't fit into our categories."

Dick's mouth dropped open in disbelief. If the grizzly bear hump on his back had been visible, I know we would have seen the hair standing on end. To avoid a scene, I asked, "Isn't there something we can do?"

"Yes, you may qualify for ADC."

"Good. Let's try for that. What's ACD?"

"A...D...C," she corrected me.

Dick began to simmer down, thinking perhaps, there was still hope.

She continued, pulling another long form from her drawer, "Aid to Dependent Children. Take this form, fill it out and go to the line right over there." She pointed to another long line.

"Can't you do it?" I asked.

"No. I'm just food stamps. Midge is ADC."

The four of us shuffled to the other line, where I began filling out an almost identical form to the other one we had just completed for food stamps. After another hour's wait, it was our turn again. We filed toward the desk and sat down.

Midge unceremoniously took our application. We waited uneasily while she glanced through it, then she looked at me. "You two legally married?"

Oh yes," I answered, thrusting our marriage certificate toward her. *Ha!* I thought. *Now we're making progress. At last I had the needed receipts.*

"And are you living together with the children?" Like a loaded gun, she aimed her question squarely at Dick.

"Every day and night, through sickness and hell of all kinds," he beamed proudly, with confidence.

"And these two children are your legal children..." pointing to Katherine and Ricky.

"Even paid for!" Dick quipped.

I could see he was happy with her questions and even happier with our answers. At last we were getting somewhere! Thank heaven, I thought. We sat quietly, expectantly.

Midge moved the paperwork to one side, "Then why are you here?"

Dick and I stared at her. "What?"

"Why are you taking up my time?" she asked, unsympathetically.

"What do you mean," I stammered. "That lady over there told us to see you."

"Can't imagine why," she shrugged, "you obviously don't qualify for anything here."

Now it was my turn to get mad. I could feel the anger in my stomach, slowly working its way to my throat. I knew my face was flushed. "How can we not qualify?"

"This desk is for deprived children. You two are legally married, living together and the natural parents of these children, are you not?"

"YES!"

"Then you don't qualify." I couldn't believe what I was hearing.

Dick sprang into action. He towered above the woman like a grizzly taking aim at a salmon. His big fist clenched white knuckles on her desk. "Are you telling me that because I'm not living in sin, that because my wife isn't a whore, and these two kids aren't legal bastards, that we're being penalized by your system?" he bellowed. Everyone in the office was looking.

"I'm sorry sir, that's the way it is. The children aren't deprived," she answered sarcastically.

"Deprived? I'll tell you who's deprived around here," he fairly shouted.

"Depraved..." I cut in, "the word is *depraved* and these people are just that." I was completely disgusted.

Dick boomed, "I guess it doesn't matter that there's no money, no food. If you don't fit into their idea of needing help, you're just screwed!" He glared at the woman, then, "We've watched people in here all day taking off expensive jewelry, cheating and *qualifying*. Well, lady, here's what you can do with all your *help*." He grabbed our application, tore it into a million pieces and threw it around the room. The pieces scattered like snowflakes.

"I wouldn't ask any one of you for the time of day. We'll make it, and it won't be because any one of you red-necked bastards!" His fist slammed down on the desk with all the might of a nuclear explosion.

Turning to me he said, "Come on, Baby, let's get the hell out of this den of snakes. I think I've picked up lice from talking to the vermin here." He stormed out, with us following close behind.

I half expected the state troopers to meet us at the door, but it never happened. I looked back to see everyone in the room sitting in a dead pan silence, as though in shock. The ride home was quiet, but steamy. Dick kept muttering about a system that penalizes a family for staying together and trying to make the best of what they have.

That rejection at the welfare office only caused us to dig our heels in harder. We vowed to make it in spite of everything. Still, we were getting close to desperate. This trip had used all the money we had; we hadn't received the help we needed and there was no food in the tent other than a few frozen carrots, potatoes and celery. None of us had any lunch in Fairbanks and we were now faced with the prospect of no supper at home. Even with the possibility of no supper, the tent and Tok looked better and better to us.

But I worried about the kids. They had been so good, such little troopers. How could we think of letting them go to bed without lunch or supper? It gnawed on me. I knew it was bothering Dick, too.

Finally we were bouncing down our own road. Dick turned into our driveway and in a forced up-beat tone announced, "Home at last!" And there, in the middle of the driveway, silhouetted in the truck lights, were six spruce hens. Supper! Dick grabbed the rifle we always carried, jumped out of the truck and shot four of the grouse. The other two flew away.

There was immediate thankfulness in the air. Dick cleaned and dressed the birds, using his homemade hunting knife and with Ricky's help I set about getting the wood stove started. Katherine helped me cut up the celery, potatoes and carrots. "Katherine," I asked, "will you go fill this pot with clean snow? Then set it on the stove to melt." With the aid of my ulu, I finished cutting the vegetables and we dumped them into the snow water.

Ricky's head popped into the tent. "Ready for the birds, Mom?"

"If they're clean."

"Yup. Naked, too." he snickered. "They were all full of spruce needles."

Great, I thought, *now the birds will taste like spruce trees*. The meat is so delicate it picks up the flavor of whatever they've eaten. But it was food.

Dick and Ricky brought the plucked spruce hens in and we cut them into big chunks and threw them into the stewpot. In a couple of hours we were all feasting on fresh stew. I dropped dumplings into the broth and it was really good. We shared an air of festiveness that night and all of us, especially Dick and I, were especially thankful for what we had. We put the Fairbanks incident far behind us and looked only to the future and survival. We ate leftover stew for several day, and went out and cut more firewood. We were able to sell another cord and buy a few staples.

Katherine's seventh birthday was December 9, and she had seen a doll at the store that was *her baby*. She had wanted that doll for months, always afraid that some other little girl would get to take her home. With some of the firewood money we'd made, Dick bought the doll and birthday ice cream. I baked Katherine's cake on the wood stove. The ice cream was set outside to keep it well frozen. When the kids got home from school that evening, Katherine was bursting with happiness.

"The whole class sang *Happy Birthday* to me, Mommy. The whole class!" She was ecstatic. *Funny about simple pleasures and how great they can be.* "Your cake is on the table," I said. She dashed over to get a better look.

"No tasting," I warned, just as one little finger poked into the icing.

"I was just testing." She looked at me innocently.

"Umm, more like tasting," I winked at Dick. These kids were chips off his block. He just looked smug, but said nothing.

After dinner we cut up the cake, sang *Happy Birthday* to Katherine and gave her the doll. She was so pleased. A million dollar bill wouldn't have made her as happy.

"Now for the ice cream," Dick announced, bringing it to the table. I opened the box and began spooning it out, or at least I tried. All I really accomplished was to bend the spoon.

"Seems to be a little hard. Flash-frozen in Tok temperatures. Maybe I'll use the ice cream scoop." That too, was unsuccessful.

"Guess we'll have to deal with forty-five below zero a different way," Dick commented. "Let's see it." He peeled the carton away from the ice cream brick, then reached for a hammer. Chris looked on, quizzically. Striking the block of ice cream several times, Dick shattered it like glass. Chris quickly retrieved an *ice cream mouse*, taking it to the corner and sharing it with Perk.

We picked the remainder of the shards up with our fingers, putting them on our cake plates, but soon found that the ice cream never softened to an edible stage. It was either frozen solid or runny like milk. There was no in between. So we ate our cake and chewed on ice cream *splinters*. They were tasty, but rubbery.

The next day we posted a list for people needing firewood. They could print their names, addresses and how much they needed and we would promise delivery. Dick figured this might lead to something regular instead of sporadic sales. More than a week went by as we kept checking our wood list, but it remained empty. One evening we made our usual check and were surprised to find four names on the list. Four customers needing a total of six cords of wood! That made our day. Soon we would be *rolling in the dough*.

Dick and I went out early the next day, cut the first cord of wood for ourselves and returned to the tent with it. Then we made another trip for the first name on the list, John Martiniuk. We cut the wood and split it with tremendous happiness. This wasn't work, it was sheer joy. Before delivering the first order of wood, we stopped by the tent. The kids were home from school and we didn't want them to worry because we'd be a little later than usual.

"Get lots of money, Dad!" Ricky called when we pulled out of the driveway. Dick winked at him as we departed in high spirits. We found Mr. Martiniuk's home and began unloading and stacking his firewood. It made a nice neat pile. We were just finishing when the owner came home.

"What's up?" John asked.

"Just delivering your wood," replied Dick.

"Wood? I didn't order any wood. I cut my own."

Dick looked at him blankly. "Didn't you sign your name on our wood list at the grocery store?"

"Nope. Sure didn't."

Dick looked at me. "I think we've been had, honey." I nodded and started to throw the pieces back into the truck.

"No, wait!" Martiniuk was gesturing. "Leave it, since it's here, I'll go ahead and pay you for it."

"You don't have to do that. You didn't order it." Dick said.

"I know. All the same, I can use it. I'll take it."

He paid us and we headed for the store once again to check out the rest of the names. We found out not one of them had requested wood. Dick told George, the store's owner, about it and George said he'd keep an eye on our list.

Someone with a sick mind had played a practical joke on us. George didn't think it was funny. Neither did we.

CHAPTER ELEVEN

Christmas

Christmas was always a special time at our house. As I grew up, my mother and dad always made it seem like each year was the best Christmas ever. It wasn't a bunch of expensive gifts that did the trick, because rarely was there anything very expensive. Rather, it was the spirit. Mother always made special cookies and candies. My dad always decorated the outside of our house with lights, Santa, reindeer and nativity scenes.

I sat in the tent, thinking back on those childhood memories, I suddenly realized that some of my most treasured gifts had been homemade ones. The doll house Daddy had made with his own hands when he was out of work and we were broke. And there was a beautiful wardrobe for my dolls because Mother had spent many hours sewing tedious stitches and sequins for some of the fancier dresses.

Maybe we could still make this a good Christmas for Katherine and Ricky, even though there would be no *store-bought* gifts. Just thinking back on my own Christmases had helped put me in a better frame of mind.

"Can I be in charge of the tree, Mama?" I looked at Ricky, such a little man.

"Do you think you can handle it? That's a pretty big responsibility, getting a Christmas tree," I questioned.

"That's just why I want to do it." he exclaimed. "It's got to be just the right one: special. 'Cause this Christmas is special."

"Well, I guess you're man enough for the job, then," Dick cut in. "Go to it. But don't go too far, and remember, it has to fit on this table. Take the bow saw and the whistle." The whistle was a safety factor. In case Ricky got lost or needed help, all he had to do was keep blowing the whistle and we could come to his aid. He quickly donned his Arctic gear, grabbed the bow saw and disappeared down the driveway.

Katherine waved goodbye until she could no longer see him. "Mama," she asked, suddenly serious, "does Santa know we're living here now? I asked Ricky, but he said I'd better ask you 'cause you'd know better."

I could have kissed Ricky on the spot for referring Katherine's question to me. He hadn't wanted to slip up and put any doubts about Santa into his little sister's mind even though he already knew this was going to be a lean Christmas for us. I turned to Katherine. She stood there expectantly, hoping for the right answer, but her face mirrored concern.

"Of course he knows, sweetheart. Santa keeps up with things like that."

"But will he know about our tent?"

"I'm sure he does. If he knows how good or bad you've been, then he must know about the tent. Right?"

She shifted from one foot to the other, mulling that thought around, weighing it, dissecting it.

"Besides," Dick cut in again, pulling Katherine onto his lap, "Santa could never forget such a good little girl as this one." He gave her a big hug. I could see she still wasn't quite convinced.

"Yeah," she paused, "but will he know how to get in and leave our presents?"

"Oh, yes. He's very smart."

"But it's dark in here at night. How will he see? Will he know which door to come in? He might stumble over the stove and burn himself! OH-h-h..." She let her sentence trail off in despair.

I put my arm around her shoulder. "Santa sees in the dark like we can see in the light. Santa has never let you down before and I'm positive he will find us. He'll probably be waiting outside in the dark, wishing the little girl in the tent would go to sleep early so he can bring her present. Besides, he's got Rudolph's nose just in case."

She let out a sigh of relief. "Oh!" A pause, then..."I'll go to sleep ear-r-ly on Christmas, Mama. Right after supper!"

"Good girl."

"Mama?"

"Yes, sweetheart." I couldn't help wondering what what troubling that seven-year old mind, now.

"Could we leave him something to eat? And Rudolph, too?"

I laughed, relieved. "You bet!"

She grinned a big broad, toothless smile. If ever there was a child who fit the song lyrics, *All I want for Christmas is my two front teeth*, it was Katherine. Only she lacked four front teeth, two on the top and two on the bottom. Thinking of his penchant for Americana and especially children, the artist Norman Rockwell, would probably have loved this face. So innocent. So typically toothless.

"Tell you what," I said, "why don't you finish coloring and pasting these candy canes and paper chains together so the tree will have something pretty on it. Okay?"

She set to work. This would be our first Christmas with no lights on our tree. I wondered how the kids would react to that when they realized we wouldn't have a brightly lit tree.

Soon Ricky was back with the tree. He was all smiles and so proud. "This is the tree!" he beamed. "Isn't it a beauty?"

"You did real good. Guess you're the official tree-getter from now on," Dick said, shaking the snow off its branches. "Have any trouble cutting it?"

"Naw, piece of cake," Ricky remarked, trying to be casual. He sounded exactly like Dick at that moment.

"You guys are two peas in a pod," I commented.

"Huh?" Dick questioned.

"Oh, never mind," I said, smiling to myself. I knew they'd never understand. I also knew that if Ricky really had run into trouble cutting that tree, there was no way he would have admitted it. Just like his daddy.

Dick positioned the tree in the stand, then secured it. Lifting the whole thing up onto the small table sitting at the end of Ricky's bed, he said, "There you go. Make it pretty."

Both kids worked diligently the rest of the evening making decorations to hang on its branches. They used everything imaginable. Paper, cardboard, string, aluminum foil, cereal box cut-outs, bits of leather, clothespins, scraps of yarn and material and lots of glitter. If we had wanted to put lights on the tree, it was so loaded there wouldn't have been room for them.

We stood admiring the tree, as the kids put the finishing touches to it. "There," Ricky said, "all done. It's a 'beaut'!"

"You both did quite a job," Dick praised, encircling my waist with his arm. He contemplated the tree.

"Penny for your thoughts?" I asked.

He pulled me closer, winked at me and said, "I was just thinking how proud Santa will be."

"Yeah," replied Katherine, jumping down from Ricky's bed. She was beaming, every bit as proud as her big brother. It didn't seem to bother them that there were no electric lights on it, they were just happy with their handiwork. This was *their* tree. It was also obvious that it was their gift to Dick and me. It brightened up the tent's interior and did wonders for our spirits. *Every tent should have a Christmas tree*, I thought.

Throughout the next week, I began to make Christmas gifts. Since funds were strictly limited, everything would be homemade. The mukluks had turned out so well that moosehide slippers were first on my list of gifts to be made. Dick helped cut the thick leather. Every morning before we went out for wood, I spent time sewing or beading on them. They turned out nicely. Next, at Dick's suggestion, was a leather camera bag for Ricky to protect his camera from the cold and tent dust and a leather drawstring purse for Katherine. They both needed mittens, so I added those to my list and soon had them in the making.

I lined the moosehide mittens with an old, woolen blanket, then beaded the backs of them for decoration. Katherine's had smiling Eskimo faces, while Ricky's were beaded with a smiling, flaming sun face. Both were trimmed with beaver fur. As a finishing touch, I added a long, leather thong which, when the mittens were worn, went from one mitten, up the arm, around the back of the neck, down the other arm and connected to the second mitten. This kept the mittens from being dropped into the snow if they were removed outside. The thong was decorated with a brightly colored yarn tassel where it attached to each mitten.

But these things, although pretty, were also practical items, so the last gifts I made were unpractical things. First, I made each of the kids a small yarn doll. Katherine's was a little girl doll with long, red yarn hair. Ricky's was a male version of the same thing. The final gifts were small, comical clothespin dolls, clothed in moosehide, material scraps and bits of yarn. Dick helped me with those. Then we wrapped all the homemade gifts and placed them under the tree. Now, it really seemed like Christmas.

Christmas Eve found us celebrating with *real* hot showers at the public showers in Tok. I thought about the last time we celebrated with hot showers and hoped we wouldn't return to something bad again. When we got home, Katherine and Ricky bounced out of the truck, their wet hair steaming, instantly freezing in the sub-zero temperature. Our wet towels, rolled up on my lap, were already frozen into hard brick-like bundles.

"I got the flashlight," called Ricky, entering the tent.

"Oh, WOW! Somebody's been here!"

I shuddered. Now what, I wondered. Dick and I expected the worst. He lit a lantern. "What's wrong?"

"Lookee!" Katherine picked up an object from the floor, just inside the tent door, and thrust it at me.

"Well, I'll be..." I trailed off, "is there a card with it?" Katherine lifted the tinfoil off the top of the bowl. It was filled with cookies and Christmas goodies, but there was no card.

"Wonder who brought it by?" Dick said, sampling a delicious morsel.

"Santa Claus!" Katherine fairly beamed.

"Well, I don't know, but it's sure nice of someone to think of us on Christmas Eve!"

I made hot chocolate for the four of us. We feasted on the cookies while the kids talked excitedly of Christmas and Santa Claus. Then suddenly...

"Listen," whispered Dick, "Sshhh." Everyone was silent. The tent roof, right at one end of the peak, was jiggling.

"What's that?" Ricky said, wide-eyed. The footsteps continued the entire length of the tent ridge. We were silent.

"It's Santa!" Katherine wailed. "He did bring the cookies. We gotta go to bed so he can bring our present!" She scurried into her nightgown. "Hurry, Ricky!" she pleaded.

Ricky looked at me. He was too old now to believe in Santa, but because of the cookies he did have an uncertain look about him, and I noticed that he lost no time in going to bed, either.

After placing our *Santa* gift under the tree for the kids, Dick and I turned out the lamps and snuggled into our own sleeping bags, our heads almost touching each other. I silently wished the little squirrel that had run across the roof a Merry Christmas. He'd never know what great timing he had or what a commotion he had caused. I made a mental note to place some crumbs outside for him as a Christmas treat.

"Quite a day, quite a day," Dick said, reaching over his head and running his fingers through my hair. I squeezed his hand, then kissed it.

"Merry Tent Christmas." Simultaneously, as seemed to be happening more and more often with us, we had voiced the same words, with the same emotion, at the same time, "... and Merry Christmas, little squirrel." We had just done it again. The tent was welding us into one person. I was so deeply in love with Dick, my heart pounded. I wondered if he felt it too.

"Feel it?" he asked, reading my thoughts.

I drew in a long breath, "Yes," I whispered.

"How does that happen, I wonder?"

"I don't know, but I'm glad it does. I'm so glad I married you," I said. This time, I reached across to him, stroking the small bald spot on top of his head.

He held my hand, whispered, "Merry Christmas. Love you," and drifted off to sleep, his hand still gripping mine.

"Ricky! Ricky! Ricky! Wake up, Ricky!"

I awakened to Katherine's Christmas-morning voice. "Ricky! Look what Santa left us!" He was rubbing his eyes, trying to focus on the tree and her extended index finger pointing at the tree.

"Oh, wow!" He suddenly came alive. Sitting under the tree, along with the homemade presents was one very special *store-bought* gift that Santa had left for them: a gingerbread house. Dick and I grinned at each other. This was the first time either of the kids had seen one close up. After admiring it sufficiently, they turned to open their presents. Neither one seemed the least bit disappointed over homemade gifts. When the opening of presents was over, I turned to getting things ready for the day.

We had been invited to spend the day at a friend's house. He was new to Tok, and so far his family hadn't been able to move from Anchorage. He was facing the holidays alone, so Bob asked us to come and spend the day at his house. All he asked was that I cook the turkey that he supplied. He didn't know how to cook. The turkey was ready to go. It had been cooking slowly in the wood stove's oven all night and smelled delicious. We transported it and ourselves to Bob's place around noon. The day was leisurely. I cooked the rest of the meal there. We enjoyed visiting, listening to the radio, relaxing. Everyone had a good time playing games.

When we returned to the tent that night, we were tired, happy and satisfied. It had been a great Christmas after all.

Before retiring to his own cot, Dick pulled my bag up around me, tucking me in for the night. "G'night, honey. Merry Christmas. I love you," he said cuddling me.

"Yeah," both kids whispered, "Merry Christmas!"

It truly was.

Little Tent, Big Tent

Denali with her mailbox

Donna and Dick working

Donna in Whitehorse

Dick on the Throne

Rick, Kath and Dick in Whitehorse

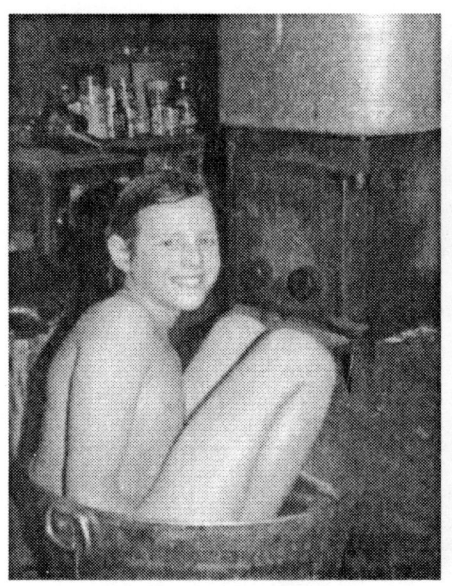 

Ricky takes a bath   Bathtime for Kath

The tent snowed in

Chris Jerk and Perk

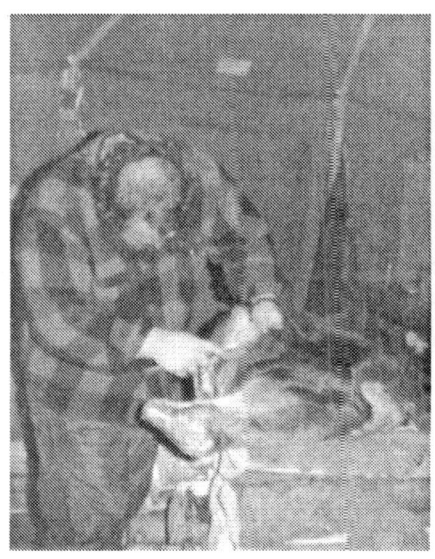

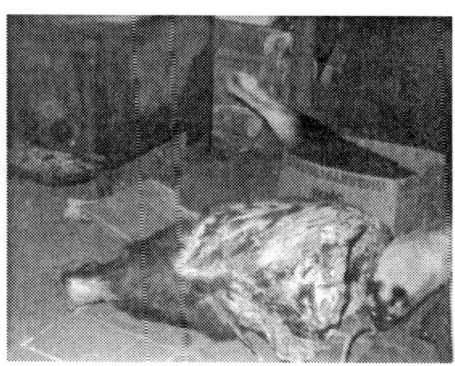

Bad moose meat

Dick cuts moose

Christmas in the tent

Kath at Christmas

Tok Cutoff Beauty

Cabin XMas Card

Dick works on cabin

VonHairy   Dick, VonHairy and bear

Howdy   Slim Pickens meets us

April 12, 1978

Mrs. Richard Bernhardt
P. O. Box 61
Tok Junction, Alaska 99780

Good Morning, Mrs. Bernhardt ...

A delight to hear from you. Let's
keep in touch.

               Sincerely,

PH:jw
enc. "Escape to Nowhere" (bd 4-11-78)

PAUL HARVEY NEWS
360 North Michigan Avenue
Chicago, Illinois 60601

Paul Harvey

VW being dug out

Valiant Stove

Center Beam

Nearly finished cabin

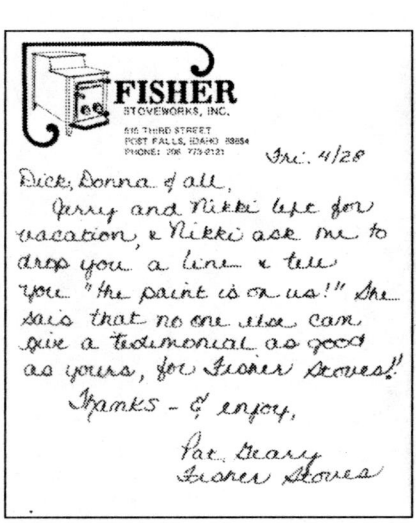

Fisher Stoveworks

Me and Perk

CHAPTER TWELVE

Poaching A Moose

"We've got to do something," Dick said, putting the last of our gas into the truck's tank. "We can't go on like this."

We were talking about food, something we had precious little of. Because of the long, dark days and this time of year being the lean months for most people in Alaska, we weren't selling much firewood. Our Christmas feast was over, jailguarding was non-existent. Now it was famine. No money, no groceries. No food stamps. It was as simple as that. Dick still bristled every time he thought about that incident.

"I don't like the idea, either, but do you see any other way?" He broke my train of thought.

"No," I said quietly, "we need the meat. It's a matter of survival, I guess. There's no money left and very little food."

Dick was cleaning his rifle. "I'll use the .223. It's not as loud. I've got several clips and the snow and cold won't hurt it. We'll go tomorrow..." he paused, studying my face, "And quit worrying. I've already made it clear in town that we need meat and I'll drop any bastard who stands between me and feeding my family, including a game warden. I don't think we're gonna be bothered."

If that was meant to console me, it didn't. It really bothered me, but I knew that Dick was desperate. We both were. There was nothing left to do but go out and kill a moose. Moose, tasty moose meat, in my opinion, better than beef and more of it on the hoof. It wasn't killing a moose that bothered me. This wasn't a matter of moose hunting. This would be moose poaching. The season had ended months ago.

In all of our years together, thirteen of them, we had never gone so far as to poach anything, even though some years were very lean ones. Somehow we'd always managed. But now it was different. No legal moose this year. It was either poach or let our kids starve.

The kids. "What will we do with the kids?"

"We'll have to tell them the truth and take them with us. It's the only way. They can't stay in the tent alone for that long, and we can't let them freeze to death while we're out getting meat to keep them from starving to death."

The words sounded harsh, but I knew he was right. Still, the skewed expression on my face must have bothered him. He cupped my face in his big hands. "Honey," he said, "do you want to quit right now? Pack up some clothes and move into Fairbanks? We could get welfare and fit into their system if we lived there." His hands dropped to my shoulders, resting there. He continued, a slight waver in his gentle voice, "Say the word and we'll go. This is stupid, you know, staying here."

One hand cupped my chin, lifting it slightly. This time, with much more conviction, he said, "No one much knows us. I don't think anyone cares. Frankly, I don't believe anyone gives a damn. The few who have heard of us are betting against us. It's an unfriendly place," he paused, looking me directly in the eyes. "It's an armpit." he said sarcastically.

I knew, once again, that he was trying to make it easier for me to give in, to give us an easy way out. I pondered his words. What he'd said was true. People in town were making bets. What were we proving? What was I proving?

For some strange reason, a variety of seemingly unrelated things went flashing through my mind including Joan of Arc. What did Joan of Arc have to do with the situation? She was a warrior. Is that how I saw myself? Certainly not. Maybe just because she and I were both redheads, I reasoned. Helen of Troy. Also another redhead. Strange thoughts, totally unrelated to moose poaching. I felt like I was in some kind of weird time-warp.

"Honey?"

The thoughts continued. *Women's lib. Bra burning.* "Haw!" I said, almost shouting. I think I must have had a smile on my face. I had never given much thought to the women's lib movement. I figured if that's what some women felt they needed to do, let them. I knew that a good portion of what they said, and the reforms they wanted, were needed. I'd also felt that for some women it was an excuse to do a lot of man-bashing, and that part of it didn't sit well with me. I was of the opinion that if those women had a man in their life like the one I had, they might not have been burning their bras. Equality was one thing, opportunism was another.

At that point, I know I smiled. I was conjuring an image of a bunch of bra-less women, living together in a tent and arguing over who was going to cut the firewood the next day. I laughed out loud. I certainly would never fit in the women's lib category.

Joan of Arc, Helen of Troy, women's lib. What was I thinking? Maybe living in the tent was altering my mental faculties. Maybe *my mind was slipping,* I wondered.

"Honey!" Dick shook my shoulders. He had a worried look on his face when I returned from my time-warp. "We'll come back in the spring." It sounded as though he'd already decided I'd had enough and would started packing.

"Dick, we don't have enough money to go to Fairbanks. We wasted it when we went there asking for help. That's the last time I ask for anything." *Did I sound bitter?* I hoped not. I hoped it came out with strength and conviction, not bitterness. Because I wasn't bitter. I was happy in what we were doing.

And that's when I made the connection. Although it may have been a far-fetched connection, it still seemed to be a connection between myself and those fragmented thoughts. What did those women all have in common? Certainly not red hair. No. Strength and conviction. Whether anyone else believed what they were doing was right didn't matter, *they* believed what they were doing was right. And I believed what Dick and I were doing was also right. I could have shouted it to the universe. Not until that very moment had it been an absolute for me. Not that I had ever doubted it, but at times I had wondered. We both had. Deep inside us we had felt this was what we should be doing, but now I knew, and I had to let Dick know that I knew. No matter how rough it was, we were fulfilling our convictions.

He was looking at me with great concern. "Dick," I began slowly, groping for the right words. "We both know Tok wasn't our first choice. Right?" He nodded while I continued, "And for some reason we were not only pointed the way by some invisible finger, but dumped here and made to stay, by the Almighty, by whatever, for some reasons we don't understand yet. Remember?" My words came faster now, as though afraid of losing my train of thought if I dared to stop for a breath. "Tok was not our choice. It was made *for* us. There has to be a reason." I didn't want to sound like a soap box preacher, but suddenly I was brimming with insight, and I felt desperate to get it across to him, just in case it hadn't fully hit him yet.

"Sometimes," Dick mused, "I think God has deserted us. Then some little thing happens and I know He's still there. But then I get to wondering where he is when the do-gooders, those who call themselves Christians, make their dutiful efforts to get us to go to their churches. Never asking if we're warm enough, or how the kids are eating, just trying to get us in their churches so we can give to them." He went on, "Hypocrites. Church membership is all they think about. Is that being a true Christian? Is that what God would do? Not once do they think of that and maybe what the other guy needs. Some of the truest Christians we've met in town don't even go to church. They're the good, honest people who really care about others. These *un-Christians* are better than the self-proclaimed ones." He looked at me, slightly red-faced. He was getting all steamed up.

"Now who sounds bitter?" I made that more of a statement than a question.

"Am I ranting?" he asked, defensively.

"Well, yes."

Dick stood there, thoughtfully, for a few seconds. "How did I get off onto this?" Lowering his gaze he simmered for a while, then continued, "Anyway, I know there's a reason we're here. But what?

You know me, I have a hard time waiting for answers. I usually need answers yesterday. Waiting isn't easy for me, especially when I watch you and the kids. It's so hard on you, day after day, trudging through the snow, packing cords of firewood in the miserable cold. No water, no lights. No nothing. Just a tent. This isn't the way it was supposed to work out." He gestured toward the beds, "And what about the kids? What kind of life is this for Katherine and Ricky? It's hard to see my family living like this. I just thought it would be easier if, well, you and the kids could stay in Fairbanks, I'll stay here. I just thought..."

"I know. And I love you for thinking, but don't think so hard. Quit already. Okay? Do you see anyone complaining? We're a family. We stay together, here, in our tent. We may not have a house, but how's that saying go? *Home sweet tent?*"

He sighed a sigh that held more than just a little bit of relief, "I think that's *Home Sweet Home* and boy, do I love you. I really got quite a package when I swept you off your feet."

I feigned an air of disdain. "'S'cuse me? Who swept whom off their feet?" We both laughed.

"And tomorrow we go get a moose," I said.

"Yup," he nodded.

".....So that's the plan," Dick explained to the kids as we bounced down the road in our truck. We had been over this road so many times that I knew when to bounce before we hit each pothole and frost heave. Dick continued, "No one will think much about the truck being out here because we cut wood every day. So if someone stops, just tell them we're out getting firewood." He was drilling this into the kids.

I prayed we wouldn't get caught. Poaching carries some stiff penalties. I hated the word *poach*. It sounded so bad, so illegal. It left no room for survival. On our many firewood trips we had seen plenty of moose. We knew right where one herd stayed. It would be easy to pick one out and kill it.

There, the easy part ended. Dick and I would have to cut it up and pack it out, uphill, to the truck, trip after trip, with no one seeing us. And this spot was easily seen from the highway.

We had one advantage though, a truck and firewood. A fact that Dick kept telling the kids. If someone stops, we're just getting firewood. The temperature was about forty-two degrees below zero. Not too many people would be out in that weather, maybe just an occasional car or game warden. Another problem. With only three hours of daylight, it would be dark soon, and harder to dress and pack out a moose in the dark, then again, we would be less easily seen.

It seemed like a bad day to me. *Wait until tomorrow*, I thought. Must be a bad case of nerves. Dick pulled off the side of the road and parked. He was telling the kids, "Remember, leave the keys on. The truck has to stay running or you'll get too cold just sitting here. Keep the doors locked."

"Go to the bathroom now," I interrupted, "I don't want either of you out of the truck for any reason." *I was probably worrying too much about my babies*, I thought. *But what the heck, that's what mothers do.*

Dick continued, "Yes, definitely don't get out of the truck. Katherine, you mind Ricky." He sized up his son, then said, "Ricky, you're in charge here. If you need us just keep honking the horn. You won't be able to see us, but we'll come back to the truck if we hear the horn. Got it?" Ricky shook his head up and down.

"Don't get out of the truck and come looking for us." I could see from the look on Dick's face that he meant it, and I wasn't the only one worried about our babies. He went on, "As soon as we kill a moose, we'll come back and get you. Then you can come and help us with it. Leave this window cracked, like this, just slightly. Okay? Any questions? Good. Now, where are Mama and Daddy?"

"Moose hunting!" Katherine giggled.

"No, they're not!" Ricky snapped at her, "They're out cutting firewood."

This was futile, I thought. Katherine would let it slip if they were asked. *Dear God*, I prayed, *let us get this moose and get out of here without getting caught. Take care of our babies in the truck*, I added while Dick and I plunged through the snow.

"Maybe an hour 'til they show up to browse," he was saying as we sat on a log resting, "should be just right. It'll be dark by then."

He was right. It was 1:30 now. Another hour and it would be almost dark. Easy enough to shoot a moose, then be cloaked in darkness while we packed it out. I drew in a deep breath of sub-zero air, exhaling it deliberately hard. The air issued forth like a blow torch of frozen fog. Smiling in amusement I did it again.

"I love you, Alaska," I heard Dick say softly.

Warming my hands beneath my parka I commented, "Yeah, boy, I love Alaska, too. So much it hurts."

"No, I meant *you* Alaska," Dick corrected me. "I mean, to me, you *are* Alaska."

"Oh!" I laughed, "You mean I'm millions of acres around, cold as ice and too wild to be tamed?"

"Naw, you know what I mean. I've said it before. I love Alaska. I love you. You are part of the Alaska I love. Look at you. You're sitting on a log at fifty below zero, out in the middle of nowhere bundled up so heavily I can't even see your freckles, waiting for supper to drop by and you're playing with your own frozen breath. Now is that Alaska or what? You're my Lady Alaska. I rest my case."

"Well, I'm just glad it doesn't mean my southern territory is too large." I goaded him.

"Nope. And I sure do love that northern territory, too," he quipped, reaching for my gloved hand. "Hey, Alaska..." He had that familiar look on his face.

With mock sternness I said, "No fraternizing with this wild country. Besides, it's fifty below and..."

"Uh, oh," he mumbled. I looked the direction his mittened hand was pointing. Five or six moose had just come out of the brush and into the clearing. Several more were behind that group. They moved out right in front of us. Beautiful beasts. Everyone I'd ever talked to called them big and ugly. Not me. I loved moose. On the hoof or on the table. It didn't matter.

"They're early," Dick whispered, "they never come out here this early."

It figures, I thought to myself.

"I could pick one off right now." He continued. "Beautiful shot."

"And anybody driving by over there on the highway in the next hour would see it," I warned. The highway was at least a quarter of a mile away, but there was nothing between it and us except frozen marsh.

"Yeah, better wait a while, I guess." He resigned himself to waiting.

I watched this man I loved so much. He peered into the distance, thoughtfully staring at a range of gargantuan mountains. His beard, covered in frost, made him look very Santa-like. I smiled. He was intent on the mountains. "Penny for your thoughts," I said, gently nudging him.

"Ummm, I was just thinking about those mountains. How rugged they are, the great earth upheavals that caused them to be eons ago. Alaska must have been one gigantic cataclysm a long, long time back."

"Probably," I said, "but even as old as they are, they're still relatively young mountains. All our mountains are so rugged, yet not worn and weathered. That's a sign of young mountains."

"Yep. And that's exactly what I was thinking about." He turned to me. "How things can be young and still be old at the same time. Hell, I'm only 33 years old, but damn if sometimes I don't feel lots older than that."

I laughed. "Yeah, you're ancient, old man."

"No, really. Don't you ever feel like you're older than you really are? Well, not older. Maybe I should rephrase that. Wiser. Yeah, that's it. Don't you ever feel like you're wiser than your actual years?"

"Sometimes, yeah." I answered "Sometimes I get flashes of what I interpret to be wisdom, and I wonder where it came from. Sometimes I think it comes from living up here all my life. You know, Alaska sort of, in some way, makes you wiser, or at least more aware of things I believe."

He grinned, part of the frost breaking off his mustache, "Yep, our lifestyle makes us more aware of things. Cripes, considering the lifestyle we're living right now, by the time we get our cabin built we oughta be *very* aware!"

Twenty more minutes passed with each of us absorbed in our own thoughts. I was getting cold in spite of mukluks, down pants, parka and a face mask. The Tok area experiences some of the coldest weather in North America with unofficial lows in the sub-zero seventies. While I was dressed appropriately enough for the cold, I wasn't moving. That was the problem. We were sitting, being very quiet, watching the moose just one hundred feet or so in front of us. At fifty below, you need to keep moving.

My rear end was numb. Picturing black cheeks, I wondered if it would be frostbitten. There was a miserable thought. I dismissed it, turning to Dick. His face was almost completely covered in frost now. Beard, mustache, even his eyebrows and lashes caught the vapor, freezing them as he breathed. He wasn't Santa anymore. Now he resembled the abominable snowman. My fingers hurt. I wondered about the kids. The horn hadn't honked so they must be all right. I couldn't see the truck from where we were.

A car on the highway stopped. They had seen the moose. Dick and I froze, hardly daring to breathe for fear of being seen. After what seemed like hours, they drove off, but the moose were also moving. The car had startled them. They were moving away from us, across the clearing. Soon they'd be out of sight and back in the trees. Dick stood up.

"It's now or never," he announced.

"No, it's too light yet. Wait."

"Can't, they'll be gone. Which one do you want?" Just then they stopped moving and began to browse again. I breathed a sigh of relief.

"Good thing. Now we can wait," Dick said.

About 30 minutes later, the daylight was almost gone. Dick figured he could still see well enough to place his shots and, with luck, the dark would close in fast enough to guard our dirty deed from view. He shouldered the rifle.

"If he runs, take note of where he goes," he told me, and drew down to fire.

"Wait!" I shouted. "Listen! There's another car coming." We both flattened ourselves into the snow. The car slowed down and stopped near our truck. We listened. A car door opened and we could hear voices. I strained to hear what was taking place. Someone was talking to our kids. My heart pounded in my ears.

Keep your mouth shut, Katherine, please. I prayed.

Minutes were ticking away; it was getting dark. Finally, we heard the car door slam, then the sound of tires moving down the highway. Just one car door slammed. That meant the kids had not opened the truck door at all. They were safe. No one had taken our babies, or suspected us.

Dick stood up. "Stupid people. They're gonna cost us this moose. It's almost too dark to aim, now. See the small bull? Second from the left? That's the one. Watch him, hon."

I watched. He aimed and fired. "Hard to see the sights," he said and fired again. The herd was moving away rapidly. Our moose just stood there.

"What the..." Dick paused. "Didn't I hit him? Could you tell?"

"Try again before he wises up and runs off, too," I suggested.

"See if you can see where I'm hitting him."

I strained to see in the failing light. It was almost dark. Bang! Bang! Bang! The moose continued to stand there.

"I must have missed him," Dick said angrily.

"I don't know. I can't tell. It's too dark to see for sure." Dick was an excellent shot. He never missed, but then, it *was* almost dark.

"The hell with the head and shoulder shots," he roared. "I'm going for any broadside shot."

And he fired, again, three times. Four. Five. Six. I couldn't believe it. I'd never seen any moose this stupid. It was almost as though he weren't real, like a cardboard cut-out used for target practice. He wasn't flinching and he wasn't running away. Finally he raised his big head and looked around, then pawed at the snow.

"Well, there's some movement," I said. "At least we know he's not a figment of our imagination!"

"Eleven shots and I've missed every time? Don't know how that's possible. Don't ever tell anyone about this. I'll never live it down." He kept firing and emptied the rifle.

I've been on a lot of moose hunts and had never seen anything like this. I couldn't make myself believe Dick had missed every shot. He had to have hit it once. Something funny was going on here.

Dick rammed another clip into the rifle. "I'll get him yet!" And he fired away. The moose began to amble toward the trees. "Might as well save a few bullets," Dick said in an exasperated tone, "it's just too dark to try any more." By now, the moose had disappeared into the snow and underbrush. We began walking across the frozen marsh. We had to see if there was any blood in the snow. Had Dick really missed all those times? I couldn't believe he had. *But if he had hit it, why didn't it turn and run?*

"Must be a really stupid moose," I mumbled, and suddenly realized I wasn't cold any longer. Too much excitement to be cold. "Here, here's where he was standing."

Dick asked for the flashlight. "There's no blood in the snow. I knew it. I wasted all that time, all that ammunition, all of this, just to miss it every single time."

"But..."

"No buts, and don't you ever tell anyone about me missing a moose thirty-six times!" We would have both laughed if we hadn't needed the meat so badly.

"Funny, I don't hear him crashing around in the trees any more," I commented.

We began to follow his trail into the trees. I wondered how the kids were doing. Ricky must be worried about so many shots. We walked and stumbled through the snow-covered brush for another fifteen or twenty minutes, following the moose prints in the trail. Here and there it criss-crossed other moose prints. In the dark, it was difficult at times knowing which tracks belonged to our moose.

Finally, we saw a few drops of blood in the trail.

"Looks like I hit him once," Dick remarked sarcastically.

"Either that or he's got a vicious hangnail." We both laughed and continued on, the flashlight beam disappearing into the jet-black night ahead of us. Entering a thick patch of swamp trees slowed our progress.

"Hmmmp..." I voiced to myself.

"Huh?" Dick turned to question me.

"Oh, nothing. I was just marveling at the way an animal as huge as a moose can get through this kind of crap, and so quickly. I mean look how thick it is."

"Yeah, pretty amazing, all right. Here, we're almost out of it now," he said, holding a limb so that it wouldn't snap back and hit me in the face.

"Oh my God!" I said, looking beyond him.

"What?" He swung around, following my gaze.

There lay a moose, right in front of us. Dead. He was on his back in the snow, with his legs straight up in the air.

"Someone else has been here before us." Dick said, dryly, "Shot and lost their moose."

I walked over to the dead moose. "He's still warm!"

"No..."

"Yes! Warm, he's still warm. Come see."

Dick was beside me now. The head of the moose had rolled to one side, half-buried in bloody snow, it's tongue hanging out.

I turned to Dick. He was just staring at it. "I don't get it," he said. "Help me roll it onto its side." That is no easy matter. In several feet of snow, an eight or nine-hundred moose is a lot to handle. We pushed him over, then gaped in bewilderment. This was not someone else's moose. It was ours.

Dick had hit it, apparently, every time he aimed and fired. One-half of its head was blown away. The first eleven shots had hit their mark after all. This was unbelievable. It should have fallen immediately. Flinched. Something!

Dick knelt down, knife in hand. "I'll start gutting and cleaning. You go back to the truck and get the kids. Bring the meat saw back, too, and the pack boards..."

He was interrupted by twigs snapping. We listened. Suddenly another moose broke clear of the trees. It was less than twenty-five feet from us. A big cow moose. Seeing us, she stopped, then just stood there looking at us with big, unblinking, brown eyes. Sleek and proud, steam vented from her nostrils in the cold air. She was beautiful.

"Shall I kill her, too?" Dick was asking, "Lots of meat"

"No. We got our moose. We can't take care of two, it's too much. Besides, it's a cow moose, not a bull."

"I know, I know, temptation though, all those T-bones just standing there." He was almost drooling.

Dick handed me the rifle. "Go." He told me, almost like he didn't trust himself with the rifle with the second moose still standing there. She turned and went back through the trees.

I headed uphill toward the truck, trying to break a good trail as straight and easy as I could find. A good one to bring meat back and forth without wasted or difficult steps.

The kids had the light on in the truck, eating vanilla wafers.

"Mama!" Both shouted at once, "Did you see him?"

"Yes, what did he want?"

"Who?"

"The man who stopped a while ago," I said panting.

"Oh, him," said Ricky, "just to know if we needed help, but..."

"Did you see him? Did you?" Katherine cut in.

"Yes, honey, I did."

"Great, gr-r-r-e-a-t big horns," she was saying.

"Oh, come off it, Katherine," I tried not to be too short with her. "Nobody has horns."

Ricky countered, "Nope. But that moose sure did."

"Moose? What moose?"

"The big, giant mo-o-o-s-e-!" Katherine had her arms outstretched, "horns this big!"

"He came up out of the woods," Ricky said. "He stood right there, eating some bushes for a while. Then he walked over to our truck, Mama, and he looked inside. Right through Daddy's window."

Katherine ventured, "....and he smoked up the window," she giggled.

"Frosted," Ricky corrected her, "he was breathing on the glass."

"You could see his teeth!" Katherine flashed hers for me. "Ricky wouldn't let me pet him an' I would've gave him a cookie, too..." She put on a theatrical poutface.

"Of course not. You did good, Ricky."

An air of superiority came over him. He was wearing an *I-told-you-so* look.

"Get your things on, all of them. Bring the cookies, Katherine, and you can carry the thermos, too. Ricky, grab the meat saw. I'll get the packboards."

"You got a moose? Yippee!" Ricky hadn't heard all those shots after all. Now he was excited.

Katherine asked if she could have some hot chocolate. I told her to wait until we got back to Daddy and our moose. It was hard walking for Ricky, but even more difficult for Katherine. She was flailing her way through the deep snow. The kids had to be with us in the field, though. We couldn't leave them in the truck at night. We still had hours of cutting and packing ahead of us.

The temperature was dropping, too. Probably another ten degrees colder. No sun. No heat at all. That's the way it was. By morning it would be colder still. We were heading into a long, cold spell. I could feel it coming.

Katherine fell headlong over a stump, buried in snow. Luckily, she had on her face mask. Couldn't afford frozen cheeks on my baby. She didn't cry, but I picked her up and carried her the rest of the way.

Dick's beard was completely encrusted with frost and his hands and gloves were already blood-soaked when we arrived.

"Oh, boy!" Ricky whooped.

"Yuk. Dead moose," was Katherine's only remark.

We began cutting and sawing. Dick's hands were so cold, he kept shoving them inside the moose's body cavity to warm them. I told him about the giant moose the kids had seen.

"Hold the front legs," he said while he sawed up the breastbone. We had already dumped out the guts. Katherine was gingerly poking them with a stick.

"Stinky, yuk."

"And plenty of good hamburgers." Ricky was the hamburger and french fry kid.

Dick sniffed, "Does smell funny. You ever smelled a moose that has an odor like this one?"

I shook my head no as he went on. "Never killed a moose in December. Maybe they just smell different at times."

We tied a front quarter to my packboard, some smaller pieces to Ricky's, then took a break.

"Did you notice the chest area?" Dick was saying, "peppered with bullet holes. I don't think I missed him once. Look at all those holes."

"It's pretty weird," I said, "never seen anything like it. He must have been completely numb."

We drank some hot chocolate before Ricky and I started to the truck with our first load of meat. Dick would remain with the moose and continue cutting. Katherine would stay with him.

It wasn't easy traveling in spite of having made a trail. In absolute darkness it was difficult not to stumble over bushes and stumps buried underneath the snow. I had Ricky walk ahead of me so I'd know exactly where he was at all times. He couldn't walk as fast as I could, so that slowed my pace and made it even more difficult. The cold was still closing in and we were packing uphill on a gradual incline. Between snow and the incline, my legs ached. The pack was very heavy. It's straps cut coldly into my shoulders. Ricky was thrashing ahead, laboring under his own load.

"Mama, are you sure all the bears are asleep now?"

"They're hibernating, Ricky. Fast asleep."

"What if one wakes up?"

"If you had a choice, would you wake up and go out in the cold, or would you stay in your nice, warm bed?"

He thought a minute, "Right!" And then he cheerfully trudged on. *Quite a kid, we've got there*, I mused to myself proudly. *Quite a kid.*

We reached the last incline, the road embankment. It was steep, probably a twenty-five or thirty foot embankment. I thought for a moment. Smarter to leave the meat at the bottom, stashed and covered with snow, than to go up to the truck each time, wrestling the meat up that incline. That way, no one snooping around would see the meat in the back of the truck and there would be no obvious blood trail up and down the slope.

"Take off your pack, Ricky. We'll leave the meat down here for now."

The way back to the moose was easy. When I got there, Katherine was starting to cry. Her hands were cold. I unzipped my parka and put her hands inside my shirt. "You've got to keep your hands moving, Baby. That's what will help keep them warm. When you put your mittens back on, play pat-a-cake or something to keep them moving." *Kids noses, feet and hands are especially vulnerable to the cold. I've got to watch them carefully,* I reminded myself.

Dick asked Ricky how he was doing.

"Fine, Dad, fine. I'm warm. I'm a man!"

"Ricky," I said, "even men get cold. Just ask your daddy."

"You better believe it," Dick responded, still cutting meat. "Being cold and admitting it. That's a man."

"Well, my fingers are a little cold, but just a little." I warmed his hands the same way I'd done Katherine's.

Over the course of the next several hours, Ricky and I made trip after trip, packing out moose meat. He was a great help, never complained and I complimented him on it. "Thanks, Mom," he smiled proudly, puffing as we arrived once more at the kill site.

The two hindquarters were too heavy for me, so we saved those until last. Dick would have to pack those out.

"You'll have to make two trips for them," I said.

"No. Strap both of them on together. This is the last trip to the truck. I'll carry them both at once."

"They're too heavy to do that," I pleaded. "I know you're strong as an ox, but..."

"I can do it. You'll just have to help me lift it up and get it on my back. Then it'll be okay."

"You're also stubborn as a mule," I pointed out. He shrugged and grinned.

I had my own pack lashed with a light load of meat: the neck, heart and smaller pieces that were left. Ricky's board contained the meat saw and thermos. We cleaned up the kill site and covered everything there with fresh snow. It would be obvious from the air in daylight, but someone would have to be directly over it to spot it.

"I'll go on ahead," Dick said, "and meet you at the truck. Once I've got this pack on, I've got to keep moving. I can't stop."

I helped him shoulder his pack. It was too heavy. I knew it. He knew it. But he was anxious to get out of there. He disappeared up the trail.

"Come on, kids. Ricky get your pack and you go first. Katherine will go between us. And don't go too fast. She can't walk very fast, remember." I took some spruce boughs and dusted behind me, covering our trail as we went. It was very slow going. Most of the time I had to carry Katherine. We stopped and rested. I was leaning on a tall stump, marveling at the utter stillness of the late evening when I heard a shout. There it was again. The kids had heard it too. We listened.

It was Dick! Somewhere ahead on the trail, in the dark, something had gone wrong. I swept up the kids, hurried up the trail and rounded a bend, my lungs burning from the sudden exertion in fifty below cold.

There he was, face down in the snow. His body askew, he lay draped over a small log, feet higher than his head, and the pack was holding him there like an anchor. One foot was caught in branches.

In the dark and snow, Dick had tripped while stepping over the log, lost his balance and fallen. The weight of the pack prevented him from righting himself. He couldn't move. I freed his foot, then dug the snow away from his body. This gave him maneuverability, but he still couldn't get up. We needed to get the pack off. I took his knife and cut the rope holding the meat. Bloody hindquarters fell to both sides, rolling into the snow.

Now that Dick was free he rested, then admitting partial defeat said, "I'll take one hindquarter to the stash from here, then come back and get the other one."

It sounded like a much more sensible plan. We trudged on to the stash. There, the kids and I waited for Dick to return the second time. Katherine and Ricky got into the truck and began to warm up while I started hauling stashed meat up the incline and into the bed of the truck.

When Dick arrived with the second hindquarter, we worked as a relay team. My part was from stash to midway up the incline.

Dick took it from there and heaved it into the truck. Within thirty minutes we were loaded, had the meat covered with a tarp, snow and pieces of firewood, and wiped away any signs of blood around the road area.

We were off! All we had to do was drive home. We hadn't been caught. The kids were jabbering about hamburgers all the way back to the tent. I leaned back and rested. My back ached, my arms and legs were tired. Ricky and Katherine even looked a little worn out. I knew Dick was tired, too. He hunched over the steering wheel, deftly guiding us safely home.

"Thank you, God," I whispered. Dick reached over and squeezed my hand, mouthing a silent *love you*.

Katherine and Ricky leaped from the truck upon our arrival, glad to be home even if it was a tent. While Ricky started lighting the lamps, Dick and I got a fire going in the wood stove. Soon it was warm enough to take off our parkas. We laid canvas and cardboard down on the dirt floor inside the tent and brought in some of our prized meat. The cats sniffed at it and backed away, their hair bristling.

"There's a city cat, all right," Dick said, laughing. "If it's not fried chicken, it isn't fit to eat!"

"Speaking of fried," I said, "let's cut off some steaks for tonight."

"Steaks, Mom?" Ricky asked.

"Yes, we earned them, don't you think?"

His head bobbed up and down as though on a spring.

Dick sawed off four nice, big frozen steaks. All of the meat was nearly frozen by now. I plopped them into a cast iron frying pan to fix later.

"I'll help you finish wiping off the meat. We'll eat after you take it in to *you-know-who*."

I was referring to one of the few friends we'd made since coming to Tok. He knew of our plight and sympathized with it. And he wasn't afraid to help a friend cut up a moose whether it was in season or out. He had seen some tough times, too, and was going to help us cut and wrap the moose meat in his small, backroom butcher shop. His generosity would save us many hours of labor. Instead of Dick and me being up all night cutting and wrapping, now there were two men, better equipment and a clearer place than the tent to take care of the meat. That gave me time to do things around the tent, feed the kids and get back to normal life.

Ricky helped Dick unload the equipment we had taken with us. Dick was in a hurry to deliver the meat, but I reminded him that he was covered with blood, wet, cold and he also smelled awful. The arms of his shirt and his gloves were saturated with partially frozen blood. It made him smell anything but good.

While Dick was changing into clean, dry clothes, I fixed a cup of coffee for him. "Whew!" I said, almost gagging. "I always thought you looked like a big Grizz. Now you smell more like grizzly bait."

"Yeah, try wearing these things," he said, holding up the bloody clothes. "These things are nasty!"

"I can't argue with that," I replied, "just put them outside the tent and let them freeze. That way they won't smell up the whole tent. I can deal with them later."

I handed the cup of steaming coffee to him. "Ummm, that hits the spot. Warms from the inside out. Guess I'd better go."

Dick left with the load of moose meat. I picked up things and cleaned the knives and meat saw, stoked up the stove once more, and set the frying pan on it to start the steaks thawing for cooking later.

Katherine had retired to her bed where she sat with a coloring book and crayons in her lap, busily creating a new masterpiece. The canvas walls around her bed were papered with her colorful efforts. Ricky spent his time playing with the kitten. Diligently trying to coax him into eating a small piece of the moose meat, but all the animated little fur ball would do was hiss at the meat. The Parka Puss wanted no part of it.

Suddenly very tired, I sat on my cot and began brushing my hair, letting go a little, forcing my muscles to relax. With each stroke of the brush my long hair crackled with static electricity. The long strands, trailing the brush, stood at a ninety degree angle to my head, held there by the invisible force. I licked the palm of my hand and swiped it down my hair. Reluctantly, the renegade strands returned to their proper place. "Dry air plus sub-sub zero," I said to myself, "equals a hair-do that does whatever it wants."

I had almost forgotten my own wet shirt. It wasn't wet from blood but rather, perspiration. In spite of the very low temperatures, and it was now around fifty-eight below, the body still perspires when active and that can become a problem. I was beginning to chill. That would never do. After changing shirts, I stood near the stove, warming my backside.

The heat felt so good I closed my eyes, mentally going back over the events of the day. A hard day. A risky day. Not a day I would want to do over again. Glad it was over. We would have meat for the rest of the winter. No more rationing food. Our babies wouldn't go hungry after all. I began to relax with the heat; tension moved out of me. I felt good. Tired, but relieved that the worst part of today was behind us. Dreamily, I thanked the Lord once more. Time slowly drifted away.

"Ricky stinks," Katherine broke my stupor-like state.

"I do not!"

"Do too."

"I didn't do that!" Ricky sounded indignant. "You did!"

Katherine responded with a loud, "Didn't!"

"Did so," Ricky growled.

I intervened, "Just a minute, you two."

They both looked at me with such innocence. "Mama did it!" Ricky teased.

My muddled brain had begun making the connection between my nose and what they were talking about. Something sure smelled bad. I could hear the meat sizzling in the pan behind me. Idly, I picked up a fork and turned one steak over. The odor rising from the pan nauseated me. Instead of the wonderful smell of a steak cooking, this piece of meat smelled more like moldy hay being fried. It was terrible. Taking the pan from the stove, I discovered the awful truth. All four steaks stunk badly. I sighed. No steaks tonight.

I wondered if we had ruptured the bile sack while gutting the moose. That seemed like the only explanation. If the bile had gotten on some of the meat, that part of the meat wouldn't be fit to eat. We had been so careful, though. How could it have happened? *Well,*

I thought, *it's macaroni again*, and started melting snow for the water.

While the kids were eating I kept thinking about that moose. I was sure we hadn't perforated the bile sack and yet ...

Katherine and Ricky were finished and ready for bed. I kissed them both good night, tucked them in and gave each one an extra big hug just for being so uncomplaining. Katherine wanted to know where her daddy was. I told her he'd be back pretty soon and would be sure to give her a kiss when he got home, even if she was asleep. She closed her eyes and before long both kids were sleeping soundly.

Couple of good kids we've got, I thought.

I made myself a cup of tea and decided to patch a pair of jeans while waiting for Dick's return. I had just cut a scrap of moosehide to a suitable size for the patch when I heard our truck coming down the road. The meat cutting had taken even less time than I had supposed it would. Dick shut off the engine. I could hear his slow steps to the tent door. They sounded tired, hesitant. Finally, the flap opened and he stepped inside. The look on his face told me something was wrong, very wrong. I wasn't sure I wanted to know.

Warming himself by the fire, he spoke, slowly at first. "Honey," he faltered, "it's the meat." He wavered again, weighing his words, heavily. He looked at me almost apologetically. "It's probably no good."

His words stunned me. I was speechless, not letting myself believe what he was trying to say.

Dick softly continued, "The meat, the stink. It's probably no good. We were cutting it up and the inner layers of it is full of holes, like pockets, and there's stuff in the pockets like sawdust. We quit cutting on it, it just smelled too bad. So we'll keep it frozen for now 'til we know for sure ..."

I felt as though my heart had stopped, like the world was coming to an end. Like a two-edged sword, his words couldn't have hit me any harder.

Dick continued, "We sent some of it, a sample, to the game biologist to see what's what. But, I'm sure in my own mind ..." he took my hand and held it, "... the meat's no good."

I blinked, trying to clear my thoughts. My head was reeling with the consequences of what was taking place. "All of it?" I finally managed to ask.

"All of it."

There was a finality in his voice. I knew he was positive. Numb with that knowledge, I stood, just staring, an empty hollow deep inside my guts. It wasn't fair. All of the hard work, the cold, the hardships on the kids. *It couldn't be happening. We needed that meat so badly. Why us?*

"I'm sorry, honey," Dick said, hugging me.

"It's not fair," I mumbled, my face buried in his chest. "All we want is to survive. To feed our kids." I looked up toward the roof of the tent. "Is that too much to ask, God?"

Dick, trying to comfort me, only made it worse. "But look here," he said, reaching into his shirt pocket. "It's not a total loss. You won't believe this, but look here."

He was brandishing a twenty-dollar bill.

"When we finally gave up cutting on the meat I was so discouraged," he said, but when I was leaving his place, something came over me, something made me walk to this row of water jugs. I don't know why. I randomly picked up one of the five-gallon jugs and there was this twenty on the floor beneath it. Just like it had been put there for me to find. He told me I found it, that I should keep it. Isn't that crazy? So we may not have the meat, but we've got gas money for tomorrow. It's got to be a good sign." He sounded almost enthusiastic.

That did it for me. In all the time in the tent, I had never been so disappointed. I had managed to bolster Dick when he began to have doubts. I had tried to remain strong and sure. At times I'd had to remind myself that I was strong and sure. But now I found myself folding. I couldn't help it. I was caving in, as surely as a river bank erodes under pressure of a spring thaw. This was my low point, and a twenty-dollar bill didn't seem like much compensation for all that work and eight hundred pounds of meat, now lost.

I cried. Great sobs vented forth. I was grateful that the kids were asleep, not witnessing their mother crying like a baby. I couldn't stop. It was as though a dam had just burst inside me.

Dick held me tightly. "It'll be all right," he said. I shook with desperation. He wiped away my tears.

When I was finally able to control myself, I retired to my cot for the night, my ribs sore from crying so hard. Dick turned out the lamps and lay down on his own cot. One last tearless sob involuntarily issued from me in the dark. He reached over, put his arm around me and whispered with conviction, "It *will* be all right."

I wondered.

The next morning we went out and cut wood with my face still red and swollen from tears. But I had cried myself out. There were no more tears left inside me.

The following week was hell. Cold, cold and more cold. Broken ax handles. A chain saw that didn't want to run. A truck that didn't want to start. Extreme food rationing for me and Dick. Our stomachs growled with hunger.

New Year's Day arrived bitterly cold. My hunch had been right about the cold spell settling in. It was still hovering in the minus fifties, day and night. We were cutting a cord of wood every single day. At night we'd unload the entire cord and stack it inside the tent. This served several purposes. First, the firewood was kept dry in case of snow at night. Second, it was handy, and with such a big tent, there was plenty of room for it. It filled up an entire corner of the tent. But most importantly, we didn't have to make a trip outside the tent every 15 minutes to keep the stove stoked. Hauling it inside eliminated many openings of the tent door and kept our precious heat from being lost. By morning, almost every log and stick of wood would be gone. In spite of an efficient stove, we were forced to cut a cord of wood a day now, just to stay warm enough to sleep.

We cut a second cord to sell in town, but the post-Christmas season was a bad time for selling wood. Everyone was broke and if we couldn't sell wood, we'd be in serious trouble very soon.

Word had been passed around about our moose meat. Dick had been right; it was no good. Our moose had a disease caused from an old wound, evidently when he was gored by another moose during rutting season. While the wound itself had healed, infection had set in and spread throughout his body. He was dying.

That explained all the gunshots. He really had been numb! And the stink. He was slowly rotting away, a living death. We had probably done him a favor by killing him. The technical name for his infection was two winters long, but it meant one thing. We couldn't eat the meat. We found out later that it was only the second moose in seven years known to have the disease and we had picked that one as ours. It made me sick to think of the other moose we could have killed that would have provided us with good meat. Our meat wasn't fit for human consumption, so we fed it to the dog. He ate like royalty, while we existed on sparse meals.

Christmas vacation was over and Katherine and Ricky were now back in school. That, in itself, was a blessing. At least, for eight hours each day, they were comfortable. And they had hot running water to wash their hands and faces, not that they seemed to mind melting snow in the tent. It didn't seem to bother them either way. They were versatile kids, those two.

Dick was just about ready to load the chain saw into the truck by now. It had taken about three hours to get the truck running, since all we had was a small two-burner camp stove as our truck starter. Dick would light both burners, shove the stove under the oil pan and lay a blanket over the hood of the truck. The heat then warmed the oil and the engine enough to get the truck started. But in these severe temperatures it took a long time for those little flames to warm so much cold metal. The truck would need gas soon. We hadn't sold any firewood and we had to have gas to go out and cut wood for our own use. It was a vicious circle. We had to do something fast. No money, no gas, not much food, little hope of any change. Things didn't look good that morning.

Dick and I had discussed it all, over and over, and yet some type of a calm peace had come over both of us, like a positive understanding. It was as if we knew that things would get better, and we let ourselves be enveloped in that feeling. At times, we projected that feeling to each other, without a clue as to the reasoning behind it. Something good was going to happen.

"Hello, the tent!"

We looked at each other blankly. Someone was here?

"Hello, the tent. Anybody in there?"

Who could it be, we both wondered aloud. Dick threw open the tent flaps and looked outside. I peered through the opening. Coming around one side of the truck were two men. My heart sank as I recognized one of them. Dave something. I couldn't recall his last name — a state Fish and Game man. We were sunk. They had caught us at last; it was all over but the prison bars. They must know about our *great moose caper.*

"You be Bernhardt?" the other man asked.

Mentally, I was already standing on the fifth amendment. Dick was nodding yes, but reluctantly. *Don't admit to it,* I was thinking. *Tell them we're the Smith's from Chatahootchie, or something. Bernhardt? Never heard of Bernhardt.*

"Could you use some meat?" Dave was saying.

"Huh?"

"Meat," Dave continued, "we're distributing Fish and Game meat." Another man was coming up our driveway with two large, heavy canvas bags.

"Fish and Game. We kill certain animals every so often for varied reasons. Biological studies, census, general overall check on how the species is doing. Stuff like that. Then we distribute the meat to local people. This here's sheep. Heard you folks might be need'n some meat, so we thought we'd just drop this by." He winked.

I stood slack-jawed. Dick was dumbfounded. Here was meat, delicious Dall sheep meat, being handed to us out of nowhere. We stumbled several times over our thanks as the men were leaving. There was enough meat here for a couple of months.

That turned out to be a good day, doubled, because we sold our first cord of wood in weeks just a few hours later.

While out cutting that day, things seemed to be going more smoothly. Maybe it was the gift of the sheep meat. Maybe it was following, our own faith in believing that things were going to get better. Whatever the reason, things were definitely different that day. Even the mountains, our constant backdrop and companions, seemed more beautiful than ever. Shrouded in snow, blanketed in cold, they loomed tall and protective around us.

Donna Blasor-Bernhardt

Through his solidly frosted beard, Dick commented, "God, look at the beauty we work in every day." He brushed frost from my bangs and hair around my face and continued, "Think about what we'd have missed if we hadn't broken away from the city. In spite of the hardships, it is worth it, isn't it? We have fresh air, freedom, a spectacular workplace and each other. What more could we want?"

How can you argue with logic like that? I felt the same way. I found myself shouting to the heavens, "I LOVE YOU, ALASKA!"

Yesterday had been hopeless. Today we had meat and gas money. Things were definitely looking up.

CHAPTER THIRTEEN

Life In The Tent

We settled into typical, routine days in the tent. This meant that everything we did was necessary for survival, if not very exciting.

The deep winter months were providing us with spectacular sunrises, though. I've never seen a sunrise more beautiful than those around the Tok area. The sun never actually rose above the horizon. All we saw was the resulting glow from below the horizon. So, dawn lasted sometimes for a couple of hours, with the sky in the southeast gradually glowing, then illuminating the frost-covered spruce trees in bright pink. The sky itself turned first fushia, followed by bright pink, then shades of orange fading into a soft salmon color.

Dick and I, out one morning starting the truck, were totally struck with the beauty around us. The sky was crimson-colored.

"Hey, look, my Lady Alaska," he stood behind me, arms reaching around my middle in a tight hug. "Look at those gorgeous mountains." The highest peak visible to us in the Alaska Range was shrouded in salmon pink-colored hues. Its deep valleys were dark purple. Rising above the tent like a great monument, majestic and regal, it proudly displayed its colors.

"Nothing like them in the whole wide world," I said softly. "What a privilege Tok has, to fly a banner called the Alaska Range."

"Yep," he said, "I never get tired of seeing them. Hey, you sound like you're getting soft on Tok."

"It's because of the country around it," I reminded him.

Most days began by getting the kids off to school and getting the truck started; then Dick and I would go out to cut firewood. In severe weather, the chain saw froze often and we would have to put it in the still-running truck to thaw out. We always left the truck running while getting firewood. It would have been disastrous to shut it off to conserve fuel, only to find that because of the cold it would not start again.

Katherine and Ricky usually arrived home before we did and their first chore, after refueling and lighting lamps, was to re-stoke the stove. We always stoked the stove tight before leaving to cut wood. Upon the kids return, there would be enough coals left for them to re-kindle the fire with the remaining firewood. Next to the stove, we left several detergent bottles filled with water. These were our fire extinguishers. After stoking the stove, Katherine and Ricky each stood ready, bottle in hand, and watched the tent roof for the inevitable hot sparks that would soon burn through the canvas. One good squeeze, properly aimed, would extinguish the tell-tale hot spots.

Next they fed the dog and cats and brought enough clean snow inside to melt for water. After that they could play or do homework, keeping alert for fire danger, until we got home. Then they helped us pack the cordwood inside and stack it.

I busied myself fixing supper while Dick fixed broken ax handles or sharpened the chain on the saw in readiness for the next day. After supper, I'd help the kids with homework or sew until bedtime.

When the outside temperature passed the 50 below mark, we could not just go to bed and expect to sleep comfortably. Dick and I were forced to sleep in shifts, usually four hour shifts, and stoke the stove almost continually. The stove was literally kept red hot to enable the rest of us to sleep. Even so, when it was my turn to sleep, I needed to change sleeping positions every 30 minutes or so. Sleeping on a cot was just too cold for me to stay comfortable. The cold air circulating underneath me was almost unbearable. After 15 or 20 minutes, the joints on my down side began to ache so badly that I would wake up. Not wanting to disturb my warm, upper side, I always tried to go back to sleep without moving. Always unsuccessfully. Another 10 minutes and, rather than go out of my mind with the pain of the cold, I'd give in and turn over...only to start the sequence all over again. I tried everything to lessen the problem. I blocked off the underside of the cot, layered blankets under my sleeping bag, layered other things like cardboard and newspapers, even switched cots once with Dick. Nothing helped. I was never able to come up with a solution to sleep warmly.

Dick didn't seem to have that problem. I can only assume that he had more natural padding than I did, therefore he was better insulated against the cold. On one occasion I pointed that out to him.

"You're probably right, hon. Us Grizz's know what it takes to be comfortable for hibernation," he said, good-naturedly.

Of course, we installed a *thunder mug* inside the tent for night use. This kept the kids from leaving the tent at night and also saved us from opening the tent door and losing precious heat.

So went a typical day. Not exciting, but then, we weren't looking for excitement. We were surviving.

Naturally, if there is a typical day, it follows that we would have plenty of typical weeks. Since the truck was our lifeline, Dick spent many hours checking every suspicious squeak, squeal or groan, preventing breakdowns and repairs. Again, when temperatures passed the magic fifty below mark, our truck routine changed. Anti-freeze will freeze in those temperatures. There is nothing you can do except keep starting the vehicle every couple of hours to prevent its freezing. Either that, or allow it to run all night. We did both. Around 50 below, since one of us was up on a four-hour shift anyway, we kept starting and restarting the truck, but below sixty below zero, even that was difficult. Many times the truck ran most of the night.

We were burning seven cords of wood in seven days in those temperatures. That meant a lot of hot coals and more spark holes in the roof to be patched. There was tremendous draft up the chimney when the stove door was opened for re-stoking. We were constantly gluing small patches to the roof.

Baths were a once-a-week luxury and chore combined. The hot water always felt good, but it took so much work to get it. All of our bathing water was snow, melted in a big double boiler atop the wood stove. Then it was dumped into a larger galvanized tub next to the stove. One by one, we each got our bath. It was a Saturday night family affair with everyone hauling snow for everyone else.

Even hauling and melting snow for simple things such as dish washing required a major amount of snow. Because of the severe cold, Tok snow has an arid quality to it. Ricky was the official snow-getter for dishes. One evening, after he had made a half-dozen trips outside for fresh snow, I noticed him standing in front of the stove, staring intently at the melting snow in front of him.

"What is it, Ricky?" I asked.

"I was just thinking ..." his voice trailed off.

I waited a minute, then said, "Earth to Ricky. Are you there?"

"Oh ... yeah."

"Well?"

He punched the snow down into the pot. "Well, Mom, I was just thinking, you know, like you do sometimes?"

"Okay ... "

"Well, just thinking about our house, the one we used to live in before the tent." he added.

Here it comes, I thought. *He's finally fed up with living in a fort.*

"...and I was thinking that when we lived in the house, we had a dishwasher and everything..."

"Yes, we did."

"...and I wouldn't even unload the dishwasher. Can you believe that? I didn't even have to wash the dishes. I didn't have to make the water for them to be washed in, and I wouldn't even unload the thing. Gosh, what at a difference."

I realized, at that moment, that Ricky wasn't complaining. He was making a simple observation and appeared to be re-evaluating himself. The way he'd said "What a difference" had pride in it. What a difference in himself is really what he was telling me.

Dick, too, picked up on Ricky's tone. 'You're a big help to us, son. I want you to know that."

Ricky picked up the pot and disappeared out the door for another snow run.

Washing clothes was worse than taking baths when it came to melting snow for water. It involved both wash and rinse water. I used a scrub board and a rapid washer. The latter looked like a metal toilet plunger and was used in much the same fashion. Both were effective, yet time consuming. After rinsing, the clothes were then hung on a line stretched from one end of the tent to the other. Some of the heavier items, such as jeans, were first freeze-dried on a line outside, then by hitting them soundly, the ice would break away from them. The ice had formed from the water in the wet clothes; removing the water that way gave them a head start on normal drying inside the tent.

Haircuts were another once-a-week thing. I would trim Katherine's bangs and keep Ricky's hair short enough that he wouldn't always have hair flopping in his face. Then I'd trim Dick's hair, too. Couldn't have him looking too much like a grizzly bear. All of the haircuts were done with a pair of scissors since we had no electricity for barber shears.

Raking the floor also became a once-a-week chore. Raking kept foot-tripping roots buried and helped improve the looks of the tent's interior. I felt like a well-groomed tent was aesthetically pleasing and anything we could do to improve the inside was worth the effort.

We had our life in the tent down to a fairly rigid routine. Surviving left little time for distraction. Because of that, there was a certain monotony during those deep winter months. One can have monotony without boredom though, and while at times tedium set in, cabin fever did not. We didn't have a cabin so how could there possibly be cabin fever?

Basically, this was our way of life throughout the winter. By the shortest day of the year, just before Christmas, we were doing everything except wood cutting in the dark. We had less than three hours of daylight. Darkness and the dust in the tent were the worst parts of tent living, even worse at times than the cold, though that was bad enough. It kept getting colder. Now it was January and we were experiencing our coldest weather yet. About ninety-nine percent of the time, I was experiencing an extremely uncomfortable, if not dangerous situation because of the cold.

Being a large-busted woman, may at times be an envious thing, however I can state from experience, that a large bosom projects further into the cold than does a small one with unenviable results. It didn't seem to matter what I wore, or how many layers of shirts or thermal underwear I put on under my parka, I could not keep them warm. Even while sleeping I still had the same problem. At times my breasts were so cold the nipples were drawn into hard knots, causing me enormous pain if I accidentally brushed them with my arm.

It became an unbearable situation, affecting my ability to help Dick with our daily wood cutting chores. I found myself spending more time in tears of pain, or constantly thrusting my unmittened hands beneath my shirt and holding both breasts for a few minutes of warm relief, than I was helping with firewood.

At first, Dick thought it was a rather comical situation, until he realized the gravity of what I was going through. "Honey," he said one day while I was desperately holding both hands under my shirt, "why don't you try a different bra?"

"I've tried everything I've got."

"Yeah, but they're all nylon or polished cotton. Those are cold materials to start with," he said in deep thought.

"Yeah, and...?"

"Well, I was thinking if you had a bra made of something that would be warm immediately against your skin like wool..."

"With wool, I'd spend all my time either raw or scratching," I cut in.

"What about a wool blend? Maybe you could make a bra that would keep you warm, maybe out of a piece of old thermal material, maybe..." He stroked his beard, a sure sign of very deep thought. "...maybe, I don't know. I'm just thinking about how thermals work: you know pockets of warm air trapped next to the skin. If we could come up with a way..."

I began to have a brainstorm. "Yes, yarn. I could crochet myself a bra. Why didn't I think of that? I've got some nice, soft cotton yarn. I'll bet that would work."

Dick was obviously pleased with himself. "Gonna try it, then?"

"Oh, yeah!"

And I did. That evening I crocheted two large triangles, joined them together and crocheted the straps onto them for added warmth and durability.

I slept in it that night and wore it the next day while we cut wood. It was the first time in weeks I was able to work or sleep without chilling pain. The relief I felt can hardly be described. While the severe cold continued to pound at us, beneath my shirt I stayed warm and toasty.

Late one night, as I was up for one of my four-hour shifts, I was reminded of the old sourdough phrase about *a two-dog night* or a *three-dog night*, etc., referring to the number of dogs one has to take to bed with him to stay warm.

After once again shoving a log into the stove, then squirting the roof, I noticed the frost had moved higher up the inside of the tent walls. I could almost see it moving. Knowing the temperature was dropping rapidly brought out my curiosity, so I decided to go outside and check the thermometer.

A spectacular night greeted me when I stepped beyond the tent flaps. The sky, absolutely devoid of clouds, was filled with stars that fairly leaped from their places in space. They flickered like swarms of fireflies attracted to the North Star Mountains glowed beneath northern lights dancing gracefully to an unheard heavenly symphony. A full moon shown over us all. Nearly bright as day, frost sparkled brightly on tree boughs. I drew in a long, slow breath of this magic air. The severe cold brought a clean crispness to the world ? the snow squeaking beneath my feet as I walked over to the thermometer hanging on a tree.

Von Hairy, our Husky, lay curled asleep in the snow, his nose tucked snugly under breath-frosted tail. A hardy breed, they prefer sleeping beneath the stars. I could understand why. Kneeling, I gently patted his big head. His tail wagged, but almost as if he didn't want to break the spell of the silent night, he didn't get up. I stood beside him, drinking in the beauty, the mystery, surrounding me, overwhelmed by the magnitude of this time and place.

Even the tent was beautiful. Covered in frost, like a house of diamonds, it glittered in the moonlight. Woodsmoke billowed from the stack. Tall and unwavering, the white column stretched toward the sky some twenty-five to thirty feet straight upward.

Not a blemish creased the air. Somewhere in the distance, a wolf howled his prayerful song. I could feel the essence of the night enfold me, wrapping its celestial arms around me, hugging me, loving me. Feelings that had stirred me as a child still stirred inside me. I realized then, as I realize now, that my love for Alaska had been born into me, that I could never *not love* this land. Full-blown now, it was an eternal love affair. I felt so blessed in having two lovers: Alaska and Dick.

My eternal lover, however, was not keeping me warm in spite of my feelings. I shuddered, gazing once more into the ethereal night, then peered at the thermometer. It read sixty-nine below.

Sixty-nine degrees below zero! Neither Dick nor I had ever experienced this kind of cold. I mused over it once inside the tent. My other lover lay asleep in his sleeping bag. Dick's chest rose and fell in time with his snoring, and with each exhale I could see his breath. Oh, yes, it was cold. I watched as frost inched its way further up the inside of the tent walls. It was a different world entirely.

Dick had remarked once, not unkindly, that Tok was like living on the moon. It certainly seemed so now.

I thought of how our life had changed and all that we had left behind – the dishwasher, television, washer, dryer, constant heat. Memories of our Anchorage life flooded over me. That life seemed so far away now, so long ago. It hadn't seemed like a life, really. It had felt more like an existence. It was here that we had found life. It was now that we were living. I felt grateful for having the chance to grow with Dick and the kids.

I sighed as I watched my family softly sleeping. With all my heart I knew we had done the right thing. Even with what we'd already been through, I wouldn't have traded it for what we had left behind.

One of the kids' school books lay nearby. I picked it up and leafed through it. Too dark to read comfortably. Stick another log in the stove. Squish out the burn holes. Now what?

I picked up a pencil on the table and idly thumped it. Why not write? I thought. About what? About the way I felt. About what we're doing right now. I caught myself mentally asking and answering my own questions in the quiet night.

After rummaging up a scrap piece of paper, which happened to be part of an old grocery sack, I began putting down random thoughts about the tent and our life here. Before I knew it, a poem was taking shape. I chuckled. Poetry? Hadn't done much of that since high school, but there it was.

I titled it (what else?), *A Tent In Tok*. It didn't seem too bad. It rhymed. It had meter. It was certainly real life and what the heck, I was just fooling around, anyway. It went like this...

> This is our "house" among the spruce,
>   The guy lines are taut and never loose.
> It's all we have; it isn't much,
> The walls are sewn from canvas duck.
> We have no floor, as you can see,
> It's made of dirt and that was free.
> The roof above is canvas, too,
> But it's a roof, so it will do.
> We heat with wood, both birch and spruce.
> The stewpot's full of rump of moose.
> Our beds are cots with bags of down,
> The walls aren't white, they're olive brown.
> Blazo boxes stacked (and there are four)
> Serve as shelves from roof to floor.
> Of running water? We haven't any.
> And trips to the outhouse? There are many!
> A kerosene lamp provides our light,
> Our freezer's a box, set out at night
> To keep things cold in winter's snow
> Or frozen solid at fifty below.
> And since we're short of electricity

Donna Blasor-Bernhardt

> We're basically back to simplicity.
> Though life is hard, it's not so bad,
> We've got more than we might have had,
> And, come spring, when winter's over;
> The fireweed blooms and so does the clover,
> We'll build a cabin of pine and spruce
> And welcome our neighbor; a big bull moose
> To graze in the yard as he did before
> And gaze again, at our front door
> But, it will be of solid, built,
> No more, a door, of canvas quilt!

Once it was completed, I thought no more of the poem. It was my turn to sleep, so I shook Dick gently and told him it was his turn with the stove.

Well, Dick turned out to be a sneaky sort. He read the poem, presented it to Beth Jacobs, editor of the local newspaper, *The Mukluk News*. She liked it and asked permission to print it. I was flabbergasted. That was something I had always wanted, but never dreamed it could happen here, under these circumstances. Yet it was just these circumstances that had brought it about. The poem ran in the next issue, and Tok loved it. Soon, Beth was asking if I had any more. I didn't, but found that I had plenty inside me, just waiting to be put on paper. That was the beginning of my own column in each issue.

Funny how things work out.

CHAPTER FOURTEEN

Fire And Futility

By February, we were noticing the days beginning to lengthen slightly. Now it wasn't dark until after five in the afternoon. Ah, thoughts of spring filled my mind. Even the pounding cold had subsided; although we were still experiencing fifty below nights, the days warmed up to ten or twenty below. It seemed ridiculous to think of twenty below zero bein "warm. But, to us, it was.

One evening when we were all inside the tent doing our normal things, the tent seemed draftier than usual. I moved closer to the stove, warming myself, then went on with what I'd been doing.

"Getting cold in here," called Ricky.

"Yeah," chimed in Katherine, "cold!"

Dick got up off his cot and reached for another log, "Geesh! What a draft!"

And suddenly, almost in unison, it struck the four of us as to what was really happening. Directly above Dick's head a gigantic hole was forming in the tent roof. Its perimeter was aglow and every second the hole was getting bigger. Just one small coal had started it. One little spark that we had somehow missed.

It was a harried, mad scramble to get outside. Quickly we began throwing snow on the hole. A four-person bucket brigade minus the buckets, we were scooping up snow with anything we could find. Dick grabbed the snow shovel, I picked up an empty cardboard box. Ricky was throwing snow using his saucer sled as a scoop and Katherine had borrowed Von Hairy's food bowl.

A moonless night, we were stumbling all over each other in the dark, but that gaping, glowing hole was not hard to see. It grinned at us, an ugly spectre rising from the bowels of winter, waiting to pounce on us and threaten our very existence. We threw so much snow around that hole you could have skied right off the roof. Perhaps we overreacted a bit, but once there was no more glow to be seen, we calmed ourselves and assessed the damage. Out of breath, Dick and I surveyed the gaping eight-foot-diameter hole from the outside.

"What a mess, Mom!" Ricky, also out of breath, called from the inside.

"All the snow's inside now, Mama," Katherine cried. "An' it's melting all over everything!"

The table was wet, as were the dishes, pots, pans, some of Dick's clothes, a lot of my own clothes, Katherine's doll, and anything else within range of our frantic snow throwing.

"We've got to get as much of this out of here as possible," Dick told us.

"Yeah, before the *melt* refreezes on everything," I said. "It's already getting cold in here."

I put Katherine to work drying up things inside with our spare towels. Dick handed Ricky the shovel and told him to scoop up as much of the snow as possible from the inside of the tent and haul it out.

While they worked inside, Dick and I worked outside. By the light of a lantern we maneuvered a large sheet of canvas. After measuring to be sure it was big enough, we swabbed glue all the way around the perimeter of the hole. Placing the large patch over the hole wasn't hard, but the difficulty came in trying to support it and keep the edges sealed down long enough for the glue to dry.

The cold hampered normal drying time. We ended up placing several old pieces of plywood over the top of the patch to help press it firmly onto the roof's surface, and then standing inside under the patch, we supported the patch and the weight of the plywood until the whole thing dried enough to hold itself. Dick and I looked like twin Atlas's, holding up the world. We were holding up our own world.

"Boy, that was close," Dick said, swinging his arms down for circulation, "a little more time and we wouldn't have had a roof left."

After that, we were doubly cautious, even paranoid, about sparks. Sometimes we used twice as much water as we really needed, drenching the roof and leaving it dripping for several minutes before we were satisfied that a spark was out.

It seemed we were destined to have things happen in pairs. We were all inside the tent again under similar circumstances, later the same week. All four of us thought we could smell something burning, but a quick check of the tent and vicinity, inside and out, had turned up nothing. Finally, even though remaining suspicious, we brushed it off as fire paranoia and resumed our normal evening's routine.

Having just finished washing the dishes, I emptied the rinse water outside, and returned inside to finish putting away the dishes. Which is what I was doing in the center of the tent when suddenly, I heard something sizzling above my head.

I never glanced up, there wasn't time. I didn't think it? I didn't will it, but I did react. My right arm, as if it were a disembodied *thing*, shot straight out, simultaneously catching the Coleman lantern in mid-air, by its handle. It was automatic and incredible. I just sort of stood there, wondering if I had really done that. I hadn't even known what was happening, so I couldn't possibly have known what I was doing. Yet disaster had just been averted.

Katherine, Dick and Ricky were sitting wide-eyed, mouths open, staring at me.

"Wow! Did you see that? Mom just reached out and grabbed it right out of the air! She never even looked!" Ricky exclaimed. "That was great!"

I set the lantern down, feeling slightly dazed. It had been hanging by a rope from the ceiling all winter and somehow, at this precise moment, the rope had burned through, causing it to fall.

Dick rushed up and grabbed me, crushing me with a bear hug. "Quick thinking," he praised. "Great reflexes!"

"I can't take credit for that *save*," I said, still stupefied. "I didn't even know what was happening until it was over. It was like this force came over me and propelled me into motion." I had an eerie feeling of not being my own self at the instant my arm shot out and caught the lamp, not by any of its hot surfaces, but precisely by the handle.

Dick looked at me, then at the kids, "Fact remains, if your mother hadn't caught it, we'd have fire all over the place right now. Kerosene would have spilled and ignited. Everything would have been gone." He was already cutting wire as a replacement for the rope.

I was still having trouble believing that scenario, but I knew I'd had outside help. I wasn't that good. Someone up there was looking over us.

Two smaller disasters were also close together, and dumb. Katherine and Ricky were playing outside late one afternoon when I heard her scream and saw Ricky burst through the door.

"Mom," he panted, his face contorted, "Katherine's caught. She can't get loose!"

"Caught? On what? In what?"

"On the truck!" We ran outside. There stood Katherine, with a big grimace on her face and tears streaming down her cheeks.

"Don't pull!" I warned. "I'll be right back. Don't move!" I dashed back inside the tent and grabbed the teakettle from the stove.

Katherine's second and third fingers were frozen to the truck's cold, metal bumper. I loosened them by pouring warm water over them. Once freed, I lectured both kids about the perils of cold metal and warm or damp skin. This wasn't news to them; Katherine had just forgotten.

Ricky's turn came the very next day. And it was Katherine's turn to come running into the tent with the news.

"Mama-mama-mama!" she spewed in one breath, bolting through the door. "Hurry! Ricky!"

I sped outside. She motioned me behind the tent. There he was, in a half-bent position, next to the tent. He had his back to me as I approached.

"What's wrong, Ricky?" I called, before reaching him.

"Molm! Iah goth thuk."

"Huh?"

"Thuk." His arms were flapping up and down. "Thuk. Iah goth thuk," he repeated, as I moved alongside him.

"Ohh, Ricky..." Katherine said, her eyebrows knit tightly together in great sympathy.

"Yeah, oh, Ricky..." I said turning away to stifle a sudden urge to laugh.

"Ith noth fun-nay!" he retorted.

"Maybe not to you." I couldn't help it. There was no way I could conceal the idiotic smile that was spreading across my face.

Still bent, arms flailing in helplessness, there was nothing Ricky could do but sputter. "Aaagh," he emphasized.

"Boy, Ricky, we may have to do something drastic here. Maybe surgery!"

Katherine's brows furrowed even deeper into her forehead.

"Molm! Quith ith!" Ricky flailed some more.

"Okay," I relented. "I'll go get the warm water."

He was still flailing when I returned with the tea kettle, freeing the tip of his tongue stuck to a metal fastener on one of the guy ropes. Other than the few taste buds that stayed on the fastener, Ricky was unscathed. Again, I lectured.

"But I didn't mean to touch the metal, Mom," Ricky said, nursing both his tongue and his ego. "I just wanted to bite the little icicle off it. Honest! Only I missed and got stuck."

"Oooh, does it hurt real bad, Ricky?" Katherine was standing on her toes, trying to peer into Ricky's closed mouth.

"No. It's okay, " he said sharply, trying to cover his true feelings. He was not about to admit any pain to his little sister. "It's fine."

It was so ridiculous, I knew neither of them would ever forget that experience.

Later that week, we received some good news. Upon checking our mailbox at the post office, we were delighted to find a letter from the U.S. Bureau of Land Management.

"'Bout time!" Dick roared, ripping open the envelope. "Yep. It's our logging permit. Took their sweet time, bunch of idiots. What do they think I can do in the middle of winter? Well, at least once spring is here we can cut *legal* logs and get the cabin finished without sneaking around. Nothing will stop us now." His eyes twinkled with delight.

He went around humming to himself the rest of the week. I hadn't realized how much that small piece of paper had meant to him. We talked a lot about our beautiful little cabin, picturing it in our minds, completed and warm, with curtains, a welcome mat outside the door and smoke curling out the stove pipe. As soon as spring arrived, we would be outside cutting our house logs again.

Ah, thoughts of spring. It still seemed a long way off. Warm air, no stove to stoke, sunshine; those were my thoughts. Dick, on the other hand, went one thought further. Food. More specifically, barbecued food.

We were discussing spring and barbecues a few days later while in Tok picking up groceries at Mike's store. Mike was always asking us about our tent life and on this particular day, he invited himself to dinner.

"If you guys aren't ever going to invite me to dinner then I guess I'll just have to invite myself," he said. Grinning, he handed me a couple of chickens, then thrust a dozen eggs, potatoes and pickles into Dick's arms. "And here's the ingredients. What else do you need?"

"Nothin', 'cept a couple of hungry guys." Dick answered.

Mike laughed, "Think we've already got those."

"Yeah, but prepare to put on a few extra pounds once you've tasted her potato salad," Dick chuckled. He patted his belly, "Nobody can beat my little redhead's potato salad! Seven o'clock, Okay?"

"Eight." Mike said. "Right after the store closes. I'll be there."

Back at the tent, we got busy. Ricky peeled potatoes and Katherine fille, and kept refilling, a large pot with clean snow. I set it on the wood stove.

"Just put the eggs in the pot, Baby. Push them right down into the snow. And when Ricky gets the potatoes peeled, you can put them in with the eggs. Okay?"

Ricky looked up from his potatoes, "Mom, how come Mike wants to eat supper in the tent?"

"Guess he can't wait for us to get the cabin built," I joked, while cutting up the chickens.

"Fire's ready!" Dick called from outside.

"Be right out." I turned to the kids, "As the snow in the pot melts down, keep refilling it with fresh snow until the eggs and potatoes are finally covered in water while they cook." I realized this wasn't exactly the way one would normally cook those items, but hey, when you live in a tent ...

I picked up the chicken parts and barbecue sauce on my way out. Sure, it was crazy. Call it cabin fever, or tent fever. Whatever. And yes, it was about thirty-five below zero out there, but what good is potato salad without barbecued chicken? And we were all dying for barbecued chicken. So it all seemed very logical, the logic of the north, anyway.

I was determined to fix it and Dick was doing all he could to encourage it. He had a good fire going in the driveway. Beneath a makeshift grill perched on two logs, the coals were just right for cooking the chickens. So I was barbecuing chicken in a snowbank at thirty-five below zero weather. So what? So this is Tok. So this is Alaska. It just seemed natural by now and we were enjoying this madness.

The temperature had dropped to forty-five below when Mike arrived, right on time. Was he a little eager? I'd say he was. The fall in temperature hadn't quelled his spirits, either. Everything was ready. And even though Mike had known we were going to barbecue the chickens, he was still a little surprised that we had actually done it.

"I can't believe this," he said more than once. "I can't believe I'm actually sitting here in a tent eating with you guys. Eating a chicken you barbecued in your driveway; barbecued at forty-five below zero." He was sitting on a cot, balancing his dinner plate in his lap. "I love it and this potato salad's great!" he said, dishing up another helping.

Dick leaned back on his elbows, patting his belly, then motioned toward Mike's belly, one of the things they had in common. "Yep, told you so. My little redhead outdid herself on this batch."

Mike helped himself to another piece of chicken. "This whole thing is just too good. I can't believe it. Wait'll I tell my grandkids about this."

"You don't have any grandkids, Mike," I said, brandishing a pickle speared with a fork, "your kids are still little."

"Well, when I have grandkids, they'll never believe it. What a great story."

I marveled at Mike. He was actually enjoying himself. I guess I shouldn't have been surprised because Mike was a good, down-to-earth person. But I had wondered if, when he finally got here, the reality of the tent, a dirt floor, no table, the cold, everything ? might not be a little worse than he cared to admit. I shouldn't have worried. He didn't seem to notice that we had a dirt floor; couldn't have cared less that we had canvas walls. He was more intent on keeping up with Dick and Ricky in their potato salad-eating marathon.

The meal was scrumptious, the company ? wonderful. Mike was the only guest ever to eat dinner with us in the tent. It was the beginning of a long-lasting friendship.

Later that week, the Indians in Tanacross, the small native village twelve miles west of Tok, began ordering wood from us. There were several native villages in the Tok vicinity, Northway to the east, Mentasta to the south, Tetlin to the southeast, but Tanacross, on the banks of the Tanana River, was the closest of the four. Selling wood to them was a real break.

One evening while unloading a cord of wood and stacking it beside his house, the old Indian man who lived there came out to greet us. He was holding one arm in such a way that it was obvious something was wrong with it. Throwing another log on the stack, I caught Dick's attention and motioned toward the old man. We stopped stacking and walked over to him on the porch. The old man pulled back his sleeve to show us his battle wound.

I jumped. I'd never seen anything like this being displayed as though it were nothing. "Oh, cripes! That's awful!" Never having been the least bit squeamish over anything before, now I felt my stomach doing a slow churn. I turned toward Dick, drew a deep breath, then turned back to the old fellow. I had to concentrate on not throwing up. "Something's got to be done about that." I told him.

Dick grimaced, "My God, man, what happened?" The old man's arm was broken, just above the wrist. Worse, the bone protruded through the skin. Swollen and discolored, infection was already setting in. He was half-drunk and quite proud of the break.

"Got in fight with white man," he explained. "Hurt him up real good!"

Getting control of my stomach, I moved in closer for a better look. "You really need a doctor," I told him.

"No. No see doctor."

"But it's already infected," I tried to reason with him.

"No. It okay."

"Look," said Dick, "I'll drive you to the P.A. in Tok. He can fix it for you."

The old man was stubborn. "No. I fix. Be fine."

"You may be fine now," Dick added, "but you could die from the infection in that later."

"Even if you don't die, you could lose your whole arm," I pointed out. " There's stuff oozing out of it. Bad stuff. Let us help you."

"No die. No lose arm. No doctor. Be fine. Boys here," he looked down the street, "look after me."

He refused over and over again. Dick and I even offered to take him all the way to Fairbanks if he preferred to see a doctor there. He would have nothing to do with it. Short of physically dragging him into our truck, there was nothing either of us could do. He would not listen to reason and there was no way he was going to change his mind. He finally turned and went back into his house.

"That is one tough old man," Dick commented.

"Yeah, and stubborn," I hastened to add. "He's going to be lucky if he doesn't die from being stubborn."

We finished unloading the wood and left. Several weeks later we learned that he had become sick enough that, at last, he consented to being looked at, but it was not until some of the villagers forced him into it. He was taken to Fairbanks where he was treated and eventually healed.

On another wood delivery to Tanacross, we had finished stacking up the wood and were invited inside by the old Indian living there. This was the second time in as many weeks that we had delivered wood to him. Dick and I wondered what he was doing with all that wood, but were glad to have the sale. I found him to be a very likeable old man, full of spirit and kind of heart.

This was the first time either of us had been invited inside. The house looked like a disaster area and half a dozen *young bucks*, as the old man called them, were milling around making a general nuisance of themselves.

They backed away into one corner when we entered the room. We recognized one as a culprit Dick had chased from our tent months before. Upon catching him, Dick had not actually done anything to him, but the young buck knew with certainty that there had better not be a second time.

While the old man dug into his pockets looking for money to pay for the cordwood, my eyes were roaming the room.

These were government-built houses. Most of them, other than the color they were painted outside, looked pretty much alike outside and inside. Except for this one. There were no cupboards on the kitchen walls. You could see where they had been, but now nothing was left but blank walls and sheetrock remnants where they had been pulled off. And the floor throughout the house was riddled with small, perfectly drilled holes that penetrated all the way through the flooring. I scrutinized walls and floor, then nudged Dick.

Dick was never one to mince words. "What happened to your cabinets?" he asked the old man.

"Young bucks," he pointed to the group in the corner, "steal my wood at night."

"I don't understand what that's got to do with anything," he said, shaking his head.

The old guy looked at Dick as though he were stupid.

Dick still questioned, "So?"

"Steal wood," the old man repeated. The look on his face was saying, "Don't you get it yet?"

Obviously, neither of us did.

"And...?" Dick urged.

"Young bucks steal wood. Got no wood. No make fire," he grunted. "No wood. No fire. No heat. Water freeze up at night. Pipes break. Water all over floor next morning. Froze. No wood. Burn cabinets, instead. Make heat, now water all over floor. Make holes in floor; get rid of water."

I had the feeling that this made perfect sense to him, even if it didn't to either of us.

The young bucks were getting a big kick out of the old man's explanation. They began laughing and slapping each other on the back obviously pleased with themselves, until Dick gave them a stern look. It didn't, however, stop them from smirking as they moved into a tighter circle in the corner.

"Let's get this straight," Dick said. "If they..." he nodded at the group still grinning in the corner, "...hadn't stolen your firewood, you would still have cupboards and no holes in your floor?"

"Mmmm," the old man nodded affirmatively.

"Well, what did they do with your wood? Where is it?"

"Take home. Burn it. Sell it."

"Is that why you had to buy wood again from us?" I asked. "Because they stole what we brought you before?"

Again, he nodded yes.

Dick had heard enough. He spun on his heels and walked briskly toward the young bucks. "You think it's funny? Ever heard of respecting your elders? Want me to show you how funny I can be? You..." he said, grabbing the familiar Indian, "you tell them how funny Dick Bernhardt can be. Remember?"

Dick looked like a mountain next to them. They cowered. His reputation had preceded him.

"Tell you what. You leave this poor old man alone. Leave his wood alone. Don't bother him anymore. If you do, and I hear about it, and I'm gonna be checking, you'll regret it. Understand? This white man means what he says. You don't treat old people like that! Got it?" he asked, bellowing in their faces. They never uttered a word. They understood quite well.

Dick turned to the old man. "This time the wood's on us," he said, "to make up for these bastards. If you use this up and need more, then we'll take your money." Dick looked over at me, "Okay, honey?" He was reading my mind.

"Absolutely."

"Now, you guys..." he shook his fist at the young bucks, "...split and don't ever let me hear of something like this again." They fell all over themselves getting out the door.

The old Indian thanked us, adding, "I hear of Dick Bernhardt. He live in tent. He good man. I tell friends. Him woman, good woman, too." He shook my hand. "Good woman take care of good man." I laughed, and Dick and I headed home.

One regular customer, again another old Indian, was a delightful character. Everyone knew him as Yukon Ben, and more often than not, he wore an old suit that gave him an air of dignity. Slight of frame, his face lined and leathered, he appeared to be as old as the earth itself. He lived alone in a small cabin in old Tanacross.

Old Tanacross lay across the river from new Tanacross. The original village, decaying and about half empty, was slowly being replaced by newer houses at the new site of the village.

Yukon Ben liked his old cabin and he always paid us cash on the spot for his wood. We never had a bit of trouble collecting from him and the routine never varied. Dick and I would unload his wood, split it and stack it wherever he wanted it. Once finished, old Yukon usually came out, inspected our work, then invited us inside. He had no electricity, so he would light a candle. Always just one, then he'd search around in the semi-dark until he found what he was looking for — a roll of money. He'd peel off what was needed and return the roll to its hiding place.

Once, in the dark, Yukon overpaid us by $20.00. We didn't discover his error until we were back in the truck and halfway home. Dick and I turned the truck around and returned it to him. He was startled to see us return so quickly.

"You gave us too much money," I told him. "Probably because it's so dark in here."

He re-rolled the twenty into his hidden stash.

"Yukon," I asked, "How come you don't have electricity? The other houses have electricity and it seems like you could afford it.."

"Don't need it," he replied simply.

"Wouldn't it be easier for you if you could just turn on a switch for light?" I was thinking more of the fire danger here in this tiny cabin than I was of light, but didn't want to seem obvious about it. And Yukon seemed so old, so frail.

"Candles good enough." he stated. "Don't worry, no fire."

He had caught me off guard. "Fire? How did you know I was thinking of fire?"

Yukon shrugged, "You woman. You mother. You worry." Then, smiling, he added again, "Candles good enough."

I guessed maybe he was right. If a tent was good enough for us, why shouldn't candles be good enough for him, if that's what he wanted.

Back at the tent that night, I caught Dick outside, just standing, staring at our snow-filled, unfinished cabin. Moonlight reflected off its log walls. He appeared to be mesmerized. I approached him quietly, not wanting to break his own moment in time. We stood side-by-side for a long while, each deep in our own thoughts.

I wondered what it would be like next winter. Surely we would have the cabin finished by then. I pictured it complete. A warm glow would fill the air, woodsmoke curling from the smoke stack. A porch in front with lots of wood already split and stacked. Good food smells inside, a real floor with carpet for extra warmth, glass windows, the kids chattering in their loft. And sleeping once again in a real bed with Dick curled around me, safely tucked in his arms. His warm breath on the back of my neck. Living happily ever after.

He slipped his arm around my waist, holding me close. "A penny for your thoughts," I said, finally breaking the silence.

"Why don't you finish it for me?" he said, still gazing at the cabin.

I looked into his hazel eyes, kissed him, laughed and said, "Okay." With my forefinger pointing at the cabin, I shut my eyes, concentrated very hard, wished that cabin finished and twitched my nose.

Without success, of course. It may have worked for Samantha on *Bewitched* but not for me. "Guess there's no magic in my twitch," I said.

"Oh, I wouldn't say that," Dick grinned, "There's lots of magic in your twitch."

"Yeah, well, not in the twitch that counts."

"I wouldn't say that, either.!" He drew me into him, smothering me in a deep, long kiss. "I'm so glad I have you, Silver Girl."

"Silver Girl?"

"Well, you look magical," Dick explained. "Standing here in the moonlight, everything about you glows. Your skin is all silvery. You look like a magic, silver girl. Maybe you are magic; a Silver Lady of the night."

I had to grin. "Lady of the night? I don't think so!"

"Didn't mean it that way. Besides you're my lady of the night."

"Guess that makes you my man of the evening." I blinked my eyes in an exaggerated *come-hither* look.

"You know," he said, "one day we'll be able to come out of the tent and the cabin will be finished. It will be standing there all silvery in the moonlight just like you are right now. When that happens, we're gonna remember tonight and then we'll know that it worked. There will be magic in our cabin because of tonight."

With one arm still around my waist, he took my right hand in his. Without a word, Dick pulled me into him and began a slow, deliberate waltz. We had never danced much together during our married life because neither of us had ever really learned to dance, but this night we moved as though we'd done it all our lives.

In the ultimate silence of the north, with only the sound of the snow squeaking beneath our feet, we danced. For an electrifying moment, we shared heartbeats, breaths ? one person in two bodies, two silver spirits merged, bonded forever beneath the northern lights. His soft, hair-covered cheek pressed into mine. He kissed my ears and his kisses moved to my throat.

His face glowed with enthusiasm and love. He swung me around to face the tent. It, too, glowed magically in the moonlight.

"This may be home this winter," he said, "but next winter there isn't going to be any tent. We will have a cabin for next winter."

"Yes," I said, "a real cabin for winter, a winter cabin. Winter Cabin. That's what we need to christen it when it's finished, Dick. Winter Cabin."

"I really like the sounds of that," he said. "Winter Cabin. No more snow home," he laughed. His remark gave me an idea. The painted *M.A.S.H* letters on the front of the tent were almost hidden in snow. "You know," I said, "those letters could also stand for something else."

"Like what else?"

"Well, since it's all covered in snow — Making A Snow Home — M.A.S.H." I replied.

"What about the '4077'? Does that have a new meaning, too?" he asked.

"Forty below in 1977!"

"Yeah, boy, does that ever work." he said, massaging warmth into my shoulders and neck.

The tent was literally buried in snow. Only its roof and door were visible. Snow and ice had been building up all winter until the snow walls were actually higher than the tent walls.

"It really looks like a giant snow cave." I said.

"Yeah, but that snow is doing a good job of insulating us against the cold," he reminded me.

"Mmmm. Guess we're pretty smart to let it accumulate, huh?"

"Pretty smart, I'd say!"

If we'd only known.

CHAPTER FIFTEEN

Of Saws And Sutures And Science

"Move over, Chris!" I demanded. "You have your own shelf." She looked disdainfully at me but made no attempt to move. The cats had long ago taken over one of my kitchen shelf boxes. They were wooden Blazo boxes stacked opposite the wood stove and caught the heat, making a nice, warm cubby hole for the feline members of the Bernhardt family. I really didn't mind because they had earned their keep by either discouraging, or eliminating, small rodents.

We hadn't had any problems with mice or squirrels trying to winter with us inside the tent. What varmint in their right mind would deliberately face a pair of cats? But this morning, Chris was busy scouting out the boxes above her own. Perk was asleep in their *official* box.

"You can scout all you want, but those three boxes belong to the kitchen." She cocked her head at me, blinking those gorgeous, crystal blue eyes. "And don't turn on the charm with me," I said, patting her head. She began purring as I stroked down her back to the end of her tail. Arching under my hand, she probably thought she had won the battle of the cupboards. "Did you really think I'd be that easy?" I asked, reversing the petting motion and going against the grain of her fur. With great indignation, she jumped away just as Katherine's voice squealed with delight outside.

"Faster, Ricky! Wheee!" The kids were playing, with Ricky pulling Katherine on the sled down the driveway. I had to smile to myself, thinking about those two out there sledding in the cold. There had been a time, not so very long ago, that I would never have let either of the kids out to play in sub-zero weather. It had been unthinkable. Now, here they were, bundled up and having a blast because of it.

Ricky had always been good about playing with Katherine. Before our tent days, I had watched as he invented a mystery horse that appeared out of nowhere at times. Conveniently, it always appeared when Ricky was not in the room. And it always had a familiar blanket thrown over it, gave Katherine a ride around the house, then disappeared. As if on cue, Ricky usually reappeared soon thereafter.

So far, in the tent, *Horsey* had failed to appear, but Ricky and Katherine had shared each other's time by coloring in the same books, or making things. Both kids were very creative, using whatever they found to occupy themselves. Old cardboard boxes became forts, or chariots and entire miniature towns had been built on castoff pieces of plywood, gluing rocks, sticks and bark to form houses, streets and trees.

In Anchorage, the kids each had room of their own, filled with toys that were rarely played with more than a few times. Here, they didn't seem to need toys. Instead, they had a great tool — imagination.

"Whee, Ricky!" Possibly Katherine had a replacement for *Horsey*. A glance through the tent flaps showed Ricky pulling his little sister as fast as he could on the sled down the driveway. From all the puffing and panting, it was clear that he was tiring of doing all the work, but there he was, still pulling, much to Katherine's delight. I wondered why he hadn't thought of hooking Von Hairy up to the sled.

I had finished doing dishes when I heard the kids calling. "Mom!"

"Mama, come see!"

After drying my hands, I slipped on my parka and stepped outside. Ricky had wised up. He had hooked the dog to the sled and both he and Katherine were sitting demurely on it.

"How 'bout that?" I said, "Just hold on real ti .. " I never got to finish my warning.

Ricky gave Von Hairy the signal and the dog leaped forward. In one swift motion, he somersaulted off the back of the sled, and the dog and the sled, with Katherine hanging on for dear life, disappeared down the driveway. "Catch him, Ricky!" And he took off after them. I wasn't worried, just amused. After all, where could they possibly go? We were the only ones in the vicinity and there was only one direction the dog could head.

In a short while Ricky returned, leading the dog, sled and Katherine.

Her eyes were wide with excitement. "Let's do it again, Ricky!"

We all had a good laugh over it. Von Hairy, being a dog bred for freight sledding, had too much power, even as a pup, for so little weight to pull. His sudden lunge in starting hadn't helped much either. Ricky was determined though. He worked with the dog, and after a week of practice, proudly showed me a pretty decent *dog sled ride*.

With the weather warming some now, I put the kids to work digging my Volkswagen out of the snowbank, figuring that now, at twenty below zero, even a V.W., which normally is hard to start in the cold, might start.

Dick had taken the truck to go to Farren's grocery store in Tok. George, and his wife, Pat, owned Tok's only other grocery store and we had become friends. The little store, alongside the Alaska Highway had a real frontier flavor. Immediately inside the door sat a wood stove identical to our own. Kept fully stocked, it was a welcome sight, and more often than not, someone could always be found standing near it drinking a cup of hot coffee or discussing the price of gold.

George often dealt with some of his customers in gold dust and nuggets. A large area north of Tok, called the Forty Mile, had been a precursor to the great 1898 Klondike gold strike in the Yukon.

Still gold rich country, active mining continued there. Miners would often come into the store for provisions, and George, obligingly, weighed up their payment in gold on a set of gold scales kept there for that purpose.

The first time I saw George, he was in the little butcher-shop part of the store, cutting up chicken. I was amazed. He looked enough like Dick for them to be brothers. Their height, weight and very build were the same and both were big-chested, bearded men ? twin grizzlies. They even smiled alike, loved joking around and had similar personalities.

And his wife, Pat, was a pretty, statuesque woman and taller than George. They had two sons and two daughters who helped them in their store. Pat looked so much like her daughters, that for a long time I had a lot of trouble telling which was which. They all looked like sisters. I never knew if it was mother or daughter at the cash register.

I'd say, and I always tried to sound confident that I knew I was going to be right, "Hi, Pat," and the tall girl would say, "Oh, I'm Gigi," or "Oh no, that's Mom. I'm Patti." It was embarrassing, but as we grew to know the family better, the problem decreased until, finally, I could walk into the store and say, "Hello, Pat!" And it really was Pat.

It somehow struck me as odd that there were so many people who looked alike: Pat and her daughters, and Dick and George. Even some of the townspeople later would ask Dick if he and George were brothers. Dick and I took an instant liking to the Farren family. Later, Dick would even call George's mother *Mom* and she'd call him her *number three son*.

Today Dick and George were away together. They were going to install a stovepipe for somebody, somewhere. It would give Dick time to be with someone else and a break from our regular routine. It also was helping someone else who needed help. Since firewood wasn't an all-important, life or death, *Gotta do it all the time* situation now, it was nice to be able to do something else for a change. Dick had been gone several hours, when Katherine and Ricky came back inside the tent.

"It's done, Mama," Katherine said.

"All dug out?"

"Yeah," answered Ricky, breathlessly. "You've got a Volkswagen again!" We went outside, where the kids proudly showed off my gleaming red V.W., completely swept of snow.

"Good job!" I said, "Boy, you guys are good."

"Think it'll start?" Ricky said, wondering.

"Mama, can we go for a ride?" Katherine was a ready-to-go gadabout. She was showing signs of spring fever.

"Well, let's see," I said, squeezing myself inside the little car. The seat was still so cold there was no *give* to it. It felt like sitting on a brick.

I had my doubts about it starting. It had been sitting there all winter and the battery was cold-soaked, but after a couple of hard cranks, it sputtered and took. I was surprised at the life in that little car.

"All right!" Ricky looked triumphant, as though, by him shoveling the snow away from the V.W., he was responsible for its ability to start.

"Tell you what. I'll try her out, to the store and back and bring you both a soda pop for doing such a good job." I didn't want to risk taking the kids on this maiden voyage, in case the engine conked out. It felt strange being cooped up in the little car after driving the truck all winter. Being used to manhandling our truck without the aid of the power steering pump for all that time, now I found myself oversteering.

I pulled up in front of the store and there, parked right in front was our truck with the tailgate open. In plain view and within easy reach in the bed of the truck, sat our chain saw. Mentally, I was already scolding Dick for going inside and leaving the saw to be stolen so easily. After putting the saw inside the V.W., I went into the store to remind Dick of his error. Only he wasn't in the store. And neither was George. They had gone in George's truck, and left our chain saw at everyone's mercy.

I couldn't find Pat, so I told some of their help to tell Dick that I had taken the saw home, deciding to go ahead and trim up some firewood and eliminate Dick having to deal with it when he got home. Naturally, the inevitable happened.

The *help* at the store changed shifts before Dick and George returned. Dick discovered his chain saw missing and inquired about it in the store, but no one even knew I'd been there. So Dick jumped to the only conclusion he could draw: somebody had stolen his chain saw.

And he was verbal about it. He drove all over Tok looking for that saw. He figured whoever had taken it would try to sell it or maybe try trading it for groceries or booze.

He told me later that he checked out the rear end of every truck in Tok and even looked through the car windows. When he pulled into the parking lot of one of the local bars, he had really worked himself into a steam. One car parked there had several bags of groceries inside. When the unfortunate Indian owner emerged from the bar, Dick demanded to know where he'd gotten the money for the groceries and the booze, since it was the wrong time of month for them to receive their government checks. He scared the poor guy almost speechless. Upon a proper explanation, and realizing his mistake, Dick apologized profusely, then explained his own situation. The Indian, from Tanacross, told Dick he would keep an eye open for the saw. Should it turn up out there, he'd let Dick know.

Dick was desperate for the saw. Without it, we would not be able to cut firewood, or houselogs when the time was right. Next to the truck, that saw was our life.

He turned and went into the bar, slammed his fist down on the bar top, let everyone know that some *dirty low-life* had stolen his chain saw and then offered the title of our truck to the first person to tell him who the culprit was. He left the bar in a rage and came home.

Dick stormed through the door, mad as hell, and went directly to his cot. He grabbed his shotgun and began loading shells into it. I looked at him, amazed, never having seen him this worked up. "What's wrong?" I asked.

He looked up in a scowl, still shoving shells into the gun. "Gonna get me a varmint. Worse than a horse thief. Take my only means of support. Wait'll I find the S.O.B. who done it. He'll be walking home, 'cause I'll have blown his car to smithereens. S.O.B...." He stood up, ready to leave again.

"Done what?" I blinked.

"Stole my damn chain saw! Right outta the truck. Lower than whale crap, somebody who'd do that to a man in the winter!"

I shifted, one foot to the other, "But..."

"But nothing," he cut me off, "if I hafta stay up all night, I'll find the bastard who stole it, an' when I do..."

"I stole it," I blurted out. Suddenly it was very quiet. "I've got the saw," I repeated.

"Huh?"

"Well, it was laying there totally vulnerable. I was afraid someone would steal it."

"How'd you get to the store in the first place?" He said that in a disbelieving tone.

I turned and picked up the saw, sitting on the floor behind me. Dick's eyes almost popped out of his head.

"How?"

I explained the whole story, then had the nerve to bawl him out for leaving it like that to be picked up so easily. "Probably would have been gone if I hadn't brought it home first," I told him. "I left a message at the store."

"Well, I didn't get it," he mumbled. His attitude had gone from anger to sheepishness. It was obvious he was feeling very foolish. "Now what do I do? Don't say anything to anybody and maybe by tomorrow, no one will think any more about it."

"Fat chance!"

Several days later we were in Farren's store again. George came over looking worried. "Look, Donna, I'll loan Dick my saw until he finds his. Think he'll take it?"

That put me on the spot. "No," I answered.

"I know you guys can't afford to buy another one. And you're going to need wood, if you don't already."

"It's O.K., George," I answered.

"No. No, I'm serious. Talk to Dick will you? I'll go get my saw..." He turned to leave.

"No, George, don't..."

"But..."

I could see George wasn't going to drop this. "Look, George, Dick found his saw."

"That's great! Where'd he find it? Who took it? How come I didn't hear about it?"

I couldn't lie to him. "It's this way..." I began, and told him the story, adding, "but don't say anything, for Pete's sake. Dick's really embarrassed over it and he's not good at eating crow."

"Sure, not a word," George replied, putting his index finger to his lips. As he turned away, I saw the mischievous twinkle in his eyes.

"Oh, no," I groaned.

George, seeing Dick at the far end of the store, shouted, "Hey, Dick! Heard you found the thief who stole your saw!"

The store was full of townspeople, who by now were well aware of the saw's disappearance and Dick's subsequent search for it.

"Yeah," Dick replied softly and cunningly moved behind a stack of boxes.

"So, Dick," George relentlessly pursued the subject, "who gets the title to your truck?"

Someone else in the store asked, "Yeah, who?"

Then another, "Who took the saw?"

That was George's cue. "Donna did it. His wife! " George broke into a series of guffaws.

The truth was out. Poor Dick. The townspeople had a field day with the story. It became a standing joke, with everyone stopping Dick to ask if he'd lost his saw lately. Dick learned to laugh with them, though. Eventually, he was telling his own version of the story to the few who hadn't already heard it.

During the days that Dick was trying to live down the chain saw incident, Ricky was diligently preparing for the science fair at school. He made a barometer and was going to do a weather project, since it seemed like the weather and wood were the two biggest things in our lives right now. He discovered immediately that the normal way to construct a barometer wouldn't work because of the way we were living. Regular colored water in the beaker and protruding straw, marked in graduating degrees, would freeze and break, even inside the tent. But with the addition of a little antifreeze, it wouldn't freeze and would still conveniently move up and down with the fluctuating barometric pressure.

Ricky made a chart and for two months, took daily notes of the type of weather we were having; snow, cloudy, clear, etc, at the same time of day. He also recorded the temperatures and his barometric readings. As the fair drew near, he charted all his findings and graphed them out.

"How does it look?" he asked me.

"Looks great," I answered truthfully. He had done a fine job, constructing a large, half-box affair, pasting his graphs on it and adding embellishments such as rain drops, clouds, snowflakes and a sun face. The beaker-turned-barometer and a handwritten report with all his findings and conclusions sat in the center of it all.

"Think it'll win, Mom?"

"I don't know, honey, but if I were judging, I'd sure give you an A for all the work you've put into your project," I said. "I hope the judges love it," I added, giving him a hug.

We loaded it, carefully, in the car and took it to the school the next morning. Judging was set for that afternoon. I helped him set up his display amid dozens of others. Big ones, small ones, impressive ones, colorful ones.

"Wow! Look at this neat one!" Ricky said while wandering over several rows and gazing down at a glass aquarium that now housed a snake. Since there are no snakes in Alaska, he was enthralled. Next to it sat another project with a half-dozen bottles full of formaldehyde carefully arranged in a semi-circle. He peered into them, squinting at their preserved contents.

He turned to me, his face skewered in torment. "I don't have a chance, Mom," he said sorrowfully. "These are just too great."

"Now wait. You aren't the judge and neither am I. Don't assume you've lost. You don't know what they're looking for. Also don't get your hopes up. Just know that you put a lot of hours into your project and it's real good. And whether you win or lose isn't the idea. You've learned a lot and had fun doing it, didn't you?"

"Yeah," he said glumly. I had the feeling I wasn't making much difference. He wanted, understandably, to win.

"You did have fun with it, didn't you?"

"Well, sure."

"It looks real pretty sitting over there, doesn't it?"

"Yeah, it sure does," he said with pride, "but Mom..."

"I'm proud of you, win or lose. Remember that." He gave me a hug and I left the school.

When Ricky returned from the day at school, he told me the judging was over, and he seemed agitated. Dick asked him what was wrong, then, "Didn't you win?"

"I don't know. Probably not." He flopped down on his bed.

"What do you mean, 'probably not'?" Dick asked. "I live down an unstolen chain saw and now you're fretting over a 'probably not'? Remember it's not the wining that counts, it's..."

"I heard all that this morning," Ricky interrupted, looking squarely at me. "They judged everything all right, only they're not telling who won, and they've locked the door to the Science room so nobody can get in and see. It's not fair!" he complained.

"I heard Ricky got first place, Mama!" Katherine chimed in.

"Oh, can it!" Ricky retorted. "How would you know? And how can I win when there are snakes in a cage?"

"Really, Mama and Daddy," Katherine went on, "some of the kids told me today that my brother had won the science fair." Right or wrong, it appeared the school grapevine was at work.

"Well, let's don't count on it," Dick said. "If it's a secret, then how would anyone know?"

"But, Daddy, I just know Ricky won!" Katherine was emphatic, determined to support her big brother whether he believed her or not.

"I remember my school grapevine," I said, thinking back many years, "and I can't remember it ever being wrong."

"Let's just hope," Dick said. "When do we find out for sure, Son?"

"Tomorrow. At lunch they're gonna open up the room for kids and parents to come in and view all the projects. We won't know 'til then," Ricky said, his arms flailing on his bed.

"Then tomorrow, at noon, Daddy and I will come to the school and we'll all go together and see. Okay?".

"Yeah, guess so."

Ricky slept fitfully that night and for the first time in ages, he had no trouble getting up and ready for school the next morning.

As planned, Dick and I met the kids at their rooms at noon. We all walked down the hall to the science room. It was already jammed with people. Anxious as he was, Ricky's face had a look of gloom and doom on it. He bit his lower lip.

"Just remember," I said, hugging him, "winning is great, but just because you don't win doesn't mean you've lost either." We stepped inside and inched our way through the crowd to get closer to Ricky's project. It was surrounded by kids and adults.

And there, on the top corner, hung a big blue ribbon. Katherine and her grapevine had been right. "Told you so, told you so, told you so!" Katherine chanted with delight. Her face radiated happiness for him.

Ricky was speechless. He stood, transfixed.

"Pretty neat, Ricky." The other kids chimed in.

"Yeah. Way to go!"

"You worked on this for two months?"

"Hey, you even outdid the snakes!"

His schoolmates had suddenly realized that Ricky was standing among them and they lost no time congratulating him.

"Told you so," Katherine repeated one more time, giving Ricky a demure, *you-should-have-listened-to-me-in-the-first-place* look.

Leaving Ricky to bask in his well-deserved limelight, we left him with his project and wandered around looking at the others.

Later he approached me, beaming, and whispered, "Mom, even if we do live in a tent!"

I was more than a little amazed at Ricky. Had he really thought our living in a tent even entered the picture? I supposed he had. Now he knew different. I hoped he understood from this example, that living conditions or anything else doesn't matter, it's what you do with those things that makes the difference.

Dick overheard his comment. "Son," he said, "I'm real proud of you. I never won anything like this in school." If anyone had asked me, who, at that moment was the proudest of all, I honestly couldn't have answered. Both father and son were pretty well equal when it came to the pride they displayed.

The next day we learned that Ricky's project, along with the second and third place projects, was to be transported to Glennallen, one hundred and fifty miles south of Tok, where all other first-second-and third-place winners from other schools around the state would be assembled and judged for the District Science Fair.

A week later, the news that Ricky's project had won second in the district fair was announced over the loudspeaker at school. Someone from a bigger school had taken first. But Ricky was elated. Winning the Tok Science Fair had been one thing, but just placing in the *biggie*, as he called it, was an honor. He was so proud at the awards ceremony.. Ricky beamed all the way home that evening, clutching his ribbons and certificates.

He looked exhausted, but happy, when he went to bed that night. It had been an exciting day. I noticed his science awards, neatly arranged, hanging on his headboard. As he fell asleep, one ribbon was still clutched tightly in his hand.

March was proving to be an exciting month. The monotony of winter had been broken by the chain-saw caper and the science fair. I wondered what it would bring next.

The weather was beginning to warm now and we could see a definite difference in the daylight. Every day there was more and more of it. The thermometer no longer gripped the mercury, clinging to the minus fifty mark. It was closer to twenty and thirty below zero now. The rise in temperature actually felt warm to us. We found ourselves running outside to the throne in our shirt sleeves, or even less. We also discovered that throughout the winter, our body hair had increased. No, we didn't resemble abominable snow people, but we could certainly tell that our bodies had *haired up*. Nature's protection system at work, I supposed.

With more daylight and temperatures on a slow rise, we began thinking more and more about those lonely four log walls out there, buried in snow. Maybe we could resume our work on the cabin before long. I hoped so. To me, even though it was hard work, that

171

very work translated into hope and happiness. I couldn't wait to get started again.

One morning, when Dick had finished checking his chain saw in preparation for us to go out and get firewood, I realized it looked different.

"What's wrong with the saw?" I asked.

"Oh nothing. Just put the longer bar back on it, that's all."

"The longer bar? The one we used for house logs?"

"Yeah," he grinned at me.

Oh, glorious day! I knew his plan without him speaking a word. We were going to start bringing home a house log or two with every load of firewood. By the time it got warm enough to peel them and work on the cabin, we would already have a stockpile of house logs waiting to be worked.

"Penny for your thoughts," he asked.

"I can see a great big pile of logs stacked in front of the cabin by spring, just waiting to be notched and put up."

"E-e-e-yep, exactly!"

Dick and I were in high spirits that morning as we set off down the road, bumping along in the truck. The sun, shining brightly, reflected off the snow. It's mirror-like glare forced us to wear sunglasses. Even so, it was still twenty-five below zero. The early March sun wasn't high enough to be very warm, but it lifted our spirits. The promise of spring was only a few months away.

We had a couple of trees already cut and limbed in the field waiting for our return. Today, all we needed to do was buck them into stove lengths and load them, leaving us plenty of time to find an appropriate tree for our first house log of the new year.

Dick quickly bucked up the firewood. The new bar and chain on the saw was longer and sharper, making the work twice as easy. He helped me load the wood onto the truck, stopping once or twice to brush sawdust or wood chips from my hair. I was so eagerly anticipating the first house log that I didn't care where, or how much, sawdust went anywhere. But wood chips and pitch in my long hair weren't a very good combination and I seemed to be getting an extraordinary amount in it.

"Slow down, will ya?" Dick said, once again picking wood chips from my bangs.

"Oh, God, I just can't help it. I just feel so alive today. Can't you feel it? It's like tomorrow's here today."

"I know, but we have a lot of tomorrows left to go. Don't burn yourself out."

"Look who's talking. You, of the longer bar/new chain clan. You sure didn't waste any time bucking up that firewood."

"Guilty as charged," he laughed, throwing the last piece of wood into the truck. "Let's go get a house log."

We drove to a different area to find our special tree for the log. "This one's excellent!" he said, enthusiastically. "Look how straight and tall she is. And a nice, even taper."

Dick was very good at finding trees for house logs. If we were lucky, we'd get three out of this tree.

"Before you cut it, I propose a toast," I said, handing him a cup of hot chocolate.

"Yeah, it is a special occasion." He took the cup. "Me first, though."

I nodded in agreement.

He continued, "Here's to our new house, and this tree, which shortly will become part of the Bernhardt household." Then he paused for only a moment, "And here's to my beautiful wife, who I love more than anything on this earth."

"And," I said, "here's to us. To new beginnings and to Alaska." I turned to him, my cup raised to his.

"I love you," we said simultaneously.

We gulped down the hot chocolate, then turned to the tree waiting to be sacrificed. It stood in a small clearing, surrounded with alder and willow. I mean really surrounded. The brush was thick. It had been all we could do to weave our way through it. I hacked a narrow path around it with my ax, so Dick would have room to maneuver while felling it.

He notched the tree trunk, then cut through the other side, causing it to fall toward the road. There would be less distance to carry the logs that way. We had to remember that our log-carrying shoulders would be out of shape for a while. The tree hit the ground with a loud crunch, smashing alder and willow as it fell, half-burying itself in the snow.

I began limbing, working from the butt end of the tree, like I had last fall, but Dick stopped me. "Forget it," he said, "I'll get it with the saw. Be easier that way."

"There's too much brush and snow around it for that, Dick. I can maneuver better with the ax than you can with the saw, especially with that longer bar on it."

"Naw, I can get it. Okay, hon," he said, smacking me on my rear. "Move your buns!"

Against my better judgment, I moved aside. I think Dick wanted this *trophy* tree all to himself. He began limbing, standing on top of it, moving up the trunk from side to side as I had. The limbs got smaller and smaller as he progressed up the tree. And the brush around it became thicker and thicker.

Suddenly, he bent to one side, cutting through a limb. The extra length of the chain and bar entangled in the brush beneath the tree, and as it did so, Dick began losing his balance. I could see what was going to happen. "Oh, God!" I thought wildly. "No!" I was already running in Dick's direction.

With spring-like action, the willows propelled the saw blade into the back of his leg. The chain was still spinning and when Dick realized what was happening, he released his grip on the saw, causing the chain to quit circling around the bar. But it was too late. I heard him shout in agony before I reached him and he sank down into the snow, clutching his injured leg.

Mentally, I was already preparing myself for the mess I would find. *How bad was it? Had the chain saw cut through the bone? Would he be crippled? Would he bleed to death?* I cursed the thought of this tree. I was so afraid for him. I couldn't face the prospect of him dying. I wouldn't let him. But would I have the stomach to see what I was going to have to see? Actually, I'd always been pretty good in that department. But now...

I reached Dick. The saw lay on its side. The motor was still putt-putting along and the chain had embedded itself in the back of Dick's jeans, just below his calf. It was tangled in shreds of blue denim and there was blood oozing everything. Quickly, I flipped the switch, cutting power to the saw, then took my pocket knife and cut the saw free from the jeans.

Dick was clutching his leg with both of his big hands. "How bad?" he said in short breaths.

"Don't know yet, can't see it. Your pants are in the way." Even though they were shredded, I hadn't yet seen the wound itself. "Hold still," I demanded, and ripped his pants leg up the seam beyond his calf.

"Oh, God," I drew in a breath. "The calf of your leg is all chewed. Mangled. There are strips of skin and meat hanging there. Too much blood to see much more. Twigs and dirt and stuff are all mixed in with the flesh." My adrenaline was working overtime. I could feel my heart pounding, yet I felt not one bit of panic or faintness. The wound didn't seem to be spurting blood, even though it was bleeding profusely, but then, Dick's tight grip on his own leg was restricting at least part of the blood flow.

"Dick, let up easy with your hands. I've gotta see if you hit a vital vein or something." He released it with a loud groan. The bleeding worsened immediately. Still, I could not see any actual spurting. I turned to the chain saw and cut off the starting rope.

"What'd you do that for?" Dick asked, confused.

"Tourniquet, just in case. We gotta get you in the truck and get the physician's assistant. Do you think it broke your leg? Think you can stand with my help?"

"Don't know, let's try."

I bent down, and using the saw, on end, as an extra crutch, helped him to his feet. With great relief, we discovered the leg bone hadn't been broken. We didn't know whether the saw had touched the bone or not, though. I helped him hobble through the brush, slowly, desperately afraid that his leg would give out or that he may pass out on me at any moment. If that happened, I'd have to leave him and go for help.

Dick did well in spite of tremendous pain. I wanted to lay him in the back of the truck, but it was full of firewood, so instead he had to climb into the seat and half lie down there. The leg needed to be elevated but it was impossible in the cab of the truck.

We were nearly twenty miles from Tok and any help at all. I floored the gas pedal and took off leaving several lengths of firewood toppling off the back of the truck. *Damn the firewood! Save Dick's leg.* That was all I could think about. "Don't die on me, Dick. Don't!" I hugged his head, laying against my shoulder.

"Too mean to die..." he tried to joke. "Owww!"

I had hit a frost heave. Every heave in the road was new pain experience for Dick. I tried taking it easy, but time was ticking away.

When we reached the small building that housed the P.A., Dick was still conscious, but there was no one around. I stopped several local cars, asking the whereabouts of the P.A. He seemed to have vanished. No one knew where or why. Maybe an emergency had come up or something.

I told Dick my findings, or my not findings. "Back to the tent," he groaned, "I gotta lay down." He looked awfully pale and was starting to sweat.

I helped him to his cot and he collapsed on it. After stoking the stove and putting some snow on to melt and boil, I turned again to Dick. "We've got to get your boots and pants off," I said. "Bear with me." I carefully removed his boots. That was another odd thing. Today he had put on his logging boots instead of wearing his knee-high mukluks. If he'd had on the mukluks, there would have been an extra layer of protection between his leg and the saw. I thought about that as I untied the boots. One boot was blood-soaked inside. Then we removed his pants. I covered all of him but the leg with a blanket. With the tourniquet removed, the bleeding increased again. This was the first good view of the wound I'd had. I still could not see blood spurting. *Could we be that lucky? Had the chain missed the big arteries*? It appeared so.

Getting rid of the chainsaw rope, I used a real tourniquet from our first-aid kit. It was more comfortable and didn't cut into Dick's leg like the rope. "We still need a doctor," I said. "This is a mess."

"Guess you're it, honey."

"Me? Uh, uh, no way." I didn't have a degree in anything, much less medicine.

"Gotta, nobody else to help," he said.

"But, it's a mess. Needs to be cleaned. Pieces of skin and stuff removed. And sewed up. I don't have the knowledge or the equipment. What if you die?"

"We've got everything you need in the medicine kit. You can do it. I could do it if I could reach back there."

Sure, I thought. And a snowball won't melt in Hell either.

"...an' I ain't gonna die. So stop worrying." He let out another groan.

"We don't have anything to deaden it from the pain."

"Just do it Let's get it over with. There's rarely been anybody around to help us when we really needed it, has there?"

There's gotta be somebody, I thought. "I could go see if Mike or George is around."

"You figure they've got some medical degree that you don't?"

"No but George is a butcher. He knows about meat."

"Oh, great. Besides, I happen to know they're both out of town. Honey? Just go for it. Okay?"

I resigned myself to what he was saying. The only alternative was two-hundred miles to Fairbanks. *And what about the kids?* I turned to the first-aid kit, muttered a silent prayer for both of us and began.

The first thing I did that made Dick half-cry was when I poured alcohol over the entire wound. But the sooner it was disinfected, the better. I soaked the little sharp pair of scissors in a pan of alcohol and washed my hands with the disinfectant soap and hot snow water that had been heating on the stove. I was ready, I guessed.

"I'm gonna start now," I warned Dick. "Here's some pain pills from the kit. Might as well take them now and get a head start on this."

"I'm ready," he said, gulping the pills. He was beginning to sweat and shake slightly. I didn't like that. Removing the pillow from under his head, I made him lie on his stomach, propping the leg with that same pillow. It was the only way to get at the wound. "Let me know if this gets too bad and you want me to stop and let you rest." He nodded.

With sterile tweezers, I began removing all of the bark, twigs and bits of spruce needles from the wound. It was pretty dirty. Once satisfied that I had most of it cleaned out, I again poured alcohol over it. This time it didn't seem quite so bad for Dick. Maybe the pills were helping. Most of the time I'd been cleaning his wound, Dick had been very still, breathing heavily, eyes shut tight. I loosened the tourniquet once more. Still no spurting, just normal bleeding. I tightened it again.

I let Dick and myself rest a few minutes before starting the next phase; that of removing the lacerated skin and muscle. These hopelessly shredded pieces were in the way and would be further cause for infection. Dick said nothing, except letting out a few groans now and then, even though I was snipping away. He was holding up remarkably well. I doubted that I could have done as well if the situation had been reversed.

When most of the small shreds were removed, I was able to see into the wound better. I peered into his calf with a small flashlight, carefully moving aside larger pieces of muscle. This effort made Dick jump or wince several times. I saw him tighten his fists, gripping his blanket. Still, he said nothing.

From what I could see, I didn't think the chain saw had made it to the bone. The thought of infection on the bone itself wasn't a pleasant one, but I was reasonably sure the bone hadn't been nicked and no ligaments had been severed either. I could see them. To be sure, I had Dick flex his foot up and down and side to side very carefully. His massive, muscular calf had shielded the vital parts from permanent damage. At least, it appeared that way.

Once more, I loosened the tourniquet, then tightened it and disinfected the wound again. Couldn't be too careful. God, how the thought of infection and the possible consequences scared me. I thought of infection, of amputation or even worse.

What would I do without Dick, I wondered. What if the worst happened? It wasn't just the thought of being left alone living in a tent with the kids. It was the thought of not having him around to touch, to talk to, to share things with, to love. I couldn't bear that. We were so close now, losing him would be the one most impossible thing to bear. That just couldn't happen.

For good measure, I poured more alcohol over his leg.

Now it was time for the part I really dreaded. Sewing up the large pieces that needed to be rejoined. We had sterile sutures and needles. I told Dick what was next.

"I'm only going to do a minimum. I'll tape the rest of the wound and we'll try to hold it together taped. There's no way I can sew it all back together again. All the surface skin is gone. Dick...?"

"Yeah," he grunted.

"Are you sure you want me to go ahead with this?"

"Yes."

"Is there anything you need before I start?"

He replied, a slight hoarseness in his throat. "How 'bout a kiss from my doctor?"

Still the same old Dick, even in the middle of this mess. I gave him a good one and also one more pain pill. While rummaging through the kit for the sutures, I discovered a bottle of antibiotics and gave him one of those. *Maybe, just maybe, we could get a jump on avoiding possible infection that way.*

I began stitching, taking care to keep the sutures and everything else sterile. Immediately, Dick was in great pain. I stopped.

"It's okay," he said.

"No, it's not. You can't see yourself. You're not okay." He looked faint; he was shaking. His face was ashen and there was a slight glaze in his eyes. I felt his skin. It was cold, yet sweaty. "You're going into shock."

"No, I'm okay, Just finish."

"Not yet," I said. "Turn over." I helped him turn onto his back, elevating his legs a bit higher. "Rest." I told him.

Taking one of the blankets from Katherine's bed, I threw it over the stove for a brief couple of moments, then removed the old blanket from Dick and placed the heated one over his body. I repeated this over the course of the next half hour, while waiting for clean water to heat for tea. When the tea was ready, I helped him up onto one elbow, and holding the cup for him, he sipped the hot liquid. Two cups later, beneath a freshly warmed blanket, the color was returning to his face.

I sat next to him, holding his hand while he rested for another half hour. He never let go of my hand. Finally, he looked as though he were on solid ground again. "How do you feel, now?" I asked, stroking his forehead.

"Lots better than a while ago."

"Shall we finish what we started?"

"Yeah, let's do it."

I helped him turn over once more, positioned his leg so I could work on it and began to stitch again. I was surprised at how tough skin is. At times it was very difficult to make the needle penetrate the skin. It seemed to go through the muscle much easier than the skin. All the pulling and tugging I was doing, and without anything to help deaden the pain, caused Dick to groan over and over. I stopped several times to let us both rest. Sweat poured from both of us. I wished there was a way to save him from some of the pain.

"I have an idea, Dick. Let me know if it's better or if it makes things worse, okay.?"

"Okay."

This time, before starting a stitch, and where possible, I pinched the flesh or muscle first, holding it momentarily, then pushing the needle through. It proved to be a much better system. The pinch helped to temporarily numb the flesh before the needle penetrated it. It worked well where there was skin to be dealt with, yet not as well on the muscle parts.

Even so, my nerves were ragged and Dick's pain level was near overflowing as I finished the last of the stitching. He had held up well, considering everything he had been through. Once finished, I taped the small pieces down with butterfly stitches and carefully disinfected it all once more.

"I'm finished," I sighed. I really felt finished. Hours had gone by. It seemed like days: bent over his leg, straining to help him, yet knowing I had been causing a good deal of his pain. My entire body ached from being tense for so long. I also had a throbbing headache, and those were only my symptoms.

I looked at Dick, still lying there, fists clenching his cot. "You can let go now," I said, as I massaged his neck and shoulder muscles. "We're done."

He heaved a big sigh of relief.

"You can turn over, carefully, and let's elevate your leg to keep it from bleeding too much. We'll loosen the tourniquet gradually, too." I fixed him a cup of hot chocolate, which he swigged down, made sure he was well-covered and warm, and then lay down on my own cot. "Let me know if you need anything, or if you start feeling worse. O.K.?"

"O.K., Hon?"

"Yeah?"

"I sure do love you."

"Love you, too, you old Grizz."

Soon he was fast asleep, a blessing considering, his body could rest and begin repairing itself. I rested, too, but couldn't sleep. I was still too keyed up.

When the kids got home, they helped me unload the firewood and stack it inside. Dick never moved. He was out cold.

God, heal him fast, I prayed that night and added a thank you for helping us through the day.

With the weather in the minus twenties, our wood consumption was down. That gave Dick time to recuperate without being forced into the field too early on his leg. When we did run out of firewood, I took the saw and headed outside.

"Where you going with that?" Dick asked me.

"Gonna cut up some firewood," I replied.

"We'll go down the road and cut some."

"No, we won't," I said. "There's wood out here, it just needs to be cut up, that's all."

"Where?"

"Out in front of the cabin."

"That's house logs, not firewood,"

"It was house logs. Now it's firewood."

"You aren't gonna cut up our house logs, when I can go cut some real firewood."

"Wanta bet?" I confronted him. "That leg still needs some time. You know it and I know it. It's stupid to push yourself when there isn't a reason to. Now, either I can take the truck and go get firewood alone, or I can take the saw and go cut up a couple of house logs. Which is it going to be?"

"Dammit, do you always have to be right?" he said, conceding defeat.

"Only when I'm right!" I laughed and headed out the door.

Every day I cleaned and dressed Dick's leg. There was no sign of infection. He made a point of getting up and moving around to keep the muscles from tightening as they healed. He was doing great. I couldn't believe our good fortune.

"But it was short-lived. Not for Dick, but for Ricky. How he did it, and where he managed to find a board with a nail in it, I'll never know. Dick was hobbling around in the tent and the kids were outside playing when it happened. Katherine was shouting, "Mama!" from the depths of her lungs.

I rushed outside to the cabin site. Ricky was leaning against one of the walls in agony. I peered down at the leg he was holding up. Attached to the bottom of his mukluk was a small board. With a nail in it embedded in his foot. He was crying.

"Ricky, I'm going to have to pull the board off your foot. It's going to hurt."

"No, Mom, don't touch it," he sniffed.

"I can't leave it there. You want to wear that board for the rest of your life?"

He shook his head. I made him sit in the snow, telling him I needed to get a better look at it.

"But don't touch it, Okay, Mom?"

"Ricky I'm not going to touch that nail if you don't want me to."

"Okay." He extended his foot.

Swiftly, before he had time to realize what was happening, I grabbed hold of the board and pulling it straight away from his foot.

"O-w-w-w-w!" He cried. "You lied, Mom. You lied!"

"No, I didn't. I said I wouldn't touch the nail. I didn't say I wouldn't touch the board."

"That's not fair!"

"Well, shall I put the board back where it was? You can wear it to school."

"Mom!"

"Let me help you into the tent and we'll take care of it." We entered the tent with him limping and leaning on me.

"Now I've got two gimps," I joked with Dick and Ricky. Neither of them thought it very funny. I had Ricky soak his foot in hot Epsom salts. Luckily, we all had tetanus shots before leaving Anchorage. Ricky limped around the next day and then, becoming bored, he went outside with Katherine to play again.

And there came another blood-curdling "Mama!" from Katherine. Once again I raced outside to find disaster had struck again. Katherine was in tears. I rushed up to her. "What's wrong, Baby?"

"Ricky," she said tearfully, pointing toward him. Ricky was sitting, straddling a partially peeled log, clutching the upper part of his thigh and looking disgusted with the whole world. A draw knife lay beside him.

There was no doubt about what he'd done. A two inch gash through the top of his jeans oozed blood. He wasn't crying, but he did exude total exasperation.

"Don't tell me," I said, "let me guess. You couldn't stand up to peel the log because of your foot, so you sat down on it to peel it. Stop me if I'm wrong. And you pulled the draw knife right into your leg."

His look told me all I needed to know. Once more, I helped him into the tent and reached for the medical kit.

Ricky dropped his pants, revealing a smooth, deep cut about an inch and a half long across the top of his thigh. I cleaned it with hydrogen peroxide, painted it with merthiolate and butterfly-sutured it together. He was quiet during the entire procedure, except to remark that it was the same leg that had the nail injury on it. He spent the rest of the day brooding over his misfortune.

Dick spent the day, between naps, putting a new starter rope on the chain saw and removed the long bar. And I spent the day helping Katherine learn her ABC's and thinking about the exciting month of March we were having.

How much more excitement could we stand?

CHAPTER SIXTEEN

Easter And The Woe Of Snow

March ended with Easter and no more disasters, although this Easter was a lot different from any other we had experienced. In Anchorage, by Easter time, it was getting pretty warm. Sometimes we'd be knee-deep in mud and spring breakup. I even remembered Easters when the snow was gone and tiny green blades of grass were beginning to show. But not in Tok.

Here, there was ample snow on the ground and the temperature was staying right around twenty below. Still, it didn't dampen the kids' spirits. Easter was Easter, regardless.

We boiled a dozen eggs on the wood stove and Katherine and Ricky busied themselves coloring them. And since there were no Easter baskets, that was another project for them. They each had their own ideas about what baskets should look like, so using bits of paper, magazine cutouts, foil and anything else they could find, they constructed their own baskets.

Proudly, they displayed them at the ends of their beds. And Easter morning, sure enough, the Easter bunny had filled those baskets with candy. Katherine still believed in the Easter bunny just as she did Santa Claus. Ricky, long ago, had learned the truth. He was good at pretending for his little sister, though.

Dick and I decided to have an Easter egg hunt for the kids. "You two stay in the tent while we hide the eggs," I told them.

"Yeah, and no peeking," their daddy wagged a finger at them.

Dick and I covered two of the eggs in tinfoil, enclosing a dollar bill inside each one. We stepped outside to hide the eggs.

"Anybody peeking?" Dick called.

"NO!" the kids shouted in unison.

We hid eggs in snowbanks, tree branches, on the car and truck, even on the tent rigging. And we added an extra embellishment. Giant Easter bunny tracks.

"Come on out," Dick called, "we're done hiding the eggs!"

They came tumbling out of the tent. Katherine found the first egg. "Got one!" she shouted at Ricky, plucking the egg that had conveniently been left in plain sight for her benefit. Then it was a free-for-all.

Egg for egg, they stayed equal until all the colored eggs had been found. In the middle of the hunt, they spied the giant bunny tracks in the snow. Katherine was impressed.

"Ooooh," she said, placing her own foot inside one of the tracks.

"I guess the Easter bunny is really a big bunny," I said. "Guess he'd have to be to carry all that candy, huh?"

"Yeah," she said in awe.

Ricky eyed his daddy suspiciously, but never let on.

"Now," I told them, "there are still two eggs out there somewhere. Special eggs. Silver eggs. Money eggs!"

"Money eggs, Mom?" Ricky asked.

"Yep," Dick answered, "got money inside them!"

They bolted into action. Both kids had passed those two eggs a dozen times. They began looking in earnest.

"Just remember," I told them, "the hardest things to see are sometimes those that are in plain sight." Dick and I winked at each other. He stood with his arm around me while we watched the kids in their quest.

Another ten minutes of searching went by. Finally, Katherine found the first silver egg, perched precariously on the handlebar forks of Ricky's bicycle where Dick had put it; silver egg against silver forks.

"Really sneaky, Dad," Ricky commented, slightly perturbed that Katherine had found it first. He looked all the harder for the remaining egg.

"I got a dollar!" Katherine crowed, "and I'm gonna find the other one so I can have two of them!" She knew how to get at Ricky.

"That's not fair," Ricky retorted, "the other one's mine!"

"Not if I find it first!" she emphasized, gleefully rubbing salt into his wounds.

"Mom?" Ricky questioned.

"Better find it before she does," I answered. Dick and I could hardly keep straight faces. Ricky was almost touching the second silver egg at that very moment.

"Maybe it's lost," he said after another few minutes.

"Yeah, Mama, lost," Katherine sided with Ricky. "Maybe it got lost in a snowbank," she said, leaning against the hood of the Volkswagen.

Dick and I were forced to look away from them in order to keep them from seeing us crack into broad smiles. They were so close.

Ricky looked at Dick, misreading our actions, "Or maybe, it's in their pockets!" he shouted.

Both kids bolted toward us. We assured them it was no where on either of us. "It's in easy sight. You just have to really see the things you're looking at."

Ricky narrowed his eyes, squinting, searching. Again, both kids walked right past it. Finally, Ricky came over and sat down on the front bumper of the V.W.

"Give up?" Dick asked.

"Do we still get the dollar?"

Dick laughed, squeezing my hand, "No, Mama does. She hid that egg!"

"Then we don't give up!" Ricky said with renewed determination. I was beside myself. I began to laugh, then Dick was caught up in my mirth and we both stood there laughing so hard tears ran down our cheeks. Knowing something was up, Ricky stood facing the V.W. He peered into the trees, scrutinizing branches, but never moved from his spot. Finally, lowering his head, his face suddenly lit up.

"I found it!" he cried out, picking the silver egg off the hood ornament. "Boy, you're even sneakier than Dad, Mom!" (Silver on silver, again. The car had a Rolls-Royce hood and the egg lay between the silver wings of the hood ornament.)

They spent the remainder of the day counting their loot and deciding how to spend their silver egg dollars.

With April fast approaching, the temperature stayed on a warming trend. At last it was zero, then higher by a few degrees. We noticed that while the snow didn't appear to be melting, it was slowly disappearing. Some of the brush that had been covered, now had its top showing. The snow wasn't as deep as before. It seemed to be slowly evaporating. What a difference from Anchorage. When it warmed up there, it did it all at once, but there was lots of water and muck everywhere. This looked like a clean breakup.

Every day Dick exercised his leg. It was mending nicely, though there would be an awful scar. The greater portion of his calf would always bear evidence to that accident, but we were thankful it had not been much, much worse.

We were nearly out of available logs for firewood, so when he felt he could manage it, we decided to go get a load of wood.

"I could go do this myself, Dick." I told him.

"No way and no need," he said. "I'm doing really good now. It just pulls a little when I stretch my leg too far, or move it too fast. Still pretty tender inside if I bump it, though. Besides, there's safety in numbers. I don't want you out there alone. S'pose I'd been alone that day?"

There was a lot of truth in what he said. It's always better not to be alone, in case something does happen. "Then let's just give it a trial run with a very small load of wood today, Okay? And see how that goes?"

"Okay, just a little load," he agreed.

Dick managed quite well. He rested often and didn't push the leg. Even so, because the days were beginning to lengthen and the light lasted longer, we arrived home before dark. He was tired when we drove into the driveway, but satisfied. Once again, Dick felt productive.

"What the...?" he said, gazing at the tent. It looked funny. Sort of lopsided. Something about it wasn't quite right, although nothing was obviously wrong from the front.

Further inspection revealed quite a different story though.

"Oh, crap!" he moaned.

I just stood there shaking my head. What was it with our luck? We had been home for days, but the first time out, we were greeted with another challenge.

"I'm beginning to wonder if we're the luckiest, or the unluckiest, people in the world," I commented.

"How can you compare the two and not know the answer?" he asked.

"Well, you sawed your leg in half and didn't lose your leg or your life. But now we've lost half our tent." The ice wall on the long north side of the tent had weakened and fallen. Not outward and not piece by piece. Oh, no. It had caved inward and the tremendous weight of that six inch thick, four foot high, sixteen feet long slab of ice had collapsed the side of the tent. Worse, it had ripped the tent almost in half.

"My God, what do we do now?" I asked.

"We fix it," Dick said, matter-of-factly.

The entire north side of the tent was nothing but a gaping hole. Inside the tent, the huge slab of ice lay like a skating rink. Everything on that side was either knocked over, pushed out of place or crushed. While the cupboards had been shoved completely across the tent, they hadn't broken. On the other hand, many of our canned goods had been crushed, but none of them were split open. Pots and pans were bent out of shape, dishes were broken and one of the kerosene lamps had fallen, spilling kerosene everywhere. The cats, while still jumpy, had not been hurt. I had to wonder if they were asleep in the cupboards when the ice let go. If so, it must have been a wild ride. In order to remove the ice from the inside of the tent, Dick and I took turns breaking it into smaller chunks by using the splitting maul. Then it could be hauled outside and stacked away from the area. We were in that process when the kids returned home from school.

"Wow, what happened?" Ricky asked.

We explained briefly and put both Katherine and Ricky to work helping us lift those big blocks of ice and removing them. Most of the evening and night were spent eliminating the snow and ice from inside the tent. We had thought the giant burn hole had been bad. Until now, we hadn't known what bad really was.

But neither Dick nor I were that upset. We were acquiring a calm acceptance of things gone sour. What good would it do to be mad? Better to just dig in and make it better. Even Ricky, though he tired of lifting heavy ice blocks, had something good to say about it.

"Dad, what are you gonna do with all this ice?"

"What do you mean? There's nothing I want to do with it, except get it outside."

"Well, can I have it?"

Dick stopped working. "What in the world would you want it for, Son?"

"Make a neat fort or igloo," he said, hopefully.

"Stick to the fort idea," I cut in, "Don't stack these things so that you're going to be underneath them."

"Dad?"

"They're yours but like your Mama says, we don't want you rigging up something that will squash you."

"Thanks, Dad."

"Can I make a fort, too, Daddy?" Katherine pleaded.

"You can help me," Ricky told her.

"Yay!" In the early morning hours we finally had all the ice and snow back outside where it belonged and had patched the enormous hole. Dick and I sewed as much of the roof and wall back together as best we could, then used more canvas to make a real patch for added strength. The new, giant patch overlapped the other giant burn hole patch.

By morning, we were able to get some. Dick was visibly tired, but still in good spirits. We all were. I was amazed at our reaction to the entire thing. I reached over my cot and took his hand, already searching for mine in the dark of tent.

"I guess we're the luckiest people in the world," I had concluded. "You've still got your leg and we've still got our tent."

"And we've all got each other," he added. "I love you."

Our tent had been through some hard times. We never did decide whether the extra warmth from the snow walls was worth this last disaster.

One thing we decided, we wouldn't let it happen again. The next day, we dug the snow away from the south side and while we were in the spirit of shoveling, we began moving some of the snow out of the cabin. With the sun beginning to warm things, if we helped rid the floor of snow, we figured we might be able to start work on the cabin again. But the first frozen log we tried spiking into place split. We'd have to wait a few more weeks.

CHAPTER SEVENTEEN

The Race Of Champions

Each winter, close to spring, Tok hosts the Race of Champions. This is usually the last big dog sled sprint racing event of the year. Champions, men and dogs alike, converge on Tok for the two-day event. Attractions include money prizes and lots of fun and comradeship.

Alaska's races attract not only mushers from Alaska, but worldwide. And since Tok had been hailed, unofficially, *the sled dog capital* of Alaska, the community was proud to host the racers.

We had always watched the Fur Rendezvous dog sled races in Anchorage and loved them. I had been rooting for my favorite mushers since the first time I saw a dog sled team in 1951. Through the years, I had decided that George Attla, a native musher from Huslia, Alaska, was the musher I most wanted to see win. And he had lived up to my wishes.

We needed a break from the tedium of our daily tent routine ?? something fun and different. The race sounded like just what we needed, so Dick and I took the kids to watch our first Race of Champions. We knew all of the big mushers' names. The entries read like a Hall of Fame: George Attla, Gareth Wright, Dr. Roland Lombard (from Massachusetts), Harvey Drake, Harris Dunlop, Tim Redington and more.

The day was bright and beautiful, sunny but not overly warm. It was still below zero. We stood in front of the crowd, watching the junior racers take off down the trail. These were kids. There were categories for them, running either a three-dog, two-dog or one-dog team. All possible future champions.

"Mama, can I be a racer, too?" Katherine asked.

"Well, not this year. We don't have a team. It's a lot of work, too, taking care of your dogs all year. You have to train them, you know, they don't just run without learning to be in a team first."

"It would be fun, too!" Her eyes were big with excitement.

"We'll see, next year." I told her.

During the first heat of the two-day Race of Champions, the trail was packed well and weather conditions were good. A new trail record had been set by Harvey Drake. He and his sixteen dog team had run the twenty mile trail in seventy-one minutes and five seconds. That was wonderful, of course, but I was still rooting for George Attla.

We were anxious, now on this second and final day to see what would happen. None of us were prepared for what did happen.

Harvey Drake went on to win the Race of Champions. His total time for the forty mile distance, a very respectable one hundred forty-eight minutes and thirty-eight seconds was a little faster than George Attla's one hundred forty-nine minutes and forty-five seconds. Doc Lombard placed third with a time only fifty-two seconds slower than George's.

Just the excitement of such a close race took our minds off the tent and its lifestyle. Watching the dogs barking, leaping and straining to get on the trail, seeing the mushers and the dog handlers, even the crowd, was exactly the diversion we needed. Without what was yet to come, it would have been a wonderful weekend.

But the best was yet to come, especially for Dick.

Katherine and Ricky were completely engrossed in the festive atmosphere around them, when a tall, familiar-looking figure walked across in front of us. He walked with sort of a swagger, wore a big western belt and buckle, cowboy boots and western hat and a bulky, warm coat.

Dick stared incredulously as the man walked past and headed over to George Attla, who was seated in his sled.

I looked at Dick. We both looked back at the man. "Was that...?" I questioned.

"In Tok? No way," was Dick's uncertain reply.

"Sure looks like him."

"This is Tok, Alaska. What would he be doing in Tok? Hollywood, yes. Tok? I don't think so..."

"It is. I know it is. I gotta find out," and I casually strolled over where the man was standing. The possibility that one of Dick's boyhood idols may be here in front of us was too much not to investigate further, I reasoned. Dick would never forgive himself if we didn't and later found that it had been him.

The man in question was talking to George Attla and Roland Lombard. As soon as I was within earshot, there was no doubt. Nobody sounded like that. It was the actor, Slim Pickens.

I hurried back to Dick and the kids. "It's him. It's really him!"

"I don't believe it," Dick said, shaking his head, "probably just somebody who looks a whole lot like him. They say everyone has a double ... look at me and George Farren."

I knew he didn't want to set himself up for a letdown, but dammit, it *was* Slim Pickens, and I knew it. Dick's two favorite western stars, all of his life, were John Wayne and Slim Pickens. At one point in an airport, he barely missed seeing John Wayne. He was still disappointed over it. He simply could not miss this opportunity.

"I'm telling you, it's Slim Pickens. Come listen to him. There's no doubt about it. Come on, dammit," I took his arm and began dragging him in the direction of Slim Pickens. Dick scuffled slowly along, still not believing, still thinking I'd lost my mind.

Mr. Pickens was still talking with Attla.

Dick's mouth dropped open. His face turned white. "I – I ... It ... it is him!" He wouldn't have been happier at that moment if someone had handed him a million dollar bill. "But what's he doin' in Tok?"

Several older kids moved closer to Pickens and asked for his autograph. Dick, like one of those kids, followed suit. He didn't presume to talk with Pickens, but just got his autograph. Ricky, on the other hand, by-passed the actor and headed straight for George Attla, asking for his autograph instead. Both men in the Bernhardt household were pleased with their treasures that evening. We still wondered why Pickens would be in Tok.

The following day, Dick and I pulled up at Mike's grocery store. Out in front were Mike's employees, standing with Mr. Pickens, having their pictures taken. We both laughed, because there Mike was, right in the middle of them.

Dick and I met the celebrity, talked with him, got his autograph again and found him to be a nice, friendly person. Later, Slim borrowed Mike's ATV, a four-wheeled, all-terrain vehicle and enjoyed driving it around Tok. We learned from him that a motion picture was being made about George Attla's life. Slim Pickens had the part of a storekeeper and part of it was being filmed in Tok. Some of the dog scenes were filmed here. The movie was titled, "Spirit of the Wind."

Pickens was in Tok for about a week while the filming was taking place. We ran into him several more times. He'd say "Howdy" or "Well, how d'ya do?" Always very amicable. And not once, in our brief *Hello's* with him, did we mention that we were living in a tent, slightly afraid he might think we were crazy. We never heard him utter an unkind word while he was here. His appearance in Tok meant the world to Dick and certainly broke up an otherwise tedious winter for all of us.

Dick told me later he knew why we'd been led to Tok to live in a tent.

"Why?" I asked him.

"So I could meet Slim Pickens," he said with a laugh. "That, alone, makes living in the tent worthwhile. And..." he added, "where else would you expect to find a great actor like that? Why, Tok, Alaska, of course."

CHAPTER EIGHTEEN

Paul Harvey Comments

Paul Harvey's commentary had always been one of our favorite radio shows. On a lark, we sent him a Christmas card with a photograph of our tent on it and a copy of my poem, *A Tent In Tok*.

One morning in early April, just after I scooted the kids out the tent door to catch the school bus, I turned on our battery-operated radio, sat down on my cot and picked up my mending. Dick was still asleep; we had planned to go out for wood later in the day.

The news came on. Nothing great or earth-shaking, but it was followed by the Paul Harvey show. I listened through about half of the program when he said something that made me listen extra hard. It started out...

"Received a Christmas card from Interior Alaska."

Could it be? I wondered. His voice continued.

"From Dick and Donna Bernhardt."

My heart began to pound. We were on national radio. I roused Dick out of his sleep, practically shaking him off the cot.

"Listen! We're on Paul Harvey!"

"Huh?" he said, groggily, then, "huh?"

"Ssshhhh!" I turned up the volume on the radio. "Listen!"

We sat spellbound, while he described our way of living, taken from the poem, and what we were doing, living in a tent with our kids in the sometimes sixty-nine below zero weather. In our wildest thoughts we never dreamed this would happen. When Paul Harvey finished, he made us promise to write as often as possible and let each know what the other is doing without.

"I'll be damned," Dick mused. "I thought you were crazy sending him a Christmas card! Never thought he'd do that!"

"Neither did I. That's really something."

Of course, it had made our day. We cut another small load of firewood that day and the time seemed to whiz by. Dick even hummed while he worked. I found myself whistling. We laughed and joked about the commentary all day. It had an immediate impact on some of the Tok people. For the first time, when I checked our mailbox at the post office that day, one of the workers who had never been overly pleasant previously, now suddenly went out of her way to be nice, calling me by my first name.

When Katherine and Ricky returned home from school that day, they were talking about it, too. Seems the bus they rode always played the radio in the mornings for the kids. The Paul Harvey commentary had been aired before they got on the bus, so Katherine and Ricky hadn't heard it, but the children already on the bus had listened to it. Since the commentary named us all, one by one, there was no doubt about who Paul Harvey was referring to. As soon as they entered the bus, the rest of the kids told them they had just been on the radio. Naturally, neither of them believed it. They thought the kids were just joking with them.

When they got to school, it was the same thing, until finally their teachers told them they had heard it themselves and yes, it was true.

"Wow, Mom!" Ricky said, "We got on the radio!"

"Yeah, how about that?"

"They said my name on it, too, Mama," Katherine added.

"Yes, they did," Dick said, holding her on his lap, "and I'll bet lots of people heard it, too."

We didn't realize just how many until the tide of opinion began changing everywhere. People we didn't even know began speaking to us. It was..."Oh, you're the tent people!" We didn't know them, but suddenly they knew us.

What a strange turn of events. Now, people were betting for us, not against us. Of course, the worst part of the winter was behind us. Maybe until now no one else realized it, but Dick and I had already known we'd made it. We still didn't have a real roof over our heads, but we'd made it through the winter with a canvas one.

We received letters from our relatives in the *South 48* who had heard the broadcast, too. One of my uncles, who lives in Denver and always was a joker, said he thought we were either *nutsy* or *gutsy*. He never did tell us which.

Yes, we'd made the winter and now we were famous.

That, and a quarter, might buy us a cup of coffee!

CHAPTER NINETEEN

Chinook

A Chinook (shin-ook) is a warm wind. It's an Indian word for a friendly wind, and that's just what we were having. The days were growing longer and now a chinook was blowing in. The remaining couple of feet of snow would melt away quickly. Without a doubt, we could start working on the cabin.

Dick's leg had healed so well that it was time to remove the remaining stitches. One morning's ceremony was just that.

"Hold it right there," I said, referring to the position of his sutured leg. Snip. There went the first stitch of many. Snip, snip. A couple more. I found it easier to clip the stitches using a pair of toenail clippers than scissors. Since the stitches had been in quite a while, they moved freely, causing Dick no unpleasantness in their removal. He was glad to be rid of them, because by now, it was the stitches hampering his movement more than the wound itself. Now he would have greater mobility.

"There," I said, snipping the last of the stitches, "all done."

"Maybe you should have gone into medicine," he teased. "You did a swell job." He surveyed his stitchless calf. "Almost good as new."

"Well, it'll never be good as new, I'm just so glad it turned out okay." I did feel good about it though, now that it was all over and the results were good. Until now I hadn't really sighed the proverbial sigh of relief. Now I felt I could allow myself to breath easyily.

"Still think you're a damn good doctor." he stated flatly.

"Yeah, or else I just lucked out. I don't ever want to have to do that again."

Each day thereafter, we worked at cutting logs, increasing the number gradually so that no harm would come to Dick's leg and he could get it back in shape with no problems. And as the weather was warming, our need for great amounts of firewood had dwindled. There was no real urgency. No feeling, literally, of *do or die* anymore.

We used the same old logging system that we had used in the fall; cutting, limbing and shouldering them to carry each log out to the truck. At first, it was almost too much for both of us. Between Dick's healing leg and my shoulder having softened up over the winter, we were pretty uncomfortable by nightfall.

There were nights when I found it almost impossible to sleep. I was actually too tired and sore to rest comfortably. The first week we resumed our logging, I could not sleep on my right side at all. Every time I rolled onto it, putting pressure on my log-carrying shoulder, I moaned in pain and woke up. The one time I didn't wake myself up, Dick did.

"Uh-o-o-h-h..." I moaned.

"What the heck's wrong?" Dick said, shaking me awake.

"What?" I opened one eye. Dick was standing over me.

"Wrong. What's wrong? You're moaning like an old cow moose in heat! You sick?" He felt my forehead to see if I had a fever.

"No, I'm not sick." I repositioned myself. "It's my stupid shoulder." I pulled my right arm out of my sweatshirt, exposing a technicolored shoulder. It was black, blue and deep purple across the top where the logs came into actual contact with my shoulder. A three-inch radius of black, blue and yellow extended outward from there.

"God, Honey, I didn't know it was that bad. Why didn't you say something?"

"What good's it gonna do?" I asked sleepily. "It's just going to have to toughen up, that's all."

"Well, let it toughen up more gradually. Pad it or something," he suggested.

"Any ideas about how to do that?"

"Lemme think on it." He kissed me, then crawled back into his sleeping bag. "G'night."

The next morning, as we prepared to go out logging, Dick told me he thought he had an answer. "Bare your shoulder," he commanded.

I pulled off my shirt.

"Here, hold this," he said, brandishing a roll of 100-mile-an-hour tape (silver duct tape). Alaskans call it that because it's commonly used for about anything, including repairing airplane wings. He produced two large pieces of padding, padding of a very feminine nature, and placed them on top of my shoulder, then taped them down. "How's that feel?" he asked.

"Bulky," I replied, "but soft. If this works, you're a genius." I slipped my shirt back on. The padding caused my shirt sleeve to ride high, and the addition of my down-filled vest on top of that, accentuated an already muscular appearance.

"You look like a lop-sided Hul," he quipped, referring to the cartoon character.

"Yeah, but I'm not green and if it does work, I don't care what I look like."

That padding was exactly what I needed. The logs, of course, were still very heavy, but the padding of a very feminine nature, enabled my shoulder to toughen up without looking like hamburger. Eventually, I eliminated the pads entirely.

Dick and I worked steadily and soon we had a large stack of logs stockpiled. The snow was almost gone, except for a few isolated spots in the shade of a mountain or shadowed by dense trees. And we were walking on bare ground again.

I still did most of the log peeling, while Dick cut and measured, then remeasured and fitted the logs just right. On weekends Ricky helped peel, too, but I noticed he had a much greater respect for the draw knife than ever before.

The walls went up surprisingly fast. Soon we were able to cut openings for the windows and door. It definitely looked like a cabin taking shape. Dick and I were happy in our work, sharing our work with each other. It was hard work, but not a chore to either of us; we were working with each other, for each other.

We found ourselves suddenly humming the same song at the exact moment the other started, or knowing by intuition what the other needed and having it ready without the other asking for it. We knew each other so well, thinking the same thoughts, that more than once, simultaneously and without prior conversation, we would voice in unison, "Let's have macaroni and cheese for dinner," or "Remember the night Ricky took his first steps?" Or, something equally so disassociated from what we were doing, that it became eerie at moments.

One sunny day, while Dick was measuring the log I was peeling, we hit our zenith of like thoughts. Neither of us had spoken for over an hour, each of us going about our work, deep in our own thoughts. Then...

"Penny for your thoughts," we said at the same time. He laughed. I laughed.

"I was just thinking..." we said again together, both of us breaking off at the same moment. I waited him to speak. He waited for me to say something. Neither of us did.

"...about the day we got married ..." Same words, same time, together again. We both stopped, startled at the other, almost in shock at what was taking place.

I rushed into my next sentence, in an effort to have my thought expressed first, "I never thought I could be happier than that day." Quickly I realized my words had a ring to them that sounded a lot like Dick's.

"This is ridiculous!" We both shouted.

"I'm even happier today than I was back then," we said, trying to out-voice the other.

"Oh, yeah, well so am I!" Together again, and very loud.

"I'm so glad I married you!" We said, unanimously. Every word had been identical, every phrase identical. It was incredible. We broke into howls of laughter, then just as naturally, stopped and embraced as though we had suddenly found each other. Without another word, he swept me into the tent where no more words were needed.

The following day we were back to building. As each round of logs was laid, I chinked the gaps. In the old days, and to some extent even now, the material used for chinking was moss, covered with wet mud. The moss filled the holes between the logs, providing insulation, and once the mud dried, it provided protection from wind drafts. Some cabins, if not sealed with mud, were very drafty. It also kept rodents from pulling the moss out and using it in their own winter nests.

I was not using moss for our chinking, however. Strips of pink fiberglass insulation was our choice of material. Not much was required between most of our logs, as Dick was doing a fine job of picking straight, uniform logs in the first place. They fit together very closely. Where there was a hole, I stuffed it with insulation using a thin putty knife, packing it tightly between the logs.

We discovered that mice, and especially squirrels, loved the insulation even more than moss. Overnight the little creatures could strip the walls of their previous day's chinking. To prevent them from stealing all our insulation, I laid a thin line of white caulk, inside and out, covering the chinking. It dried to a tough, windproof, water tight, yet pliable consistency, and was far more pleasing to the eye than dried mud. Our cabin was going to be a tight, draft-free, cozy fortress against the cold. Not even the squirrels were going to get to us.

Finally, we were finished with the walls and had spiked down three cross-logs to support the loft. Ricky helped us nail down the rough sawn wood for the loft floor, while Katherine supplied nails and brought us drinks in paper cups. We had a little seven-year-old *gofer*.

The front and back peaks were standing, supported by, as well as supporting the purlins, long rafter-like logs spanning the length of the cabin. Now we needed a ridgepole; a center beam to support the peak of the roof. It was the very heart of the cabin. Our keystone.

The ridgepole had troubled me from the outset. We knew it had to be bigger than all previous logs, because it needed to span the length of the cabin and porch, and bear the weight of the roof and sod. We didn't want a sagging roof. It had to be big. It would also be too heavy for us to shoulder. Something that size would take a dozen men. We began scouring the area around our cabin for just such a tree and found our ridgepole growing about two-hundred and fifty yards directly behind the cabin site. This was further away than we had hoped to find one, but there were no other suitable ones closer that measured up to what we needed. It stood in a tight thicket of other large trees.

After sizing up the tree, Dick decided we would be able to cut four to six short logs off the butt end. These would be used as rollers under the large log. We intended to push the ridgepole through the woods to the cabin by means of placing and replacing these rollers as we inched the massive log forward. It seemed like a good plan and we had the kids to help us push. Every little bit of muscle would be needed.

Once we had it figured out, all we needed to do was fell the tree and get started. With the kids well out of the way, Dick notched the tree. Standing to one side, I watched as he began cutting the back side. No wind was blowing, not even a breeze and the tree was already leaning naturally in the right direction. There should be no problem getting it down, I thought.

I should learn to quit thinking.

"Timber!" Dick shouted and backed away as the huge tree began to fall. Limbs began snapping. Crack! Crack! Snap! Crack! CRASH!

Without warning I felt myself being pummeled into the ground, face first. All around me was an explosion of dust and tree branches breaking. The ground beneath me vibrated. It roared in my ears. I lay there, gasping for air, the breath knocked completely out of me, my face buried in moss. I couldn't move.

Dick was there immediately. His voice had an odd echo to it. It was strangely high-pitched with fear. "Honey?"

"M-m-m-pf," I uttered.

"You okay? Say something!" His voice was nearing soprano.

"M-M-M-PF!" I tried again, louder.

"Don't move!" he shouted.

HA! There was a concept. How could I possibly move? I was pinned down. "M-m-mo-o-ve? C-c-an't" I managed to say, trying to free my mouth from the ground. My arms, neck and parts of my back were beginning to burn and sting. I turned my head right into a spruce limb. It was then that I realized there was a big tree on top of me.

"TRR-rr-ee?" I questioned.

"Not our tree," Dick shouted down to me, "another tree. Couldn't see it because they're so thick. Behind you. Must've been leaning on our ridgepole. When I cut our tree, the other one fell, too. You're under the second tree, not our ridgepole."

There wasn't much consolation in that. The bigger tree probably would have killed me. Still, this tree was big enough that Dick could barely see me under it. He had to cut it in pieces, lifting them away to free me. The kids had moved in for a closer look.

"Daddy, is Mama dead?" I heard Katherine ask.

"No, I'm not dead," I said, muffled beneath the tree, trying to regain air in my lungs.

Dick cut a large upper section away to free my head and shoulders.

"Boy, that's a big tree, Mom," Ricky declared.

"P-t-ooey! Thanks, Ricky, I really needed to know that!" I said, spitting out bark and spruce needles.

"Ricky, help me pull these pieces off your mama. Very carefully. Ready? One, two...lift!"

I was afraid to move once freed, fearful of finding broken bones. My eyes teared from dirt and debris.

"Mama's crying. There's blood..." Katherine wailed.

"Honey, how do you feel? Where do you hurt the worst?"

"Mom?"

Lord, how I ached. The feeling was coming back into my body, feelings that had been temporarily disconnected when I slammed into the ground. Still lying on my stomach, I ached everywhere. My ribs hurt, my shoulders hurt, even my face hurt. Carefully, I turned over. The bright sun blinded me. I shut my eyes and took inventory of myself. I felt as though I'd been run over by a bull moose.

"Mama's dying!" Katherine wailed again.

"No, I'm not. I'm okay," I reassured her.

To reassure myself, I sat up with Dick's help. Nothing felt broken. A miracle. The tree hadn't done any serious damage, but it had done a good job of ripping the back of my shirt. It was shredded, as if a wildcat had attacked it. The burning sensation on my back, arms, neck and buttocks came from large scrapes. Pitch from the limbs made them sting even worse. Blood slowly oozed from the deeper ones. But they weren't cuts, they were scrapes. Bandages would be needed, but not stitches.

What had saved me? The forest floor itself. I thanked the Lord for His great gift: a ten inch layer of soft, mossy tundra, which acted as a pillow and buffered me from any real damage. Oh, but I was sore, scraped, bruised and would remain so for a few days.

The best thing for soreness and stiffness, though, is movement. In our case, work. After a brief trip back to the tent, where Dick cleaned up the scrapes on my back and bandaged them for me, and after gulping down several aspirins, we returned to the ridgepole tree.

After limbing it, we soon had it cut and on top of the large log rollers. With all four of us pushing and replacing the rollers, back to front, it took us all afternoon to get the log to the cabin. The very moss that had saved me was equally a hinderance to roll logs through.

The next day, April 30th, we shored up the back wall and peak of the cabin to ensure that the peak, which was partially self-supporting, would not cave inward under the weight of the ridgepole. We would be using a block and tackle hooked in front of the cabin as we dragged the ridgepole from behind the cabin, over the back peak and forward to the front peak where it would rest and be spiked into place.

Everything went according to plan. I had envisioned the entire wall collapsing, but after all my worrying, none of my fears presented themselves. Everything went right. Soon, the ridgepole, with its two foot butt and thirty foot length, sat smartly atop the peak, overhanging the front wall by five feet to allow for a porch.

Our hardest, heaviest work was now complete. We found several small trees which were gnarled with burls and used them as decorative posts, helping to support the overhanging beams on the porch.

All we needed now, were glass windows, a door and wood for the roof.

What a fine looking cabin this was going to be.

CHAPTER TWENTY

On Privvies And Privacy

Ah, May! The beautiful month of renewal, when nature again restores to earth a variety of colors, gently pushing aside winter's dull shades of whites and blacks.

This was a beautiful May, when Dick and I would go out and cut a leisurely load of firewood, for the nights were still cold enough to need heat. In all truth, it was harder for us to get firewood now because the warmer daytime temperatures made us sweat profusely while we worked. Not that we were complaining, but we had become so acclimated to the cold, that now in forty above zero weather, we were too hot. Though we both worked in our shirt sleeves and logging boots, the mountains were still clothed in white.

One day we brought sandwiches with us and were taking a short break before loading the wood. We had a blanket on the tailgate of the truck and were sitting there eating, just enjoying the warmth of the sun. Snow buntings and chickadees darted from tree to tree, chirping their joyful spring welcomings. A snowshoe rabbit popped up and over an old stump, then disappeared quietly into the forest. Mountains rose against skies of brilliant blue. The world was as it should be.

I put my sandwich on its baggie, laid back in the bed of the truck and closed my eyes. The sun felt so good. So warm. I melted into the blanket. I could have fallen asleep right there with the sun lulling me into drowsiness, and would have, except for Dick. I guess the spring weather got to him, or maybe I was just too inviting. The next thing I knew, he had intruded in my truck-bed boudoir and we were rolling around like a couple of kids in the woods.

It was a completely idyllic day. The entire of month of May was like that. With the cold gone and no pressure to get house logs, Dick and I finally had time to enjoy life and each other. My birthday was during one of those days, May 8. We spent it at Broken Bridge, south of Tok.

The fishing was excellent. The river abounded in trout and grayling, and upstream, at the lake, one could almost count on catching northern pike. We spent the day there, with me doing the fishing.

"Come on, Dick," I said, "grab a pole. Fish!"

"Naw, you go ahead," he said lounging on the riverbank. "To me, holding a pole and hoping for a fish to bite isn't fishing. It's poling. Now, fishing, is when..."

His philosophizing was cut short. The pole in my hand bent quickly toward the water and the reel whizzed so fast, it may have smoked if not for the sudden *ping* of the line snapping. My light trout line was no match for the northern pike striking the lure. I reeled it in, rigging a new lure on the line. Then cast out once more.

"As I was saying before I was so rudely interrupted," Dick continued, "fishing is..."

Another strike! My pole lurched forward. I let out more line.

"Don't lose him!" Dick shouted.

I hadn't changed the line, only the lure. And I had another pike on. I eased the line out, playing the fish.

"Give him more line!" Dick croaked, "you're gonna lose him. Gimme the pole..."

"No way, Bernhardt! This one's mine! And there isn't any more line..." I began walking up and down the riverbank, giving the fish more room, more play. After a good ten minutes of running up and down the river, I was able to slowly begin reeling in the fish, taking care not to do anything that might cause him to suddenly make a mad dash for freedom and snap my line.

"By God, I think you've worn him down," Dick said with excitement. "Reel him in carefully,"

"Look, Bernhardt, I haven't lost him yet and I don't intend to. You better get the net ready, 'cause when I get him near the bank I won't be able to land him without popping the line."

Dutifully, he picked up the net, then waded into the ice cold water. "You don't have to freeze your feet off," I said.

"No damn way, I'm gonna let you lose that fish!"

He scooped the pike into the net. "Nice going," he said, "really nice." He removed the hook from the mouth of the fish and carried it up the bank. "Not huge as pike go, but any bigger and he'd have taken the line and the pole with him." He laughed. "An' maybe you, too."

I cast my line out again. The lure had barely hit the water when I had another fish on. This was not a pike, though. This was a grayling, more suited to the light-test line I was using.

"'Nother one on," I called.

"I don't have the first one cleaned, yet," he replied, laying the pike down to come look at the second fish. That was just the beginning. The fish were biting, fast and furious. I kept Dick so busy pulling fish off my line, he never had time to get his own line wet. He finally retired to the riverbank and built a fire. Cleaning some of the grayling, he put them over the fire to cook. I just kept reeling in fish. When I quit, we had plenty of grayling and trout, and one nice pike. I had used everything in my tackle box. Eggs, lures, dry flies, wet flies, you-name-it. They were biting on anything that hit the water. Even a bare hook. It was incredible.

We feasted on the fresh fish, cooking some extra to take with us when the kids came home from school. The rest we would preserve by smoking, drying and canning.

Dick leaned back against a stump, obviously full, and obviously pleased with his chefsmanship. "Ummm, nothing like fresh fish," he said.

"I'll second that," I said licking my fingers. "By the way, what is it you were trying to tell me about fishing? You know, when I hooked into that pike?" *I knew exactly what he was going to say, but this is where I was going to get him.*

"I said holding a pole and waiting for a fish to bite isn't fishing...it's poling. Fishing, on the other hand, is when you've got a fish on the line and you're pulling him in." He looked at me sheepishly, "Which, of course, you did."

"Well, Dick, to me, fishing is standing there with the pole in your hand waiting for the fish to bite."

"Yeah? Well, then what do you call what I call fishing?"

"Oh, yes, I had him, catching," I replied. "You can't 'catch' if you..."

"...don't fish first..." Dick finished my own sentence for me. "You got me, didn't you?" He smiled.

"Yep, gotcha!"

"Got a lotta fish, too," he added.

"What are we 'catching' tomorrow?" I asked.

"Think we'll uncrate the big stove. You can cook the pike on it."

He was referring to my pride and joy, an old, wood cook stove that had been sitting outdoors in its crate all winter because I hadn't needed to use it. However, now the heat from our regular wood stove was too much for daytime use inside the tent. The very dark canvas absorbed the sun's heat making it hot enough inside without adding to it.

"Good idea," I nodded enthusiastically.

The next day, with the crate removed, my beloved stove shone majestically in the sunshine outside the tent. It had a water reservoir on one end, a roll-top upper warming oven, a lower cooking oven, towel bar and two hot plates that could be lowered from the back to keep pots warm. It was beautiful: a Valiant S & Q brand, made in 1868. The date was stamped right into the metal.

And how it cooked! I baked the pike, stuffing the interior cavity of the fish with chopped onions, mushrooms, salt, pepper and butter, then wrapped it all in foil, letting it slow bake for several hours. A real delicacy. There wasn't a leftover morsel of that fish. Dick picked at it all evening, as did the kids, until nothing was left but the bones. And how refreshing it was to cook on a stove out-of-doors. I could cook and watch the kids at play, or watch Dick as he measured and contemplated logs. I loved it. Both cats and the dog loved it, too, sitting nearby waiting for me to slip them a treat every now and then.

With the warming weather, we again watched flocks of geese, swans, ducks and cranes flying overhead. Only now they were flying north for the summer. And the squirrels were out scavenging for food, building nests and having babies. They learned that the shortest distance between two points was in direct relation to a line running the length of our tent roof. All day long they used the tent roof as a highway.

Chris and Perk became wise to the squirrels and before long, grand games of *tag on the tent roof* ensued. The squirrels, being *it,* ran for their lives with two cats close behind. The squirrels had the advantage, though, as Chris and Perk weren't built to run gracefully atop a canvas roof, which at one point held under their weight and then suddenly would sag, dropping them. But pity the poor squirrel that tried shortcutting through the inside of the tent.

There was nothing, for the time being, that we could do to further our cabin building, and no one was interested in buying firewood now, so we turned our thoughts to other projects. One such project was prompted by an experience Dick would never forget.

He had exited through the back of the tent to the out house. I was in front gathering wood for the cook stove when a small plane passed overhead. Not thinking much about it, I absent-mindedly stuck the wood in the stove and then realized that the plane had circled back, this time making a lower pass. Hmmm, that's odd, I thought, and then it hit me: the pilot had spotted Dick out back sitting on the throne! I rushed around the corner of the tent in time to see Dick looking red-faced and trying very hard to be inconspicuous.

"Here he comes again!" I shouted. Dick looked up. Sure enough, the plane had circled once more. This time it was flying at tree-top level. The pilot passed directly over Dick, and tipped his wing tips, side to side, in a grand salute. I laughed and laughed while Dick kept muttering things like, "No privacy left in the world," and, "Gotta get a real outhouse built."

Starting a new permanent outhouse was a good idea and we had plenty of time. Mother Nature had other plans. Even though the snow was gone, and the wild purple crocus were beginning to bloom in the tundra, a foot or so beneath, the ground was still frozen.

That being the case, it looked like there would be no privacy in the near future.

CHAPTER TWENTY ONE

Credit And The Tough Cookie

"BERNHARDT!" From what had been a peaceful sleep, the booming voice made us both leap to our feet.

"What the hell?" I heard Dick knock a flashlight off his cot in an attempt to grab it. "Crap!"

"BERNHARDT!" It boomed from outside again, sounding strangely metallic.

I found my own flashlight and switched it on. Dick was halfway to the tent door.

"BERNHARDT!" The voice was louder this time, and agitated. "You wanna come get your dawg?"

I, too, was on my feet. Dick and I peered through the tent door. A moonless night, the light of the flashlight shone like a beacon halfway down the driveway where it collided with the beam from a pair of headlights.

"Come get your dawg, Bernhardt!"

We ran toward the lights. Suddenly bright red and blue flashing lights lit the sky above the headlights.

"G-r-r-r-r."

The growl was coming from somewhere beyond the headlights.

"G-R-R-R-R-o-w-f!"

Dick and I reached the trooper car. The state trooper inside switched off the headlights, leaving only the flashing lights on. His face, through the windshield, showed strain and agitation.

Von Hairy was standing on the driver's door on his hind feet, growling. Both front feet were planted firmly on the top of the car door window. His teeth were bared, hackles up, intimidating the trooper inside.

Dick and I broke into similar smirks, trying to contain a full laugh. It didn't work. We broke out into a series of belly laughs.

"Bernhardt, you wanna contain your d-a-w-g?" the trooper inside said, emphasizing his point over the P.A. system.

Dick reached over, patting Von Hairy on the head. "Good boy," he told the dog.

"Would'ja quit encouraging him?" The trooper's voice boomed once again.

I called Von Hairy to my side. Even standing on all fours, his head was as high as my hips. A winter of eating moose meat had not stunted his growth.

The trooper started to open his door, thought twice, stopped, and partially rolled down his window instead. "Need a jail guard, Dick," he said, "can you come?"

"Sure, just let me throw on some clothes."

"...and Bernhardt, couldn't you put him," he pointed toward Von Hairy, "on a chain, or something? There's no way he'd let me get out of this car to come get you in the tent. That's why I had to use the P.A. to get your attention."

"Naw," Dick replied. "Wouldn't want to spoil his fun!"

Dick and I turned to go back into the tent. Von Hairy moved closer to the car door. The trooper hurriedly rolled up his window. The dog sat down, next to the door, still guarding.

"And would'ja hurry, Bernhardt?" the metallic voice said. "I think he wants to eat me!"

Inside, Dick dressed quickly. "Don't know what it is about those troopers," he commented, "but Von Hairy sure doesn't like them." He laughed. "Probably the only thing they've ever been intimidated by." He stepped back outside and headed for the trooper's car. The dog greeted him, tail wagging. "You take good care of

Mama, okay, Von Hairy?" The dog licked him affectionately. "Good boy." Dick added.

I noticed the trooper lost no time backing down the driveway.

The same scene occurred every time they needed a jailguard after that. Because we had no telephone, the troopers had to come all the way out to the tent to let Dick know there was work. And for some reason, Von Hairy hated those troopers. He never let them out of their car. Dick and I speculated that it might be the uniform the dog didn't like. He had never behaved that way with anyone else. Whatever the reason, it was always good for a laugh. At least for us.

By mid-June, Dick and I were beginning to feel frustration setting in again. After a beautiful, unrushed month of May, and taking a breather from winter, we were ready to get on with things. Katherine and Ricky were out of school and loving every minute of it. But all Dick and I could feel was time slipping by, with no money as usual, and no lumber for the cabin roof.

Dick found a few odd jobs and he and I took turns as guards at the Tok jail. I disliked jailguarding with a passion, and Dick wasn't especially fond of it either, but it was a job and it kept us in grocery money. We couldn't complain. A steady job would have been nice, but in this small community there weren't many jobs available. It was a slow summer compared to other summers and most jobs were seasonal. Those that were available had been filled with returning employees.

In our off time, Dick decided we should go to Fairbanks, scout out the lumber yards, and see if, by some lucky chance, we could find someone to give us credit for our roof, door and window materials.

"This is really crazy," I said, "no one in their right mind would give us credit without security or jobs."

"Well, maybe we'll find somebody in their left mind, then," he quipped, then added, "you got my sleeping bag in Whitehorse, didn't you?"

"That's different."

"Same thing," he countered, "we just gotta try. I don't want to spend another winter in the tent, do you?"

"No comment," I said. "I'd throw the tent over the cabin and use it for a roof first."

"Eggs-zactly..." he sounded a little like Slim Pickens, "whut're we a-waitin' fer?" Now, he definitely sounded like Slim Pickens.

"Well, Pilgrim," I tried to sound like John Wayne, "if ya weren't standin' here a-jawin' ah guess we could git on are way."

"We-ll doggies! Head'em up and move'em out!" He said, motioning to the kids.

Katherine and Ricky were eager to make the trip. Ricky helped Dick hitch the little utility trailer to the back of the truck while I counted our pennies. And coupons. I had cut out some *two-for-one* hamburger coupons in the newspaper, good at Burger King in Fairbanks. With what money we had on hand, I estimated we had enough for gas and about four of those coupons. We took sleeping bags, a tackle box, fishing pole and, of course, Dick's rifle and knife. They were standard equipment any place we went.

The weather was good, the kids were happy thinking about *real* hamburgers at Burger King, and Dick was hopeful. I was a little less than hopeful, but it was good to be doing something different. I enjoyed the freedom and beauty of the wildflowers growing randomly along the road. A cacophony of color decorated the roadside: bright yellow Daisies, purple Lupines, blue Jacobs Ladders, pink wild Roses, white Yarrow and orange, yellow and white Alaskan Poppies, fushia Fireweed, growing, apparently, anywhere a seed dropped on the dark green boreal forest floor.

We stopped at every lumber yard we could find in North Pole and Fairbanks. The answer, understandably, was always the same,"Sorry." We had about given up hope.

"Dick," I said, "before we leave town, let's go see the University. What do you think?"

"The University of Alaska?"

"Yes. We've never seen the Fairbanks campus."

"What the heck, why not? Maybe one of the kids will go there one day." He made a left at the next intersection, heading toward the University.

"I thought we were going to have hamburgers," Ricky reminded us.

"After we check out the University," I assured him.

"What's a una-ber-city?" Katherine asked.

"Un-i-ver-sity." Ricky corrected her. "A big school where you go..."

"Wait! There's a lumber yard we missed." I exclaimed as we passed it.

Dick swung the truck around, heading back to the lumber yard.

"What about the un-i-ver-sity?" Katherine wailed.

"What about our hamburgers?" commented Ricky, forlornly.

"We'll get to the hamburgers, maybe not the university," Dick said, parking the truck. "Wait here."

We waited. And waited. The kids were clamoring to eat and play, fighting back and forth in the cab of the truck.

"I'm hungry!" Ricky complained.

"We'll eat as soon as Daddy gets back," I promised him. "He won't be much longer. They're probably going to tell him no, too."

Katherine squealed. "There he is!"

"Well?" I asked.

"Well, they didn't say 'no'...," Dick paused, "...and they didn't say 'yes.'"

"What's that supposed to mean?"

"The credit manager's name is Pat, but she's not here today. We have to talk to her and she'll be here tomorrow."

"Great," I said, "are we ready to go home now?"

"After the hamburgers!" Ricky screeched, almost in a state of panic.

"Don't worry about the hamburgers."

"No, I think we'll put Plan B into operation." Dick said, after pondering a minute.

"And Plan B would be?"

"We'll use two of those coupons and get four burgers and fries. Then we'll go out to Salcha River and camp overnight. It won't cost us anything, the kids can fish and tomorrow morning we'll come back in and talk to Pat."

I really thought he was crazy, but what, other than time, did we have to lose? We had been turned down so many times today and yet, here Dick was, clinging to a delayed no. But he had his mind set. And I couldn't think of a good argument against it.

We bought the hamburgers and went out to the Salcha, pitching a tarp for the night. Katherine and Ricky played around the campground. I fished. Sure enough, a couple of grayling hit the line, and Dick was soon cooking them. He and I ate them, but the kids had eaten enough fish lately. They feasted on commercial hamburgers.

We were fortunate that night, without a tent, that the mosquitoes hadn't yet come out and it didn't rain. Dick slept with his rifle, in case a bear just out of hibernation might come upon us.

As soon as the lumber company in Fairbanks opened the next morning, we were there. Instructing Katherine and Ricky to stay in the truck, Dick and I went upstairs to see Pat. Dick did the talking. He explained our situation while she and the other office help listened quietly to our story. I noticed some of them take quick glances at me, as if thinking, *Did she really go along with this tent stuff?* Finally, Dick finished.

"Let me re-cap this." Pat said, eyeing us both, "You stayed all winter in the tent, have no jobs, no security, no roof, and you want me to give you credit for lumber to finish your cabin?" She looked incredulous.

"Yes, ma'am."

"I have no reason to believe you're ever going to pay us back. What would I repossess? A tent?"

Oh boy, I thought, *here it comes. This is one tough cookie.*

Suddenly, Dick blurted out, "We were on Paul Harvey." He told her the story. The office girls were impressed, but not Pat. She countered with, "Will Paul Harvey pay your bill, if you don't?"

We're dead, I thought. *Yep, she's a very tough cookie.*

"No," Dick replied honestly. "But if you give us the lumber, one way or another, I'll repay you, I promise." He stood there, nothing left to be said.

"You know," Pat started, "my files are full of hard-luck stories and deadbeats..." At that moment, Katherine came bounding up the stairs, interrupting her.

"Did she say no yet, Mom?" Ricky asked, directly behind Katherine.

"What are you two doing here? I told you to stay in the truck."

"But I have to go to the bathroom, Mama," Katherine said, tugging at me. *bad,* she pulled me down to her level, whispering in my ear, "...and there's no outhouse."

The office girls all snickered, but one of them showed us to the bathroom. When we re-entered the office area, Pat was telling Dick, "Okay, you can go get your lumber. I'll write out a voucher and you can give it to the yard man." She sighed.

"Why?" I said, afraid to believe. "Why would you stick your neck out and give us credit? Nobody else did."

"I don't really know," she said. "I'm trusting my intuition here. But you're my last hope for honesty in humanity." We were dumbstruck. If I had been Pat, even I wouldn't have given us credit. We thanked her, gratefully and bounced downstairs.

Since the utility trailer was small, we couldn't get everything we needed in one trip. Dick and I loaded several sheets of plywood, a case of nails, and most of the roof lumber: six-inch-wide tongue-and-grooved hemlock boards, twenty feet long. We were given an especially good price on them because no one wanted that length and they had been in stock for a long time. They were perfect for us because they would allow for a nice long, overhanging eave on both sides of the cabin.

That was all the little trailer could stand. It was loaded to the maximum and we would have to go slowly on our way home. But the length of the trip didn't matter and we could always make a second trip later for the remainder of the materials. We had gotten the break we needed.

Bless that *tough cookie,* Pat.

CHAPTER TWENTY TWO

Bear Country

We spent the rest of June working on our roof. Dick and I found that there were enough boards in that first haul to cover about two-thirds of the roof. And what a beautiful ceiling they made.

Dick was about as good a painter as he was a *fisherman* and I wasn't about to try and varnish all those boards once they were nailed up. I had visions of varnish dripping down my elbows, so before we began putting them up, Ricky helped me lay them, good side up, in the yard. I varnished them right where they lay, then, once dry, we nailed them up on the roof. And as soon as we had them up, offering partial protection from the weather to the inside of the cabin, we covered the rough floor boards with plywood. Then I began varnishing the log walls inside.

Outside, Dick applied a clear log preservative. It would protect the logs and not peel away in the weather like paint or varnish.

July found us ordering our windows from the Montgomery Ward catalog. I was so excited. Just that one item, windows, meant more to me than anything else. It signified that cabin completion wasn't far away.

Katherine and Ricky began digging a new permanent outhouse hole, for now the ground was thawed. This was a big, four-foot-diameter hole and would be approximately twelve feet deep. In the meantime, we nailed two pieces of plywood over the *throne*, A-frame style. At last, privacy from airborn spies. Once again, we had used all our materials, so another trip to Fairbanks was in order. We cut out more Burger King coupons, hooked up the trailer, loaded our standard gear and headed back to Fairbanks.

Dick made sure he had plenty of ammunition for this trip, predicting a bear kill somewhere along the way. We could certainly use the meat. Black bear, so plentiful in this area that there was no closed season, would make a welcome addition to our diets. We found, from experience, that a bear that has a diet of salmon tastes like fish. If it's a bear that consistently rummages through roadside garbage cans or dumps, that's the way the meat will taste. The ideal bear meat comes from a bear that stays in the woods and swamps, eating berries and roots. That's some sweet-tasting meat.

All the way into Fairbanks we saw no bears. We did see several moose, including a cow moose and her brand new, wobbly-legged twin calves. They were so ugly, yet so cute. But no bears.

After making a brief stop at Santa Claus House in North Pole, fifteen miles south of Fairbanks, so Katherine and Ricky could have some fun looking at all the toys — and our ritual stop at Burger King to trade in our coupons, then we were back at the lumber yard. This time we picked up the rest of the tongue-and-groove, several large rolls of plastic which would cover the outside of the roof, a solid birch door, staples and more nails. Again, our little trailer was loaded to its limit when we left Fairbanks. It would be another six-hour trip home.

About forty miles from home, on an otherwise uneventful trip, I remarked, "Guess there isn't going to be a bear this trip, either." Dick was driving. He glanced over at me. "No, this is a bear trip. I can feel it. We're gonna get a bear right around that next corner..." there was a pause as he guided the truck around the curve winding through a swamp, "...and there he is!" he shouted suddenly.

Looking past me, out into the swamp, he saw a good-sized blackie. Dick slowed the truck, and I readied the rifle. I handed it to him and took the steering wheel. He bailed out of the still-moving truck and headed for the swamp.

I brought the truck to an easy stop just as the bear stood up on its hind legs. He'd been calm as long as the truck was moving, but as soon as it stopped, he knew something was amiss. He stood facing our direction, head held high, sniffing out information born on the air. Dick took aim and fired. The .375 H&H magnum sounded like a cannon. I watched as Dick's shoulder jerked back from the powerful recoil. The bear dropped in its tracks.

We stood, watching. I used a pair of binoculars for a closer look. Nothing moved. We waited and watched for any sign of life from the bear. Nothing. Dick had already ejected the first shell and slammed the bolt forward, ready for another shot.

The first rule of bear hunting is never wound a bear, kill it. The second rule is, if you wound one, find it and kill it. You never leave a wounded, angry bear on the loose. Extremely dangerous once wounded, they will attack anyone or anything in their rage.

"See anything?" Dick asked me after a few more minutes.

"Nothing," I replied, handing him the binoculars.

After several minutes he was satisfied. Dick and I began moving toward the animal, rifle ready. The kids were instructed to stay in the truck until we gave them the *okay* sign.

We stepped off the road and sunk to our knees in soft moss. This swamp wasn't the wet kind. It was an old swamp, already grown over in moss, blueberries, cranberries and other vegetation. Very little water remained. Tall columns and hills of moss, called Arctic tussocks by forestry people and always known as *niggerheads* in old-time Alaskan vernacular, though I never knew why, stuck up everywhere. Some of them were waist high. We foundered in the muskeg, never losing sight of where the bear had dropped, a quarter mile away.

Upon reaching the bear, Dick eyed it cautiously, suspiciously, poking and prodding the critter. No life. The big blackie was lying face down, his thick black coat stained with blueberries. This was a big bear — his paws large, ending in long, curved claws. We rolled him over, exposing his large barrel chest and pig-like nose. Centered between his eyes was a big bullet hole. Dick's aim had been perfect.

"That's some mighty fine shootin', pardner," I drawled in a western accent.

"Yup, if I don't say so myself," Dick drawled back, throwing both hands on his hips, then blowing across the rifle muzzle, like a gunfighter with his trusty pistol.

I signaled the kids to come, and watched as they leaped from the truck, foundering as we had done, in the thick moss.

"So tell me, sir," I changed identities — from cowpoke to on-the-spot reporter — holding a thick stick as a pretend microphone up to Dick's face, "your wife has already told us that you knew this bear was here waiting for the showdown. Is that correct?"

"Sure 'nuff," Dick replied, also switching identities, putting on his best *old sourdough* act.

"Then tell me," I continued, "just how did you know he was here? The world awaits your answer," I said, gesturing to an invisible television camera.

"Well, see," Dick said, stroking his beard, "another bear tol' me."

"I beg your pardon. Did you say tol' uh …, told you? How does that happen?"

"Yessir, tol' me. I been livin' in these here mountains for nigh on seventy-odd years. I'm blood brother to the grizzly, ya know. An' blackies is second cousins to them grizz, an' they don't like each other much. This big grizz happens by the cabin one day as I wuz throwin' out some ol' fish heads an' he tol' me this here black bear was a waitin' fer me in the swamp. He's a mean one, he wuz!"

"I see," I said, turning toward an invisible audience, "You've just heard an on-the-spot interview with Big "Grizz" Dick Bernhardt and his version of the Great Bear Showdown. Remember folks, you heard it first on B-E-A-R, Channel 29 news. Film at eleven."

I turned back to Dick, switching back to my own identity. "You really do look enough like a bear to be blood brothers, you know."

He unsheathed his knife and propped his rifle against a mound of moss. "Guess we better get to it."

Dick knelt beside the bear as I stood watching, and started cutting through the thick black chest hair, then down the belly. Blood oozed from the three-foot-long incision. He wiped his brow, then bent over the bear again, placing one hand on its chest for balance.

As he did so, the bear let out a loud grunt. Dick sprang back from the blackie, clearing several mounds of moss in one giant leap. His eyes were wide, staring at his rifle, which lay out of reach.

I had jumped back, too, but only out of Dick's contagious reaction. I had known what was about to happen, but still I jumped. Bears are scary animals. Then I began to laugh. Dick stood there panting, his face beginning a slow crimson as the truth began creeping up on him.

"Damn bear," he muttered.

"Well he got the last word, didn't he?" I laughed.

"I won't do that again. Scare a man out of a few years growth!" Dick yammered as he approached the bear once more.

"I guess that big ole Grizz didn't warn you about this, huh?" I ribbed him.

"Nope, guess ah won't be throwin' him any more fish head treats, jest for that li'l oversight." he said, good-naturedly.

What Dick had done, was force air through the bear's windpipe when placing his hand on its chest, thus making it sound as though the bear were suddenly alive and growling. Even though I'd seen it coming, and the belly guts of the bear were completely exposed, that artificial grunt had caused me to jump automatically. I could only imagine what had gone through Dick's mind in that instant.

Like I said, bears are scary animals. Dead or alive!

The kids reached us about that time and joined in the merriment, marveling over how a dead bear could still speak. It was tough getting the meat carried out through the hilly muskeg. But with Katherine and Ricky helping, we took everything — meat, skin, head and organs and heaped them on the pavement beside our heavily laden trailer.

"Only one place to put it," Dick said, mentally figuring.

"Guess so. I suppose it won't be the first time roof boards were christened with bear blood." We draped the hide over the boards, then loaded the meat on top of that and headed slowly home. Now we carried a double load: meat and roof.

First priority once home, of course, was taking care of the meat. The roof could wait. We hung the bear from our porch uprights, finished fleshing out the hide, then salted it down and rolled it up to be tanned later. Some of the meat was cut into roasts and other servings and hung to dry. I cut long pieces of meat and made jerky from them. The jerky proved to be an all-time favorite with the kids and Dick, too. We canned most of the meat. Von Hairy and the cats got the entrails and the bones; the wild birds gave them competition.

The best parts of the bear were the two *hams*. I cured them just as if they were pork. They were a delicious treat, once cured and smoked. Smoking the meat gave us two advantages: in addition to tasting great, it helped keep obnoxious black flies off the meat while it dried. At first hint of a kill, those black flies appear, seemingly out of nowhere, and if the meat isn't watched closely, the flies lay their eggs in it. A kill can be lost to flies if adequate care isn't taken.

After several days of working the bear meat, we finished nailing our roof boards. Some of them were stained with bear blood. Those boards were put over the porch, where the stains still can be seen.

One evening, while re-salting the hide, Dick seemed to be lost in thought. "Penny for your thoughts," I said.

He turned to me, a big grin on his face. "You know the old Alaskan tradition?"

"Which one?" I asked.

"About breaking in a bear rug the Alaskan way..."

"You mean making love on it the first night it's brought into the home?"

"Yeah, that one..." he paused, tenderly wiping my hair away from my face, "...that is gonna be a night you'll never forget. I promise. We not only have a new rug to break in, we'll have a whole new cabin, and a brand new bed to christen. We may have to start a whole new tradition — a Bernhardt tradition. What do you think about that?"

What could I say? I love tradition.

CHAPTER TWENTY THREE

The High Price Of Credit

By early August we had learned and accomplished a variety of things. One of the big eye-openers, to us, was the nature of interior Alaska's summers. Typically, they are gorgeous and hot and this one had been no exception. While fishing, digging a new outhouse hole, working on the cabin or anything else, we had enjoyed a wonderful summer.

For the most part, day after day, the skies were cloudless and blue, the sun hot and never-setting. We found ourselves still up and working or talking, the kids playing at midnight, without a clue that it was so late.

Everyone in Tok seemed to take advantage of the light at night. People went about daily routines far later than any normal place on earth. The difference in distance north, between Anchorage and Tok, made a considerable difference in noticeable light. In Anchorage, it got dark at night. In Tok, it never even reached twilight for a good portion of the summer.

And the difference in weather was enough to make us smile over and over again. Anchorage, being coastal, had more rain, humidity and general overall lower summer temperatures. Tok, was dry and hot. Eighty degrees above zero was not uncommon for Tok. It seemed to rain mostly in the early hours of morning, just enough to keep things green and beautiful. Tok, after all, wasn't that bad a place, we had discovered.

Now we had all the roof boards up and nailed, although we had not yet put the plastic waterproof sheeting over them. Our outhouse was finished. We had black bear meat in storage. We had also set a fish net in the Tanana River and put up some canned and smoked salmon. We were both still working off and on as jailguards for gas and grocery money. And we had overcome the *stigma* of living in the tent. Now, it seemed, we were well known around town and developing some good friends.

But we were still broke.

There didn't seem to be anything permanently available in the way of work and we needed to outfit our cabin. And where were our windows? They were taking a long time getting here. Dick had hung the door on its frame and made a latch from scratch steel. Now all we needed were our windows and the plastic on the roof. Then, once the stove was installed, the cabin would be livable. How we looked forward to that day. We had vowed not to move in until everything was ready. Temptation to do otherwise was already present.

As usual, our lack of funds dogged us, and we had to keep our word to Pat and pay for the credit extended us. With much soul searching and brain racking, Dick and I found a solution for paying off our lumber.

"We'll just have to sell some of our stuff." Dick was saying. "I can sell my portable Lincoln welder. That should net us a fine penny."

"The welder? But that's your pride and joy! Besides, it will take more than that." *What other big item did we have that we could sell,* I wondered. Oh, no. Not that. My thoughts wandered. No, no, no. I hadn't verbalized it yet. But my brain was already fighting my heart.

"The cooking stove," I said slowly. "We can sell my stove."

"Your stove? Not your stove. That's your pride and joy." Dick protested.

"I don't see any other answer," we said in unison.

Sounds familiar, doesn't it? We both looked at each other, knowing the sacrifice the other was making. And knowing there was no other way. His welder. He had wanted one forever. We had bought it two years before and now he would sell it. My stove: its water reservoir, towel-drying bar, lower, oven, two pot warmers, upper rolltop oven, all that chrome. My beautiful stove.

"Guess that's that." We said, again simultaneously, and with finality.

I would never tell Dick, nor would I let him see the tears, but the decision to sell my stove was an enormous one for me. Several times I disappeared into the privacy of the woods just to let the tears flow freely down my cheeks in an effort to get it out of my system. I needed to put on a supportive face for him and I was convinced that tears had no place in that support. Until I caught him by surprise one evening, sitting beside the welder, misty-eyed.

"I'm sorry," I said, "I didn't mean to spy on you. Are you okay?" I wiped his eyes with the sleeve of my shirt.

"Yeah, just got something in my eyes," he said.

"Uh, huh. Probably the same thing I got in my eyes."

"What's that?" he asked.

"Tears for a couple of good friends," I motioned toward my stove and back to his welder.

"They're just *things*." He tried to sound casual.

"Yes, but they are *friend things*. They've already been very good to us. I'm going to miss them." My eyes were beginning to tear again.

It was contagious. Dick's eyes began looking a bit too misty. He wiped mine with his shirt sleeve, then with his own. "This is really dumb," he said, trying to laugh. "We'll buy new ones later on some day. Okay?"

"I know," I said.

We walked down the road quite a distance that night, silently hand in hand, each weighing ourselves, our thoughts, our decisions. When we arrived back at the tent, it was obvious that once again, we had climbed that proverbial wall and reached the other side in our own way. Each of us, separately yet together, had made our peace. We were ready to get on with it.

Dick and I gathered everything extra that we didn't need and tried first to sell them in Tok, but there were no buyers. Not that there wasn't interest, just no money. It was then that we made our decision to go back the three hundred and fifty miles to our old Anchorage stomping grounds and sell the stuff. There wouldn't be a problem with sales in the city.

We loaded our truck and trailer with Dick's welder, my cook stove, five Coleman lanterns, a gas-powered water pump, car battery charger, miscellaneous tools, a load of firewood and a load of raw, unpeeled diamond willow.

We knew there were people in Anchorage who were always on the lookout for the willow, since it didn't grow near there. Unique to Alaska's interior, it really is a willow tree, but when peeled, the wood is white with bright, dark red diamond shapes around the knots. It's a beautiful, ornamental wood used for railings, walking canes and lamps. We could count on selling the willow in Anchorage, and the firewood would pay for our trip.

Here was another adventure for Katherine and Ricky. We were traveling again, if only temporarily. It seemed strange to Dick and me to be headed toward Anchorage, loaded to capacity. A year ago we were going the opposite direction, fully loaded.

Heading south, we traveled through some beautiful country. Through Chistochina (Chis-toe-cheen'-uh) past Glennallen and through Eureka. The road wound up and down, in and out, back and forth past bright blue glaciers, through high arctic pastures of caribou, past salmon and gold-bearing rivers, through mountain passes of Dall sheep and mountain goat, into lush, fertile valleys. Dick and I never ceased to marvel at the beauty of the land around us, and in Alaska there is so much land to be surrounded by.

The trip went smoothly until about one hundred miles from Anchorage. We were traveling a section of highway paralleling the glacial waters of the Matanuska (Mat-a-noos'-kuh) River, where rock slides are common. Loose rock and sharp shale had fallen down the mountain and onto the pavement.

Road crews had picked up most of it, but some of the small pieces were left on the roadway. Dick slowed to a snail's pace as we rolled over them, but fifty yards down the road, one of the rear tires went flat. We pulled off the side of the road and Dick got out to change the tire. Our spare wasn't the same size as our oversize tires, but it was close enough to get us to Anchorage. However, the flat tire would not be repairable. A four-inch slice in the tread and sidewall had ruined it. The sharp shale had done a wicked job. We would have to replace the $200.00 tire. Dick took it in good stride and soon we were rolling again.

But not for long. The Bernhardt law of averages seemed to be at work again. Ten more miles and the truck let loose with a loud, ominous-sounding "THUNK!"

"Now what?" Dick asked as we pulled to the side of the road. I got out with him, knowing that neither of us liked that kind of sound, especially when it came from our truck. Dick crawled underneath to get a better look. I shifted from one foot to another in awful anticipation, wondering how much this trip was going to cost us after all.

"Couldn't have been a freak rock or something," he said from underneath, "Honey, hand me the tool box."

"What is it?"

"Well, we're gonna be here a little while," he replied, "the rear U-joint is broken. I'll have to temporarily disable the truck to pull the front one and replace the broken rear joint with it."

"Will that work?"

"Yeah. Just makes me have to crawl around under here more, that's all. Guess I'll live through it, but we won't have four-wheel drive."

It did take a while. Katherine and Ricky played, while I was Dick's gofer, handing him usually before he asked, whatever tool he needed. And when he finished, thankfully, the truck rolled right along as though nothing had happened. We arrived in Anchorage much later than we'd expected, of course. Our good friends, Bob and Carol, had dinner ready and were waiting for us when we got to their house.

We put an ad in the newspapers for our sale items, and used Bob and Carol's home as our operations center, displaying our sale items in their yard. The kids leaned the diamond willow against the fence, putting a different price tag on each piece. People, driving by would stop and look just because of the willow. Dick took the load of firewood right downtown, parked, put a *For Sale* sign on it and sold the entire truckload within two hours.

"Felt just like a gypsy selling my wares," he boasted.

"Yeah well, Mr. Gypsy, you still look like a grizz," I teased him.

Bob and Carol backed me up on that statement.

"Sure does," Carol said.

"Well, he always did. Now..." Bob paused, looking at Dick, "...even more so."

The newspaper ads had definitely paid off. My cook stove was an attention-getter, with its gleaming trim shining in the sunlit yard.

Even the late Ray Genet', the world-famous mountain climber from Talkeetna (Tall-keet'-nuh) came by to look at it "A beauty," he told me, "opening the roll-top oven. A real beauty. You probably don't really want to sell it, do you?"

"How could you know that?" I asked him.

"It's in your face," he replied. "You love the stove."

"Yes, I do. But we need to sell it." I explained about our tent and the cabin roof, giving him a brief overall view of our finances.

"I'd buy it cash-on-the-spot right now," he told me. "I'm looking for a good wood cook stove, but this one is too big. Just too big for what I need. I'm sorry," he said with great expression, "But it's a beauty, and I will tell my friends about it."

"Thank you," I told him.

"And good luck to your family," he added, walking off down the sidewalk.

"Who's the little Frenchman," Dick asked, stepping out of the house.

"Ray Genet'."

"The mountain climber?"

"Yes."

"He's a lot shorter than I thought he'd be," Dick remarked. "Ray Genet'. I'll be darned." We had no way of knowing, of course, that a year or so later Genet' would die on Mount Everest.

Bob and Carol put up with people milling around their yard looking at our stuff for several days. They were wonderful hosts.

We had pizza parties on the lawn while people browsed through our sale items and everything sold at better prices than we had expected.

Dick and I were able to buy many needed items, including a new tire, the U-joint for the truck and still pay off our lumber bill. Our load was heavier leaving than upon arrival. We bought a hide-a-bed couch for the cabin, two four-inch-thick foam mattresses for the kids and enough carpet and linoleum for the floor and loft. The kids also got new winter clothes, candy and gum treats.

Bob and Carol had helped us enormously. Without them, the sale of our things would have taken much longer. Perhaps we might not have sold it all. *Good friends*, I thought. *Real good friends to let us barge in on them like this and turn their home into a flea market.*

Bob disappeared into the garage, returning with more items: cans of paint, an old pair of bunny boots for Dick, odds and ends of stuff he thought we might be able to use.

"Better take it," he told us, "It's stuff I'll never use, but I'll bet you'll find a use for all of it." He stuffed it into the truck.

"And here's a pair of good scissors to keep the brush from growing too thick on Dick's face," Carol laughed.

Thanking them, we waved good bye.

Before leaving Anchorage, we took in the only little piece of *civilization* we had all missed: a movie, complete with soda pop and popcorn.

Then, with four happy hearts, we were homeward bound.

CHAPTER TWENTY FOUR

Windows And Stove Black

Upon arrival in Tok, the first thing we did was swing by the post office. I went in and purchased money orders to send to Pat for our lumber credit. It was a good feeling, knowing our debt would be paid.

On the way out I checked our mail. We were hoping our windows would be there waiting for us. They had been ordered from the catalog long before, so there should have been a good chance of picking them up.

"Are they here yet?" Dick asked me.

"Nope, but we do have a letter here from Montgomery Ward."

Dick ripped open the letter, "Ah, crap," he said in a disgusted tone and handed me the letter. The letter related how the windows had been mailed, gotten all the way to the Tok post office, and someone there had realized they were over the postal regulations size limit. Instead of simply giving us our windows, since they were in Tok already, the order had been returned to Montgomery Ward.

The letter went on to tell us they'd be happy to sell us the windows if we could tell them by what other means to ship them.

"The windows were right here." I said, flabbergasted.

"Bureaucracy, red tape. Without it the world might fall apart," he said dryly. "And it makes me wonder about the mentality of whoever it was who sent those windows back, or their motivation."

"Well, there go the windows. There's no other way to get them here. If we'd known earlier we could have bought them in Anchorage. You know what really bugs me?"

"No," Dick said, "what?"

The letter says they were just one inch oversize. One stupid inch!"

"Yeah, for want of a horse, the kingdom was lost, or however it goes. Anyway, you know what I mean."

We went home, determined not to allow this setback to dampen our spirits. The cats eagerly awaited our arrival. They followed us all over the yard, rubbing against our legs and purring. And Von Hairy's tail never stopped wagging. It's momentum, at times, drastically swung his rear end from side to side. One would have thought we'd been gone for months, rather than a few days.

Later in the week I returned with a surprise for Dick. Pulling into the driveway, I stopped the V.W., stepped out and, trying to imitate the troopers said, "Bernhardt! You wanna come get your windows?"

He stepped out of the cabin, where he'd been working. "Huh?"

"BERNHARDT! You wanna come get your windows?" I shouted.

He raced to the car. "Windows?" He said blankly.

"Yes!"

"They came after all?"

" ... Uhhhh, not exactly," I pulled the front seat forward, exposing the window-filled back seat.

Dick pulled them out, struggling some in the cramped space. "How the hell...?"

Rushing into an explanation, I replied, "Saw them stacked alongside a building in Tok. Went up and asked the owner if he wanted to sell them. Six bucks each he told me. They're not new. Came out of some old military barracks. I thought what the heck they're windows."

"I didn't mean," he said, still trying to pull the windows from the tiny back seat space, "how'd you get them. I've learned not to wonder when it comes to getting things. I meant, how'd you get them in here!" He freed one of the windows.

"Well, I was afraid he'd change his mind if I came home for the truck, so I just stuffed them in. There's six altogether."

"Yeah, three windows, doubled into thermopanes," he said. "Good thinking. By God, that'll work!"

Dick unloaded the other five. They were ancient things, but the glass and wood were sound. And they were thick with layers of paint. Many years, many coats, many colors.

"Must be a dozen different layers here," I remarked the next day to Dick while stripping off old paint. 'Look here. A layer of white, one of green, one blue, a brown, another white, even orange. We could call them rainbow windows."

"Yeah, or Hertz windows." Dick interjected.

"Hertz windows?"

"Yeah, they've got a lot of mileage on them."

When, at last, I got down to bare wood, some of the glazing was chipping away. The many thicknesses of paint had been holding the glaze and the glass in place. I reworked it all. They looked like new windows.

"So what color are they going to be now for our cabin?" Dick asked.

"Red. Scarlet red. And red trim around the eaves, too," I pointed upward.

"Oh, ho! How 'bout a red light over the door? We'll have a real *scarlet house* then," he joked.

"Dick Bernhardt!" I laughed. We did have a red lantern, though.

After the windows were finished, Dick assembled them into pairs, sandwiching them in frames before installing them in the cabin walls. Homemade thermopanes, with a two-inch airspace between the glass as extra insulation against the fierce winter cold. Gosh, they looked grand. Just the addition of the windows suddenly turned an empty shell into a homey cabin.

Next, was the wood stove. Dick and I huffed and puffed with it until we got it moved out of the tent and into the cabin. It sat on its cement, shale and garnet hearth, but looked pretty sad. No part of it was black any longer. The extreme heat and many nights of the metal being red-hot in the tent, had burned the black away. Now it was ashen gray. The stove had been guaranteed for life against metal warpage, burning through or splitting, and had stood the test as far as we were concerned. Not one side or its top showed any sign of bowing. Just the color looked bad.

Dick was unable to locate a stove black, so I wrote to the Fisher Stove Works in Post Falls, Idaho. That's where our stove came from. After a detailed letter explaining that we owned the *Mama Bear* size and were in need of a can of stove black, I asked if they could possibly send us a price, or better yet, mail us a can C.O.D

In the days that followed, all four of us worked at finishing the log walls. We applied more coats of the clear preservative to the outside and varithane to the interior. Our logs were to remain the way they looked, naturally peeled, just a nice clear coating to protect them and make dusting easier. Katherine and Ricky finished chinking a few extra spots between the logs. We all worked. This was our home.

A large package arrived from Fisher Stove Works, far bigger than we expected. Eagerly, we opened it. Inside were four quarts of stove black, enough to last for a long, long time and a very nice letter.

It read, in part, "The paint's on us, no one else can give a testimonial this good."

We knew they were right.

CHAPTER TWENTY FIVE

Katherine Takes A Dive

Our temporary money windfall was just that temporary. After mailing the money order to Pat in Fairbanks to pay off our lumber, we were faced with the same old problem, lack of funds. Dick was lucky enough to find a temporary truck driving job working for Mike hauling groceries.

It would mean he'd be gone for several days. It wouldn't be the first time in our lives that he'd had to work away from home. He had spent a good deal of time working elsewhere when we lived in Anchorage, but this would be the first time we had been separated since moving to Tok.

Almost tearfully, I bade him goodbye. I could barely stand the thought of not having him nearby. This parting was particularly hard. I had gotten so used to being with Dick twenty-four hours a day, being a team and loving it, that this parting was nearly unbearable.

In Anchorage, while neither of us liked him being gone, it didn't bother us all that much. We had been a close couple, yes. But now, we were one with the other in an unexplainable way. As though our very atoms were combined. He felt it. I felt it. In the years to come, we would never lose that closeness.

Katherine, Ricky and I would carry on, doing whatever we could while he was away.

What became an immediate priority was the cabin roof. The weather all summer had been beautiful, but Dick was barely out of sight when I noticed big, black, nasty-looking clouds.

We'd seen storm clouds before, but they usually went around us, the Alaska Range acting as a barrier to bad weather. Soon, however, a wind began picking up force. Rain was on the way. While the roof boards on the cabin were nailed in place, there was nothing yet covering them to make the cabin waterproof. At this point, rain would saturate the inside of the cabin, soaking its plywood floor, carpet and padding rolled up in the corner, the hide-a-bed and a lot of other things that could be ruined.

"Ricky!" I shouted, "grab the staple gun. I'll get the Visqueen, plastic sheeting. We'll stretch it over the roof so the rain will run off. Hurry!" Wrestling the heavy roll of plastic, I climbed the ladder and got it onto the roof. Ricky was close behind. After unrolling it and measuring, I cut the first twenty by twenty foot sheet with my pocket knife.

Small droplets of rain were already beginning to fall. This storm was moving in fast. Ricky was on one end of the plastic and I was on the other, when a big gust of wind hit. Acting like a sail, the plastic unfurled and almost lifted us both from the roof. I didn't have to tell Ricky what to do. By instinct, we threw ourselves flat on it, using our combined weights to hold the plastic down until the wind had passed and we could tack it to the roof boards with the staple gun.

Ah, the staple gun, as I discovered after dispersing half a dozen staples, was empty. And the only box of staples Katherine could find was also empty. We did have tacks, though. That would work temporarily, until the rain, now falling in big, heavy drops, quit and I could find the staples and do a better job.

"Okay, Baby, bring them up to me. And a hammer. Carefully!"

I could hear her rummaging around inside the cabin while Ricky and I kept the plastic from blowing off the roof. We were both beginning to get very wet.

"Doing okay, Ricky?" I shouted above the wind.

"Piece of cake, Mom," he shouted back, hanging on for dear life.

"Hope it's sponge cake, Ricky. That way we won't get so wet."

He snickered, "Me, too, Mom."

I heard Katherine start up the ladder.

"Be very, very careful," I warned. The rain, worsening by the minute, was beginning to pound down in big splats on the roof. Everything was wet. Even the bangs on my forehead were dripping water into my eyes, and the wind was picking up again.

"Don't slip. And don't stand up when you get up on the roof," I called to Katherine over the sound of rising wind and plastic snapping under me. "Stay on your hands and knees when you get up here!"

I glanced toward Ricky. He was soaked to the skin, but fiercely hanging on to that plastic, as though he dared it to try and blow away. The sky was dark. Angry clouds boiled above us. *Hurry, Katherine,* I thought to myself, *before we all blow away.*

Her head cleared the eave and she was quickly halfway up the roof, carrying a sack full of tacks and the hammer.

"Good girl! Now bring me the hammer." Forgetting everything I'd just told her, she stood and began walking up the wet, pitched roof. Ricky and I stared at her in dismay, afraid to yell at her for fear of startling her and causing her to fall.

My fears were well-founded. Another gust of wind hit and her feet began to slip on the slick surface. She dropped the hammer and tacks, allowing them to slide down and off the roof. I could hear the hammer thump below on a log. Still sliding backward, Katherine dropped to her knees. Her descent increased.

"Mama!" She yelled, panic-stricken. There was nothing I could do fast enough, to help her. Her eyes were wide with fear.

"MA—MA!" She pleaded, still slipping.

"Flatten out! Flatten out!" I yelled back, hoping that the more body surface she had on the roof, the more likely her body was to act as a brake. She flattened on her stomach, arms outstretched, trying desperately to grasp the roof. But Katherine was beyond help. Momentum and gravity had her in their grasp and increasing her speed. I saw her look behind her and spy the ladder. Lord! I thought. Don't grab the ladder.

Screaming at her, I got her attention away from the ladder at the last minute, just before she would have grabbed it, pulling it down on top of her.

"KATHERINE!"

"M-A-a-m-m-a......"

My baby disappeared off the edge of the roof, screaming all the way down. There was a thud. Then silence.

"Katherine!"

Only silence and the sound of the wind greeted my ears. I strained to hear her voice. Nothing. *Dear God, don't let her be dead,* I prayed. *Please.*

I told Ricky to hang on and stay put, as I carefully started down the slippery roof. My mind raced through the objects Katherine must have landed on when she hit the ground: sharp tree stumps, nail cans, axes, spikes, drawknives, unused logs.

Please, God, I pleaded, and peered over the eave. Katherine was lying on her back, arms and legs outstretched, wide-eyed, staring into the rain.

"KATHERINE? Baby! Are you alright?"

No movement. No sound from her. She lay there, staring, unblinking, into the rain. I couldn't tell if she was dead or unconscious. I eased down the ladder, finally reaching her.

She was breathing. Slow shallow breaths. No recognition of me in her face.

"Katherine?" I touched her face, her forehead. I wanted to pick her up and hug her to me, yet I was afraid to move her if she was injured.

"Katherine, Honey? It's Mama. Katherine, are you alright?"

Silence. Staring. I broke into tears, instinctively grabbing her up. Hugging her. Holding her.

"Ma-ma?"

"Baby! Are you Okay?"

"Ma-ma, I fell off the roof all the way."

Her eyes were blue pools of fright. I began checking her over. Her breathing became normal.

"Mama," she repeated, "I fell off the roof!"

"I know, Baby. Do you hurt anywhere?" It didn't appear to me that anything was broken.

"Uh..."

"Move your arms and legs for me."

"I fell off the roof!" She repeated again. "Slick. All the way, WOW!" She smiled weakly at me.

As the moments passed and I checked her over, I realized that, miraculously, she was unhurt. The breath had been knocked out of her and I knew how that felt. She was either too scared or too surprised to cry, but she was all right. The only possible safe spot to land was exactly where she had hit. No tools, no stumps, just that beautiful, cushiony tundra.

"She's not hurt, Ricky!"

"Way to go!" he shouted over the rain. Then I heard a muffled snicker and Ricky broke into a full-blown belly laugh.

It perturbed me to think of him up there on the roof, laughing at Katherine's mishap. And I told him so.

"But Mom," he said, trying to control himself, "come look!"

I set Katherine on a log and went back up the ladder. He was pointing to the area where she had, moments before, been sliding. Even I started to laugh. Katherine's curiosity couldn't be curtailed. She joined us on the roof for a look, and before we knew it, all three of us were laughing like idiots in the pouring rain. There, etched for eternity in the roof boards all the way to the eave, and looking like cat-claw scratches, were Katherine's fingernail marks.

Ricky and I managed to finish tacking down the rest of the plastic without Katherine's help. She returned to the tent and changed into clean, dry clothes. We joined her as soon as we could.

What a story we would have to tell Dick when he returned a few days later.

And, all the while, our cabin stayed dry.

CHAPTER TWENTY SIX

The Finishing Touches

In early September, Dick had another chance to go truck driving and he took it. This time, he would be gone a week. And this time, before he left, we put three more layers of plastic over the entire cabin roof. Now it truly was waterproof. Aside from the dirt that would go on top of it, the roof was finished.

Dick had nailed the trim boards along the eaves and I had already painted them red, matching the windows. We'd decided a long time ago on dirt and sod for our roof covering as it would blend with our natural surroundings, and couldn't be beat for its price or its insulating value, both summer and winter.

Before he left, Dick told me we would work on the sod when he returned, but I had other ideas. I wanted to surprise him, so Katherine, Ricky and I literally dug in. We made trip after trip down the road with our truck, shoveling dirt and sod into its bed, hauling it home and then carrying it, bucket by bucket up the ladder and dumped it on the plastic-covered roof.

It would take a tremendous amount of dirt to sufficiently cover the roof. After a couple of hours trudging, puffing and panting up and down the ladder, Ricky and I sat back and took stock of the situation. We were getting nowhere fast.

"If we could get the dirt closer, Mom," he was saying.

I studied the situation.

"Or if we didn't have to go up and down that ladder."

I mused some more. "Hmmmm," I said, deep in thought. "You know, if we pulled the truck up even with the front of the cabin, put the back end right up to the porch, we'd be closer. And if you were in the truck with the dirt ... hmmm. Yes, Ricky! Grab the bucket. Let's tie a rope to the handle and ..."

"Yeah, Mom! And I can fill the bucket and you can be on the roof and pull it up."

"You got it." I said, pleased.

It was still a very physical system, but much better than the old way. Quicker, and less work overall. I wore out several pair of work gloves that way, but the kids and I made good, steady progress. When Katherine wasn't giving Ricky a break from filling the buckets, she kept us supplied with Kool-aid. My cup came up perched in a bucket of dirt. It never tasted better.

Perhaps two-thirds of the way done, the weather turned sour and snow began falling. Snow! I couldn't believe it. We were still living in the tent, finishing the cabin, and here we were being snowed on again. *Were we to have another early winter?* The snow didn't stick that first time, but it marked a definite change in the weather and put a new drive into our souls. It was a warning. Winter was on the way. Again.

We put our hearts, minds and aching muscles into finishing that roof. Both kids and I worked right through snow flurries, frost and below-freezing weather. I never heard a complaint from either of them. They knew we must finish that roof. If we waited until Dick returned, it could be too late.

When the last bucket of dirt was dumped and spread, we all felt great relief and congratulated ourselves over and over.

Dick was gone longer than expected, so we used the extra time to prepare for winter.

Katherine swept sawdust and log peelings from the floor inside the cabin. I gave the stove a second blacking. Ricky hauled in firewood, and we fired up the stove for the first time since moving it into the cabin. The smell from the stoveblack seasoning permeated the air. Heat radiated into the log walls, drying out all the dampness.

"Feels good, huh, Mom?" Ricky said, backing up to the stove.

"Sure does, Ricky," I agreed. It was already feeling cozy inside.

"Daddy's home!" I heard Katherine call from outside.

He had only been gone a little over a week, but gosh, he looked good. My big ol' grizz! How I had missed him!

Dick couldn't believe what we had done.

"How'd you..." he began, stopped, then looked squarely at me. "Never mind *how*...I've learned not to ask how you do anything anymore. I'm just amazed that you did it."

"I didn't do it alone," I said, "the kids were a big part of this. I couldn't have done it without them." I explained how our system had worked.

"It even snowed on us, Daddy," Katherine volunteered.

"Snowed? It snowed here?"

"Yeah, Dad," Ricky spoke up. "Great big flakes. We didn't even stop for that!"

"You guys did a grand job," he hugged them both. "You've saved us a lot of time, you know. Yep, it'll be a *Winter Cabin winter* this year...not a *Tent in Tok winter*, anymore. And I'll bet Santa's taking notes about the Bernhardt kids." He winked at Ricky.

Several times over the course of the afternoon, as though he had to keep reassuring himself that it was really finished, Dick climbed the ladder just to survey the six-inch deep expanse of dirt. He marveled at our accomplishment. And yes, I'll admit it, we were proud.

"Got a present for you," he told me after dinner.

"A present? Really? What?" I said excitedly.

"Here," he thrust a sack into my arms. I opened it slowly. With Dick I never knew what to expect. In previous years I could think of a great many things he had brought me from his journeys, all in some sort of bags or sacks; peat moss for my greenhouse from Kenai (Keen'-eye), an ivory bracelet from Haines, gold nuggets from Talkeetna, an empty Sake' bottle and Russian glass fishing net floats he had found on the beach out in the Aleutian Islands, even a live baby snowshoe rabbit orphaned when its mother was killed. I had raised it and returned it to the wild.

And so it was, that I carefully peered into the bag. Inside was a gorgeous, light-blue, baby-doll shorty nightgown.

"Wow," I said, "it's beautiful." I held it up. Its blue satin straps shimmered in the light as I moved it, "But..."

"But what?"

"But I'll freeze to death in it!" I said, holding it next to my chest.

"I guarantee you won't," Dick said, his eyes sparkling. "It's for a special occasion. You can't wear it 'til then."

"'Til when?"

"The first night we spend in our new cabin. Since we never had a honeymoon, we'll make this our honeymoon. We're starting a new life in our new cabin. So, even if it did take almost fourteen years, I feel like it's a honeymoon and housewarming, our own private housewarming. I like the sound of that. Nope, my Lady Alaska, you won't be cold." His eyes were fairly glinting.

"You really are a romantic devil, know that? Are all grizzlies like you, or are you just one of a kind?"

"Naw," he laughed, "we're all alike. We just have to keep up appearances so we look tough. The Mrs. Grizzes are bound to secrecy, though," he teased. "Can't tell no one we're really romantic fools."

"I promise," I said kissing him.

In the following days, Dick and I installed linoleum and carpet on the cabin floor. We did a good job: it was clean, soft and never developed any wrinkles.

Katherine and Ricky helped us part of the day, played and did schoolwork. They were taking correspondence studies. Neither had gone back to Tok school this fall. By the time school had started, they already had their books: Katherine's for second grade and Ricky's for sixth grade. I was their teacher, so in a way, I had a double work load, but I didn't mind. There were things I wanted my kids to learn, like the basic principles of *reading, writing and arithmetic*, that I felt weren't being properly applied in the public schools. Ricky was very weak in math. I felt I could bring it up to speed by teaching him myself. And Katherine didn't want to go to school without Ricky, so both were on home study courses.

Alaska has a terrific correspondence system for first through twelfth grades. I took advantage of it. Everything was free. Books, paper, materials for art, science projects, music, everything came through the mail.

As the home teacher, I did the teaching and corrected all daily work. The daily work, along with their tests were mailed to Juneau, where the tests were graded and returned. The home teacher had answers only to lesser tests, not major grade, counting ones, so there wasn't any room for cheating. Each student was allowed to work at his or her own pace, even though the courses were set up for a nine-month period. A fast learner could progress quickly, completing nine months of study in five or six. A slow learner could take ten or eleven months. The idea was to learn, and the courses were quite difficult, not to be taken as an easy way out. Katherine and Ricky did very well.

With the carpet on the floor, the cabin really looked inviting. The kids loved to sit on the soft floor when reading their school books.

Mike, our tent barbecue guest, had an old dropleaf table at his store that had been used by the previous owners. He showed it to us. "Want it?" he asked. "Thought you guys might be able to use it. It's not much, and the top's pretty bad, but..."

"You bet," we replied, since we didn't yet have a table.

Its top surface was scarred with water rings, cigarette burns and numerous scratches, but I figured I could fix it. I set to work, sanding and refinishing. The cool fall weather lengthened the drying time of the varnish, but other than that I had no problems restoring it. And I discovered, after removing a lot of gunk, that it had brass feet on the legs. When done, the table looked new. When Mike saw it later, he didn't believe it was the same table.

He was also discarding a small, ancient refrigerator. Off-handedly he remarked, "Don't s'pose you could find a use for this, could you? It still works," Mike said, plugging it in to prove his point.

Dick and I grinned at each other.

We didn't have electricity, but, of course, we took it, with no intention of using it as a refrigerator or with electricity. During the winter we would stock it with meat, like a freezer. Nature would keep it frozen and the refrigerator would keep out animals.

The hide-a-bed couch we bought in Anchorage was already in the cabin, and while I sewed curtains, by hand, for the windows, Dick made log stools, their tops covered with three-inch foam rubber and cloth or leather. There were four of them in graduated sizes.

"Reminds me of the story of the three bears," I told him. The stools were lined up proudly around our refinished table. "A big one for Papa Bear."

"One for the Mama Bear, "Dick said, patting my rear end.

"One for Ricky Bear and one for Baby Bear."

We carpeted the loft floor to make it soft and warm for the kids. They busied themselves dragging the foam rubber mattresses up the ladder and onto the loft floor, placing them pallet-style for their beds. Milk carton plastic crates, strategically placed, served as book shelves. Katherine and Ricky had detailed discussions about the arrangement up there before deciding which half of the loft belonged to each one. Territorial rights were being established.

"But Ricky, I want that side." Katherine complained.

"No, it's mine."

"Mama!"

"Dad!"

"Okay, okay, " I said. What's the problem?"

"I don't want this side, Mama, I want that side," Katherine said, pointing to the side furthest from the ladder.

"What's wrong with this side?" I asked.

"Ricky! He'll be coming through my side all the time to get up and down the ladder!" she said, faking a pout.

"She's got a point there," Dick reminded me.

"Yes, I see your point, but..." I thought a moment, "on this side, you would be closer to the ladder at night if you have to go to the outhouse. Also, it's closer when I tell you supper's ready."

Katherine's expression changed. Her blue eyes narrowed. "Yeah," she said, weighing what I'd just said.

"Besides, Katherine, you know Ricky's a terrible housekeeper. If he has the ladder side, you'll have to climb over his junk."

That cinched it. Katherine began moving her belongings back to the ladder side of the loft. "That's your side, Ricky over there," she said, pointedly.

Ricky quickly stacked his things on that side, a look of triumph on his face. Both kids were rightfully excited. This would be our first night in our new home. The air was electrified with anticipation.

Dick and I moved our things in, too, and that evening we all ate our first meal inside log walls built with our own hands. The kids were content in their new loft room upstairs, eager to spend their first night in new beds.

Mike stopped by that same day. He had been our only dinner guest in the tent. Now, as it turned out, he was also the first guest to enter our complete cabin. Sitting on one of the newly finished stools, he looked around, admiring our handiwork.

"Swell little cabin," he said, sincerely.

Dick nodded enthusiastically.

We still would be hauling water, using an outhouse, having no electricity and none of the frills. But as Mike said, "My gosh, look what you've done. Look what you've got!"

Yes. Look what we had. Freedom. Alaska. Each other. Our kids. Our cabin. No one could possibly appreciate our cabin more than we did.

Von Hairy lay curled in the corner of the front porch, guarding our new home. Even the cats seemed appreciative. They lost no time making themselves at home. Chris soon became queen of the cabin.

It had been more than fifteen months since we'd had solid walls and a real roof overhead. Thirteen of those months, three hundred and ninety-six days exactly, had been spent living in the big tent. During those thirteen months in the tent, we had burned one hundred and twenty cords of firewood. Neither Dick nor I had any idea of how many more we had cut and sold, but we had put one hundred and twenty cords through our own stove. We felt well seasoned.

Reflecting on the time since we'd left Anchorage, we still weren't sure why we felt we had been pointed to Tok, why we felt compelled to stay, in spite of the odds. Somewhere, in the vast plan of things, we just knew we were part of it.

And when it comes right down to it, I don't think there was ever a time when we seriously thought we wouldn't make it. We just wondered how bad it could get and how long it would take before we did make it.

I felt compelled to write a short poem about our new cabin, sort of a sequel to the *Tent In Tok* poem. It went like this:

THE CABIN
A cabin, complete;
The tent is no more.
At last we can open
A real, solid door.
Our floor is now wooden,
The walls are of log,
Our ceiling is solid
And covered with sod.
A railing of willow,
And windows of glass,
The door is of birch
With knocker of brass.
The porch, out in front,
Of pine and spruce burl
Smells of fresh air
And wispy smoke curl.
This winter will be
Much better than last
For the days of our tent
Are gone in the past.

"And also gone in the past are two separate cots for beds," Dick echoed after I read the poem to him. "Slip on your new nightgown."

Dick pulled our new bed from the couch. We lay there a long while, quietly drinking in the beautiful patterns dancing on the walls and ceiling in the lamplight. Finally he said, softly, "Happy honeymoon, my Lady Alaska." Taking my hand, he gently led me from the bed. The black bear rug lie waiting on the floor.

Dick gathered me in his arms. Outside, the northern lights danced in the sky. The glow of the kerosene lamp that reflected the soft warmth off those walls, was nothing compared with the honeymoon/housewarming Dick and I shared late into the night.

Our cabin was a home at last.

EPILOGUE

Farewell, But Not Goodbye

They say you can never go back. I've found that to be untrue. You can leave a place, a time, situation, or person and return to it years later, completely unchanged in your heart. For it is there where all that we hold dear remains untouched, unscathed and forever a part of us.

I had not realized how true this would be until the writing of this book. Even as I sat at the computer writing our story, I was back in the tent reliving all the moments as we experienced them. Though surrounded by cozy log walls with a fireplace blazing next to me, I still felt the bone-drilling cold of the tent nights, laughed at Ricky's tongue stuck to the *little icicle*, panicked as Katherine slid down the roof and cried as I stitched Dick's leg.

This is how it should be. If we could not go back, in our hearts, what good would life be? How could we grow? How would we accomplish things if we could not still feel those important milestones in our lives?

It is this thought that brings me to the epilogue, and you, the reader, into the present.

Our little log cabin remained one room, with the loft, for half a dozen years. The kids stayed on correspondence for several years. As they grew, each developed a circle of friends who adopted our cabin as their second home. Many nights when their friends slept over, we had wall-to-wall kids in sleeping bags on the floor.

Dick finally landed a steady job with the State of Alaska as a heavy equipment operator on the North Slope, keeping the road to the oil pipeline open. We boarded up Winter Cabin and the kids, still on correspondence, and I joined Dick there. We had vowed never to be separated by anything, ever again. Dick and I were too much one person, too totally in love to allow it. I was the only woman in camp. After a few months there, he was able to transfer to Tok, working as a diesel mechanic.

We were truly home, at last.

While working for the state, he injured his knee and required several surgeries over the course of the next few years.

With the income generated from the state job, we added on to our little cabin. Again, using logs and doing the building ourselves, we built two rooms, a kitchen and a bedroom for Dick and me. He built a real bed for us constructed of four by six foot posts. No longer would we have to sleep on the hide-a-bed couch. Winter Cabin was growing.

Dick realized a lifelong dream when, in 1985, he quit his state job, drew out his retirement, took out an additional loan and built a huge log garage. Obtaining a Goodyear tire dealership, we opened a family business selling tires and repairing vehicles in Tok. Ricky began learning a trade under Dick's tutelage and Katherine and I helped with the paperwork and sales. We hired Judd, a high school student, to work afternoons in the garage on a work/learn program sponsored by Tok School. The new business was a struggle, but once again, we were pulling as a family for something we wanted.

Ricky married an Athabascan Indian girl from Northway. They moved into the apartment built above the garage. The business provided an income for us as well as for him and his new wife. Soon, they provided us with our beautiful grandson, Kenneth.

And I continued my poetry column in the Tok newspaper as a hobby. I did a lot of writing, but wasn't serious about doing anymore with it than the column.

Dick and I, the kids, and our extended family, including a young man who was now living with us, and friends shared a lot of love throughout those years. Winter Cabin was more than a home. It was comfort, love and refuge for anyone who entered.

With the building of the garage, we did bring electricity into the cabin. It was Dick's idea, not mine. I fought it at first, then later gave in when he bribed me with a fancy electric typewriter, encouraging me to write more often with it. He told me he thought I'd eventually become a famous poet or novelist, so I needed the electricity to get started.

George Farren sold his grocery store. On our off days at the garage, Dick and I began driving a freight truck to Anchorage and back, picking up groceries for the new store owner. In 1986, we were involved in a bad truck wreck on one of those runs, totaling the semi-truck we were in and almost totaling ourselves. Dick had on a seatbelt. I did not.

Once again we were to hit hard times. Business was sporadic in the winter, and now Dick and I were both injured too badly to work in any capacity. Ricky had to drive my van to Palmer, where we were in the hospital, to bring us home. There was no insurance to help us. Dick would lay on the hide-a-bed couch for months afterward in pain while I did the same on the recliner next to him. Due to our injuries we were unable, for a while, to share the bed he had constructed. He could hobble to the garage to verbally help the boys, but was unable to physically work or remain on his feet for very long periods of time.

I was too badly injured to cook or clean. At first, I needed help even in getting to the outhouse. I would spend many months in a C-collar and using a walker. The boys took care of the garage and kept our wood split. The girls did the cooking, cleaning, laundry, and kept the wood stoves stoked. Dick and I spent our hours holding Kenneth, watching him learn to walk and reading to him.

I began the writing of this book while Dick and I were recovering. We sat reminiscing about the tent days, while I took notes with pad and pencil. It took our minds off our pain and laid the groundwork for the completion of these chapters.

Four months after the accident, Dick had back surgery. His recovery from the surgery was long, but successful. My back, neck, hips and one leg had been badly injured, and I, too, needed surgery, but since it wasn't life or death surgery, I opted to wait until we could get Dick on his feet and back earning an income in the shop. We didn't want both of us home recovering from major surgeries at the same time. The kids already had their hands full helping us, and Dick still had one more surgery left to go — knee surgery.

Financially, we had reached the end of our rope and were dangling by a slim thread. We decided the smart thing to do was combine our two separate bank loans into one, opting for one lower payment spread over a longer time and using Winter Cabin as collateral. Dick and I filled out the paperwork.

The kids took Dick to the hospital for his knee surgery. On the way, they stopped at the bank where Dick dropped off the paperwork, voiding the old loans and initiating the new one. I remained at home to help direct Ricky with the garage business.

A terrible feeling of dread engulfed me. I couldn't shake it. The feeling was all-encompassing and soul-jarring. I cried. I chastised myself for being so paranoid, for having this unreasonable dread.

Dick's knee surgery was successful. His doctor, a good friend, had performed it with competent precision. I called the hospital that evening and spoke with Dick.

"Hey, my Lady, I've got a bionic knee, now," he joked. "When I get better I'll be able to chase you faster."

"Better watch out," I said, "you might catch me!"

"I'd love to," he told me, laughing, then, "I'm getting pretty sleepy, Hon. I love you..."

"I'll call you tomorrow. Get some sleep and get better fast. I miss you already, you big, old Grizz. Love you forever." I hung up, feeling pretty foolish about the misgivings I'd had concerning his surgery.

"...I love you, Alaska," I awoke with a start, expecting to see Dick in bed next to me, then remembered he was still in the hospital. But I was sure I'd heard his voice in the dark of the bedroom. The clock read just past 5:00 A.M. I decided I must have dreamed it, but it didn't feel like a dream. I lay there for an hour in the dark of the cabin, unable to go back to sleep.

Car lights appeared in the driveway followed by footsteps on the porch then a knock on the door. The state trooper standing there informed me that Dick had died; the doctor wanted me to call him.

What had happened? He didn't know. The doctor told us Dick's surgery had gone fine. He was okay when the doctor made his rounds that night. He and Dick had even joked about his bionic knee. The hospital had called him shortly after 5:00 A.M. with a Code Blue. He was there within minutes. Dick was dead when he arrived. Still, they tried to revive him, but Dick was gone.

The next week unfurled like a black flag, hurtling me in the wind, snapping me into the eye of a dozen hurricanes and dropping me into a thousand different realities.

With Dick's cremation, the finality of our life together hit me full bore. I sat with the box containing his ashes in my lap for hours the day I received them, not wanting to believe this was all that was left of the only man I'd ever loved. My big old Grizzly bear. *How could I possibly go on without him?* I felt as though I hadn't only lost him, but a part of myself, as well. How can you separate souls so permanently bonded? My heart was in shreds; the threads of my life were unraveling.

Dick's death came fifty-one weeks after the truck accident. I was still so badly injured I could not work. I could get around, but could not work. And now, I was even more determined not to have surgery. I may walk with a limp and hurt forever, but I vowed never to have surgery.

I had a family to take care of, a business to run and no money coming in. Tool and equipment payments, mortgage payments and car payments. Car payments — we had four cars, all General Motors cars, all less than a year old, all financed by GMAC. Normally, they only finance up to three vehicles. When we needed to add a shop truck, General Motors, because of our good credit record, had made an exception for us.

I called the GMAC office to find out what paperwork I needed to fill out in order to have the insurance pay them off.

"What insurance?" they asked. "None of the cars were insured against death."

"But they must be. We always insured our cars in case something happened to either of us."

"Not this time," they said, and hung up. Another thread had just unraveled.

I called the tool suppliers. No, they wouldn't take back any tools, even if they were still unused and in their cases. It was the same story with equipment. And a four thousand dollar welder/generator mounted on a trailer and still in the crate. The kids had picked it up and brought it home when they had taken Dick to the hospital. No one would take anything back, and in February, no one was buying anything, either. More threads were unraveling.

My next call was to the bank.

"What do I have to do to get our mortgage loan paid off by the insurance company," I asked.

"Well, Donna ... " There was an uneasy silence on the other end of the telephone, "we're awfully sorry about Dick, but, the truth of the matter is your new loan isn't covered by any insurance."

"Why not? What about the old loan's insurance?" I asked.

"The old loan insurance terminated with the voiding of those loans. When you combined them, it's a whole new package."

"Then what about the insurance on the new loan?" I asked again.

"That's just it. There's a ten day waiting period for the insurance on the new loan to become effective. Dick's death occurred only four days into the waiting period. It's not covered. We're really sorry."

I couldn't believe what I was hearing. I could see my life as a tapestry, being hung outdoors. Someone dark and ominous was out there, beating the life out of it. Threads were dangling precariously, dropping to the ground. Everyone was sorry, but no one wanted to work with me. They all wanted their money. And some of them wanted it all, on the spot, because they knew Dick was gone and were afraid they wouldn't get it. Or, they thought there was plenty of insurance, so they should be paid off. There wasn't. And I couldn't.

Everywhere I turned, nothing went right.

Ricky tried valiantly to keep the garage running, but without Dick's expertise, he did not have the knowledge to take on the high-dollar repairs we needed to feed all of us.

The girls and I put up housecleaning and babysitting ads to bring in extra income. Katherine had just turned sixteen. She quit school to take on odd jobs in an effort to help. I began juggling payments, making a payment on something one month, and not the next. It was all I could do.

I returned three of the vehicles to the General Motors dealer, with my apologies and before they were due to be repossessed, in an effort to save our credit. It didn't matter, I had defaulted. My credit was destroyed anyway.

I made interest payments only on our new bank loan. It was winter. We had to eat. Times were meager. Once again, our family was pulling hard together, only this time it was without Dick. I knew he would have hated what we were going through.

My heart ached for Dick. I missed him so. Missed his big, burly hugs, the twinkle in his eyes every time he looked at me. Missed telling him I loved him. Missed cooking and caring for him. Missed his presence. The bed was cold. The cabin, even though full of kids, was lonely. His death made no sense to me. I felt empty. I could dig in my heels, but I could not heal my heart. I could try to save Winter Cabin and keep a roof over our heads, but I had not been able to save Dick.

Dick's death was shrouded in mystery. We still were not positive about what had happened.

I racked my brain trying to come up with a way to save Winter Cabin, and us, from bankruptcy. I still couldn't work and I couldn't face the thought of losing everything Dick and I had worked so hard for.

Why had we ever come to Tok in the first place, I asked myself. *Why had we so determinedly stayed a winter in the tent, only to possibly lose everything that came out of that winter? Why had Dick and I been allowed to melt ourselves as one, only to feel his loss with that much more impact? Why had we spent our last year together in pain and confined to a recliner and a couch? Why, why, why?*

Donna Blasor-Bernhardt

The more I thought about it, the more I realized there was only one thing I could do, considering the wreck-imposed limits forced on my body, that didn't cause me physical pain and that I could do well. That was writing. Poetry, specifically. In my desperate situation, I never stopped to think how preposterous selling poetry sounded to anyone other than me.

I borrowed money from a friend, and with it, self-published several volumes of poetry, with each volume using the *Tent in Tok* somewhere in their titles. I began writing articles, as well as my poetry column, for the newspaper and freelancing in other areas.

We resurrected the tent in Mukluk Land, a theme park just outside Tok. I furnished it with the original cots and beds that we had actually used. I wondered what Dick would think about this turn of events as I smoothed his sleeping bag on the cot.

By summer, still wearing a C-collar and walking with the aid of crutches, I had set myself up as a tourist attraction in Mukluk Land and around town. Gift shops were selling my little books of poetry and I was busy talking with tourists, showing them through the tent, reading them my poetry, doing one-woman shows. It was working.

It was difficult, at times, for me to talk about Dick and our life in the tent. Often, tears welled in my eyes as someone, not knowing he was gone, would ask what Dick was presently doing. At times it was almost unbearable. I missed him so. I wanted to run home and tell him how much I loved him, tell him the tourists were asking about him, tell him how my day had gone.

I returned home late one evening with news awaiting me. We had confirmation as to the cause of Dick's death. He had died of a morphine overdose. I was stunned beyond belief. We had suspected it, but until that confirmation, I had not allowed myself to believe such a thing could happen. Not to us. Not to my big old grizz.

The operation had been a success, but the patient had died. Our doctor friend was completely exonerated. Not so, the hospital. Following surgery, Dick had been put on a morphine pump. As a post-surgery patient, his vital signs were monitored regularly and duly recorded by the nurses on duty. The pump was tested. It worked correctly, administering the proper amount of morphine it was set to administer. *How then, could this have happened?*

The night shift of nurses weren't paying attention. Making their rounds, taking his vital signs, recording them, they weren't paying attention to what they were recording. Dick was going deeper and deeper into sleep. His respiration slowly slackened, blood pressure kept declining, heartbeat became slower and slower. His life was slipping away over the course of the night, as morphine built up in his system, and they were letting it happen. When they went in to take his vital signs and there weren't any, *then* they called the doctor. The hospital records, in their own handwriting, bore the awful truth.

The most awful truth was still to come. I learned that Dick was the second patient in less than a year that this identical thing had happened to. Same hospital, same operation, same shift of nurses, same time of morning. *How many more times was this going to happen?* I wondered.

I initiated a lawsuit. Medical lawsuits are tough to win in Alaska, even in a fairly open-and-shut case. Money was not my objective. I wanted to stop this from ever happening to anyone again. The kids and I were put through tearful times, broken hearts and terrible depositions over the course of the next couple of years.

And through it all, as we had in the tent, we pulled together. Ricky and I built another room onto Winter Cabin — a writing room. I produced two more books, increased the number of shows I was doing in the summer, met more tourists and media people. As the story of the tent spread, I was interviewed by more of the media, including Charlie Rose on *Nighwatch*.

Katherine took her GED test and passed with almost perfect marks. She enrolled in college and earned a degree in Business.

We were told the lawsuit could go on for many more years. I finally settled for a small monetary sum with the stipulation that the nurses involved in Dick's care and ultimate death would not be allowed to practice nursing in the hospital any longer. Also, the use of the morphine pump was to be used only on terminal patients. I was sure Dick would have approved of my decision. I couldn't put myself or the kids through anymore.

Using the settlement money and stretching it as far as it would go, I paid off the most outstanding debts, regaining ownership of Winter Cabin. I knew Dick would have been glad for that. In order to settle up the rest of the bills and make ends meet, I still needed to work and paid them all off one by one as I could.

The summer day we spread Dick's ashes was a gorgeous one. Sun shone through the cockpit of the little Cessna 206, caressing its occupants. We taxied down the Tok airstrip, lifting gently into the air. I was seated in front next to the pilot. Dick was on my lap. I cradled the bag, knowing it would soon be empty. Yet a feeling of anticipation, even hope, filled my thoughts.

The pilot banked a hard left heading for the Alaska Range and loomed over Tok. Only one mountain, in sight of Tok, still had snow on its peak. That was going to be Dick's. It had to be the tallest, the whitest, the biggest of all, to be a fitting place for my eternal lover to rest.

The little plane climbed above the mountains, making big sweeping turns as we looked back toward Tok and Winter Cabin lying in the Tanana valley. We could see the Tanana River, winding back on itself, and the Tok and Little Tok Rivers. Campers and RV's bustled back and forth on the Alaska Highway.

To the left was Tanacross and Moon Lake. To the right, the area Dick and I had traveled so many times to cut wood while living in the tent. And behind us, miles and miles of more mountains and glaciers, ridge after ridge after ridge. They were magnificent in their grandeur. Sunshine glinted from the peaks, the sky so clear and blue we could almost see Heaven itself. I looked back at Katherine. She smiled at me, almost radiantly.

This was the view from Dick's mountain. It was right. It was good. I nodded to the pilot. He circled the peak once more, dropping closer to the mountain top.

Farewell, my love, I thought as the ashes trailed behind, sailing freely in the wind.

I could almost hear him saying, "Hey, my Lady Alaska, a penny for your thoughts!"

"You'll always be in sight of Winter Cabin," I told him, "and you'll always be in my heart."

I felt good as we landed. Like I had just done something really good for Dick. The afternoon was bright and warm. I felt warm inside, full of love for Dick and Alaska, an overwhelming love that had been buried beneath lawsuits, debts and hard times. I hadn't had time to think of much other than survival for me and the kids for a long time.

I had buried myself in my writing in order to keep us going. I had pushed myself almost beyond physical limitations in an effort to heal my body without surgery. I had climbed that proverbial wall once again. I'd made it to the other side and a gentle peace had settled into me.

And I wrote a poem, dedicated to Dick, about that flight:

ONE LAST FLIGHT

One last flight with those I love
Over the lakes and high above
Rivers, ridges, birch and spruce,
Caribou, sheep and mating moose.
Carry my ashes and scatter them far,
Eternally to rest on a river bar
Or snow-capped peaks and tundra bed
While the sun goes down and the sky turns red.
One last flight, Farewell my friends.
See you again where the river bends.
This land I loved, a part of me
Part of it, I now can be.
Do not weep; I'm free at last.
I sail in the wind without a mast,
Free to fly when the north wind blows;
Free to be where the wild rose grows.
One last flight on metal wings weathered,
Freed from bonds, at last, untethered,
Think of me as I kiss the wind
And I'll meet you at the river's end.

Donna Blasor-Bernhardt

I included this poem in one of my books (there are thirteen books under ten covers and three tapes/CD's altogether now), and it has quickly become a favorite of the tourists. I still write in the winter and do shows every summer and have become Tok's and the Alaska Highway's poet laureates.

Tok's population has increased to around 1,500 now, and because of its geographical location and the important roll it plays in the Alaska Highway's tourism, by Governor's proclamation, it was declared *Mainstreet, Alaska* in 1992.

Little did I know, when my grandpa told me years ago that I was going to the end of the world, when I left with my parents for Alaska, that the *end of the world* would actually be Mainstreet, Alaska.

With a writing partner, I wrote, produced, and performed an audio tape of stories, songs and poetry that tells of my trip as that child going to the end of the world. With the same partner I cut another tape about Gettysburg.

Yes, I still write. And I will continue to write about the wonders that fill my life, for there is not a day goes by that I don't marvel at something, or that I am grateful for my kids and grandkids. I have a movie script of our life in the tent completed and another book detailing the pioneers who built the Alaska Highway finished. And a half-dozen or so other screenplays finished as well as a few film festival awards under my belt. Writing is as much a passion for me, as Dick was, or as Alaska is. I still love all three.

And I realize now, that only in Tok would I have been able to do what I've done, accomplish the things I have and continue what I love. That if it had not been for the tent and that winter, Dick and I would have missed so much of each other, of our family, of life itself. We all gained strength through that experience. I was able to draw on that strength, even when I lost him. And I continue to draw strength from it.

I still live in the cabin he and I built. Its log walls surround me with comfort and love. I share it with my cat, as the kids are grown and have their own places now. Katherine is the proud mother of a 6 year old girl, Brianne, and a set of two-year old twin boys, Michael and Erich. Rick's son, Kenneth, is grown now, graduated from the Tok School and is attending the University of Alaska. Rick and his wife split up last year and he has now begun a new life with a new lady. I still heat with that wonderful Fisher wood stove, I don't have running water and I don't have indoor plumbing. The dash to the outhouse at night often reminds me of the night Dick and I danced together beneath the northern lights.

The mid-winter pink sunrises still set the skies aflame, and as I sit at my desk in Winter Cabin, I watch as the tallest peak, Dick's Peak, catches the first rays of the day. As its purple snow-covered valleys burst into life, I find myself thinking of Dick and the love we shared, the love we still share.

But I don't live in the past. Life goes on and that's the way it should be. Several years ago, at a New Year's Eve party held at a friend's cabin on a mountainside, the group was discussing, naturally, the past. One of the party goers, it turned out, was Dave, the fish and game man who had brought the sheep meat out to me and Dick in the tent.

Dave, (Kelleyhouse) is the former Director of the Division of Wildlife Conservation for the Alaska State Department of Fish and Game and has been embroiled in the wolf hunting controversy in the state.

The evening of the party, he made the remark that they had brought the meat out to the tent to prevent Dick from poaching a moose.

Not sure I had heard him right, I said, "Wait a minute. Did you say you brought the meat out to keep us from poaching a moose?"

"Yes," he replied, "we knew you guys were hungry and Dick had made it pretty clear he was going to go get a moose. We didn't want to have to arrest a guy who was living in a tent for poaching a moose. So we brought out the meat."

I laughed and laughed. Then I told him we had already poached the moose before they came out. He was stupefied.

"You already had the moose? We never knew that."

"Yes, and when you showed up, Dick and I thought you knew it. At first we thought you were going to arrest us, then you gave us the meat and we thought you were just being nice.'

"Then you didn't really need the meat..."

"Yes, we did. Our moose was sick. We couldn't eat it."

A slow dawn of realization spread across his face. "That was your moose?"

"Sure was," I laughed.

"Well, that Dick Bernhardt was some kind of guy," he said, laughing.

"Yes, he sure was,"

So, dear reader, you see, you *can* go back into your heart. And it is in going back that we are able to move forward. That sunny summer day, as Dick's ashes sifted through the heavens, finding their way to whatever part of the Alaska Range suited him best, I bid him farewell. But because he remains in my heart, it will never be goodbye.

The northern lights are ablaze as I turn out the lamp in Winter Cabin and crawl into the bed that Dick built for us. I look at his photograph smiling at me from the wall. And once again, I can hear him saying, "A penny for your thoughts, my Lady Alaska."

My thoughts?

I think everyone should have a tent in their lives and someone like Dick to share it with.

GLOSSARY

ALASKA - The 49th state. A great place to live as long as you're willing to put up with her idiosyncrasies and challenges. You either love it or leave it. There seems to be no in-between. We love it.

BARBECUE - A form of outdoor cooking. Occasionally done at 35 degrees below zero, when it tastes better anyway. You also don't have to worry about refrigerating the chicken or potato salad.

BLAZO - Type of fuel widely used in bush areas of Alaska. Comes in handy five-gallon metal cans, which when empty, are as valuable to an Alaskan as the fuel inside.

BLAZO BOXES - Solid wood crates the Blazo cans were packed in. The very backbone of early Alaska. Entire cabins, including the roof, walls and particularly kitchen shelves, were made from these boxes. Unfortunately, Blazo no longer comes in these handy boxes, so they are considered a real "find" today.

BREAK UP - Or *spring break up*. A natural occurrence every spring when the snow melts, uncovering lost tools, ice scrapers, anything lost throughout the winter. Usually creates small lakes referred to as *puddles* of water. Sometimes the unwary may find themselves in half a foot of muck or mud on an unpaved road. In our case, *break apart* or *spring cave-in* would seem more appropriate.

BUSH - Any area of Alaska not considered city.

CABIN - Most beautiful word in the English language.

CABIN FEVER - Occurs only when one has one. Phenomenon of the North, when people cooped up in a cabin all winter begin to go a little crazy. Only two cures are known, the month of June and the islands called Hawaii.

CACHE - A safe place to stash food supplies. Humans stash their food to keep out the animals. Presumably, animals do it in reverse. Log caches on high pilings were used by early Alaskans. We should have had one to keep the animals out, too.

CHAIN SAW - Usually used for quick, efficient cutting of trees. To be used with great caution as it does the same to human parts. Not recommended for cutting anything other than logs.

CHINK (or CHINKING) - A layer of insulating material between logs. Squirrels and mice find it convenient that humans provide them with it.

CHINOOK - A warm, friendly wind. Not found in the depths of winter, but greatly looked forward to come spring.

CITY - Anything not considered bush.

CUPBOARDS - Usually used for storing dishes and/or groceries. In our case, they were also sleeping quarters for two cats.

DIAMOND WILLOW - Decorative, ornamental wood and a good way to finance a trip.

DRAW KNIFE - Long, heavy bladed knife with 90-degree handles on each end. Grasped and pulled along a log, it will quickly debark a tree (or anything else in its path).

FROST HEAVES - Also known as *Texas Mountains*. Buckled ground on a paved highway, caused by permafrost melting and allowing the newly thawed ground to move. These are Alaska's own roller-coaster system.

GRAYLING - Small member of the trout family with a high dorsal fin. Especially good cooked over an open fire alongside a riverbank.

GRIZZ (or GRIZZLY) - A type of bear, also known to me as Dick Bernhardt.

HULK - A green, muscular cartoon character. In my case, I was neither green nor a cartoon character. However about those muscles.

HUNDRED MILE AN HOUR TAPE - Silver duct tape. Used by Alaskans for anything from holding an airplane wing together, to binding books and patching snowmobile windshields, or patching a parka. Sometimes even used on duct work.

LOVER - Man? Mountain? Grizz?

M.A.S.H. - <u>M</u>any <u>A</u>laskan <u>S</u>ourdoughs <u>H</u>ere. Eventually expanded to <u>M</u>aking <u>A</u> <u>S</u>now <u>H</u>ome.

MONEY - Something elusive.

MOOSE - Largest member of the deer family Big, brown, beautiful and ugly. Good eating. Except for ours.

MUKLUK - Leather and fur boot at least calf-high, worn by the Eskimos or anyone else wanting to keep their feet warm.

P.A. - Physician's Assistant. The only medical help available, or not available, in Tok.

PERMAFROST - Ground frozen solid for more than two years without thawing. This is opposed to SEMI-PERMAFROST, found growing on Dick's beard most of the winter.

PLASTIC MILK CRATES - Normally used by milk suppliers to contain milk cartons. Also used by Alaskans as the new *Blazo box of the North*.

POETRY - Something that just happens beautifully, like my life with Dick.

ROOF BOARDS - The boards used to cover or create the roof of a house. In Katherine's case, a very slick and quick slide.

SCIENCE FAIR - Ricky defines this as something that can be won even if you live in a tent.

SOURDOUGH - An old-time Alaskan, not necessarily old in age. One who has spent at least one winter in the North, as opposed to CHEECHAKO (tenderfoot). Yes, we are sourdoughs.

THE STATES - Also referred to as *Outside* or the *South 48* and *Lower 48*. A nice place to visit. Any part of the United States, not including Alaska and Hawaii.

TENT - Usually something useful in camping. In this case, necessary for survival. Not recommended for permanent, long-term housing ... especially at 70 below zero.

THRONE - Generally a regal chair for royalty to sit upon when receiving the public. The Bernhardt throne was also sat upon when receiving the public.

THUNDERMUG - Also called honeybucket. Indoor potty bucket, usually metal. So named because of the sound made accompanying its use.

TOUGH COOKIE - Generally a very chewy, sweet, cake-like treat. To the Bernhardts, one very sweet credit manager named Pat.

TUNDRA - Rolling moss plains indigenous to the northern latitudes. Makes a nice bed, too.

TWO-DOG NIGHT - No, not a rock group. About 20 degrees below zero, one dog being needed for extra warmth for every 10 degrees below zero while sleeping. A five-dog night is pretty cold.

ULU - A half-moon shaped Eskimo woman's knife, used for scraping animal hides, filleting meat or fish, or cutting vegetables. Very effective and very sharp.

VISQUEEN - Heavy, clear plastic sheeting. Used for everything from covering roofs and greenhouses, to dwellings in the North. Also makes a good sail in a brisk wind.

WELFARE - Not in our vocabulary.

AUTHOR'S NOTES

A script for Waltz With Me, Alaska has been written and is available as a screenplay. The screenplay won the quarterfinals at the Moondance Film Festival. At WriteWay In It was a winner. If you're interested in reading the screenplay for possible film production and development, please email my agent at: hartliterary@verizon.net or visit http://www.hartliterary.com

AUTHOR BIO

Donna, her husband and two children, lived the story of the tent outside of Tok, Alaska, in 1977. They had the land, the tent, a dog, a cat and each other. There were approximately two hundred and fifty people in and around Tok at that time. Donna still lives there in the log cabin she and her husband built. She has since built three other cabins around her house and rents each one in the summer as a Bed & Breakfast. Her place is known as WinterCabin. Donna would like to see her screenplay, which is based upon this book and has won two screenplay awards, developed into a movie. There are nearly fifteen hundred people living in Tok now. Both of her children have since grown up and have families of their own, including a set of twins.

Donna is a writer by profession. She writes for the local newspaper and has self-published five books of poetry, two short historical books, two recipe books and a children's book. Donna has narrated an audio tape of her poetry, performed and recorded two nonfiction audio tapes and CD's. Two full-length, nonfiction manuscripts have been optioned once, but not yet made into movies. One tape and CD is the story of her coming to Alaska with her parents over the Alaska Highway when it was newly opened in December/January of 1950-51. The second tape is about the battle at Gettysburg.

She's been featured in countless newspapers and magazines, from the *Anchorage Daily News* to the *Seattle Times* and the *Dallas Morning News*. Donna is poet laureate for Tok and the Alaska Highway. She enjoys writing, oil painting, her children and grandchildren, living in her log cabin and simply being an Alaskan.